The Basilisk Solution

William J. Kelly

Hammonasset House Books LLC

Hammonasset House Books LLC

Mystic, CT 06355
http:/hammonassethouse.com

Library of Congress Cataloging in Publication Data

I. Kelly, William J 1935-
II. The Basilisk Solution

LCCN: 2007943113
ISBN 978-0-9801894-7-6

Manufactured in the United States

1.Fiction-Fantasy/Contemporary 2.Fiction-Humorous
3.Fiction-Mystery/General 4. Fiction-Visionary &
Metaphysical 5. Fiction-Religious

To my wife, Lynn

Chapter One

Bad things happened to Roscoe Duffy when it rained. His potbellied pig got killed by a pit bull. He broke his left leg when his new sneakers slipped on wet leaves. Last week, a storm-blown tree crushed his 1996 Volvo. He had come to dread wet weather.

Now, his burly frame slumped in the back of a cab, he was traveling through rain to respond to a frantic call from Lotti Spielmacher. Her brother, Benny, was in trouble. She was too distraught on the phone to be very coherent, but Roscoe had a bad feeling he knew exactly what kind of trouble. He and Benny had been partners on the Lake City police force before they retired.

Roscoe vainly tried to push aside his awful certainty that rain always brought him bad luck. Deep in his heart he knew the spritzing he was getting through an uncloseable gap in the right rear window was a foretaste of bad things to come.

He tucked his chin into the upturned collar of his raincoat just as the Pakistani cabby suddenly turned onto the wrong thruway. Roscoe shouted several times to get the driver's attention and then struggled to make him understand the route he should be taking. By now his raincoat was uncomfortably damp. *Here we go again.*

The cab finally let him off in front of the yellow-brick apartment building where Benny shared a condo with his sister. The building dated to the 1920s, when large rooms with mahogany woodwork gave young couples affordable space for raising a family and entertaining with a bit of style. It somehow survived the wrecking balls that broke the neighborhood down to electronics marts shuttered at night with accordion steel fencing, narrow bars with drink specials, Asian fast-food, and balloon graffiti.

Lotti answered the door. She was in her late forties, short, with a round face pulled tight by a spinsterish bun. She wore a black sweater over pendulous breasts, and green slacks stretched to their limit across her broad thighs. Years ago a rabbi had courted her but she had ended that relationship for reasons never revealed. Lotti had never warmed to Roscoe. A drinking buddy at the Galway Bay suggested she saw him as a rival for Benny's affection. That's possible, he thought. Or maybe she thought a divorced guy was a bad influence on her bachelor brother.

Without even a "hello," she led him to a large living room with a faded oriental rug. Theater posters and photographs of famous stage actors covered the walls. A *History of the American Theater* lay open on a worn leather couch, and beside it, a book entitled *Play Production.* Books on play directing, costuming, and set design were scattered on flanking leather chairs and piled next to a tarnished brass lamp on an end table. Benny's suppressed desire to produce a Broadway show blossomed into a mania after he retired. With an eye to economy, he focused on works that were out of copyright. Thus far he had had no luck with proposals and solicitations. No one showed the slightest interest in making a musical of *Pilgrim's Progress,* or staging a modern version of *The Golem.* The only financial backing offered him so far had been five dollars from an elderly secretary in a producer's office who misconstrued his pitch for *Lost Horizons: The Musical* as a solicitation for a home for runaway girls. Despite the rejections, Benny was optimistic. Tomorrow was another day. Tomorrow he would find that one backer who loved his proposal and would bankroll the whole thing.

At the moment, he looked as though he were auditioning for

the part of a corpse. He sat in a rocking chair facing the television set, dressed in his walk-about clothes: plaid pants, a yellow shirt under strain from his ample belly, a blue nylon warm up jacket, and a Yankee cap that covered his bald crown. The cap also concealed the lump Roscoe put there with a rubber mallet two days earlier. Benny's head tilted back against the chair, his eyes closed, his hands cradled limply in his lap. Only the barely perceptible rise and fall of his chest showed he was alive.

Lotti's voice quavered: "He's been gone since yesterday," she said. "He said he was going for just a few hours. I just *know* he has screwed up and can't get back. Damn astral travel! Damn *you* for showing him how to do it!"

Roscoe checked the impulse to defend himself. She was in no mood to believe how hard he resisted teaching Benny the protocol, but how he finally had to give in to Benny's begging and wheedling. Who could deny anything to a guy you've eaten doughnuts with for 23 years?

He tried to reassure her that Benny was okay.

"Probably just found something interesting that detained him. He'll pop back any minute," he said, not really believing it. There were dangers in the etheric, even for the most experienced traveler, and Benny was a greenhorn. Roscoe had made him promise never to go on a trip without him, but he knew in his gut his old partner wouldn't keep that promise if something excited him. At 48, Spielmacher was still an impulsive kid who wanted to do things *now*, no matter what. It was also possible, Roscoe thought, that he went alone just to spite me for surprising him with the mallet. *He still seemed a little pissed off after I explained why I had to do it.*

Lotti fixed him with an angry stare. He braced himself for what he knew was coming.

"You're responsible for this. You have to go bring him back!"

The damned rain never fails.

3

Roscoe Duffy got into astral travel because he couldn't stand retirement. With no job to go to every day, he felt lost. He didn't miss the bureaucratic bullshit and the politics of police work, but he missed being a detective. That's all he ever wanted to be. In his fantasies he identified with detectives in the crime novels he read so avidly. Every now and then, to amuse himself, he'd inject a snappy line of a fictional detective into his conversation. It was the closest he ever came to being the equal of his heroes.

The truth was he had been a mediocre detective. His superiors knew it and he knew it. When he reflected on this depressing fact he concluded he probably was as smart as the more successful detectives, but lacked their self-confidence. He was afraid to follow his instincts. He avoided decisions he would have to answer for. He found it difficult to back his deductions with persuasive argument, especially when his superiors challenged his conclusions.

And so he had been given the low-priority cases usually assigned to rookie detectives, and he had settled for being less than he wanted to be. As he grew older, the knowledge that he was squandering his life ate at him, but he could not manage to change anything. Now, at 49, feeling he had betrayed himself most of his life, and without the distraction of his detective's job, Roscoe felt old and useless and frightened.

There didn't seem to be any alternatives. Working in security for an agency or corporation didn't appeal to him—more of the same crap he'd left behind. Nor could he see himself as a private detective sitting for hours in a car, urinating in empty coffee cups while waiting to film some guy kissing his bimbo outside a motel. Then, a year ago, he ran into Martin Eckert, a psychic who'd helped him find a couple of bodies during Roscoe's precinct days.

Eckert was Roscoe's height--about six feet--but gaunt. His dark eyes were set deep in a narrow face elongated further by a van dyke beard. Over coffee in a doughnut shop, Eckert listened sympathetically as Roscoe complained about how he missed being a detective. Eckert's response was to recommend astral travel. It was exciting, even dangerous, he said, and above all it took you into the realm of the ultimate mysteries we all ponder. He shrugged and spread his narrow hands apologetically as he added that you couldn't make much money as an astral detective, although you could do pretty well if you specialized in finding bodies, stolen jewelry and missing pets.

Low pay did not concern Roscoe. He didn't need much money. He no longer had to pay alimony to his ex-wife, Barbara. His retirement income paid for his small apartment and other necessities, and left him with a comfortable amount of walking-around money. The astral idea excited him. Maybe he would search for a body now and then--Jimmy Hoffa came to mind--but surely there had to be more fascinating challenges than tracking down dead people, stolen jewelry and missing pets! He persuaded Eckert to tutor him.

All went well during six months of "pre-flight" training. His one anxious moment came at the end of this period, when Eckert suddenly announced he would have to fire a bullet into Roscoe's head or hit it with a mallet. Before Roscoe could protest, Eckert explained:

"Astral travel requires a faculty that was active in ancient people. Except for a very few individuals who still have that gift--and you are not one of them--that faculty has dimmed in modern man. Vestiges of the hard wiring remain, but they need to be shocked into wakefulness. In my case the wake-up call came in 'Nam from a bullet I took in the head."

There was a pause as Roscoe weighed the options. "I'll settle for the mallet," he said at last, overriding sudden doubts about proceeding with this astral stuff.

"A sensible choice. No surgery, bone fragments or collateral brain damage to worry about. Only thing is, if one whack with the mallet doesn't do it, I will have to keep whacking you until the faculty kicks in."

"How many of these mallet jobs have you done?"

5

"Actually, you'll be the first. I always used the gunshot method until I had a bad experience with the last guy I treated. My aim was a little off."

A chill gripped Roscoe's heart. "Off" meaning what? A miss or a *fatal shot?* He decided not to inquire. If it were a fatal shot, he would have to ask himself: Is Eckert guilty of manslaughter? Is he a serial killer? Is he crazy? And if he is any of things, is it wise to let such a man hit you in the head with a mallet? But if he, Roscoe Duffy, truly wanted to become an astral traveler, the prudent course would be to avoid these worrisome considerations altogether, and put one's faith in Eckert. *After all, the man looks sound enough. No buck teeth or protruding ears. Eyes are a little spooky, but not too close to the nose. No Neanderthal brow or protruding jaw. Canine teeth not extended over the lower lip.*

Eckert overcame Duffy's remaining qualms by assuring him he had read everything written on the technique and that nothing could possibly go wrong. And so Roscoe Duffy, former detective in the 31st Precinct, bent his head to the rubber mallet. It was not a complicated procedure. Eckert simply clocked him behind the ear hard enough to put him out for several seconds. When Roscoe came to, his head hurt a little but he definitely felt different.

"Tell me what you're thinking." Eckert said.

"I am repeating my name, and doing that calls up the name *Chester Conklin.*"

"The silent movie actor who played the heavy in several Chaplin films?"

"Right. But there's no reason for the association. *Roscoe Duffy, Chester Conklin. Roscoe Duffy, Chester Conklin.* It's weird."

"Excellent! One whack and that superrational sense has kicked in. It's out there in the Collective Unconscious making meaningful connections, even if you don't understand them. You're ready to go!"

Eckert gave him the numbers of a few sites he would find interesting. A site number is merely a number chosen by a previous astral traveler to mark a place he may wish to revisit, or which others may wish to visit. The number itself has no significance, but once assigned, it ever after marks the location of that site in the Collective Unconscious or, as some preferred to call it, The Divine All. And that was how it began.

Now, riding home from Benny's, Roscoe mused that even after a year of astral travel he still did not understand why thinking of his own name immediately called up *Chester Conklin.* Maybe he would understand the connection someday. Right now he had to focus his energy on finding Benny.

Roscoe's one-bedroom apartment conformed to the modern developer's first rule, that small and boxy makes more money than ample and cozy. The galley kitchen and dining area shared a space barely large enough for a car. A tiny balcony overlooked a littered Yates Avenue four stories below. The kitchen/dining space extended left into a square, windowless living room which crowded together a couch, a television set, and an overstuffed chair for visitors. A short hallway, narrowed by a low bookcase filled exclusively with detective fiction, led past the closet-size bathroom to the bedroom.

The bedroom walls would be entirely bare had not an overnight guest named Maxine suggested the place would be more conducive to lovemaking if it were softened with decoration.

"Bare wall is so *blank* when you are searching for inspirational thoughts," she told him. One wall now bore a color print of Man-O-War. Across from the foot of the bed hung a still life: a shotgun resting on a table near a bowl of pears and two dead pheasants with blood-speckled breasts. The wall behind the bed presented a blowup of Joe Louis in a fighting stance.

Roscoe opened the refrigerator, which held two cups of yogurt, a six-pack of beer, moldy multigrain bread, mayonnaise, and three slices of bologna turning green in the middle. He selected a strawberry yogurt and a beer and consumed these while standing beside the stainless steel sink.

Only a few things needed to be done before departing. Having passed on, his pot bellied pig, Snorty, did not need a baby sitter. The rent was paid, there were no newspaper deliveries to

7

cancel, and his mail would sit in his post office box until he picked it up. It was possible his nosy neighbors, Mrs. Chatworth on the right, and Elmo Denker across the hall, would notice his absence and pretend to worry about him so the janitor would let them in to snoop for gossip material. For this reason he pinned a note to his shirt : "Do not disturb. I am not dead, only gone for a while. The pig you hated so much is gone, too. He won't be back at all. Up yours."

Roscoe made sure his medicine stone--a gift from Eckert--was in his pants pocket. He also loosely wrapped two Krispy Kreme doughnuts in wax paper and stuffed them into a pocket of the red nylon bowling jacket he wore. Then it was time to go. He reclined on the couch with arms folded across his chest. He breathed deeply several times, then concentrated on visualizing 215, the number of the site he wished to visit. He fell into a trance, and within minutes felt the sudden vibration of his consciousness leaving his body and floating into the ineffable.

He was traveling head first at ballistic speed through a swirling vortex. His phantom body did not feel the ether rushing by, nor the heat his speed would normally generate. The walls of the vortex hummed like an electrical turbine generator. A small light gradually emerged at a great distance. As he drew closer, it got larger, becoming at last a portal at the end of the vortex. He hurtled through it with the small popping sound of an object bursting through a thin membrane. It took him a few seconds to realize he was no longer in motion. He stood in a white mist. His astral body looked exactly like his earthly self, right down to the stitching on the red bowling jacket. Bullets, knives and punches would pass harmlessly through his phantom body. The greatest threat he faced was being absorbed by more powerful spirits and transformed into something hideous.

Eckert had warned him about this location. Site 215 was the beginning of Chaos, the most dangerous dimension in the Divine All. Neither Heaven nor Hell, it was the unregulated realm between the

8

two where hideous evil spirits prowled in search of souls that blundered into their realm. Roscoe had been here at the edge once before, staying for just a few seconds to satisfy his curiosity before moving away to more benign locations. The dangers of Chaos had kept him from venturing through it to the heavenly dimension. But now he had to make that perilous journey to search for Benny. His friend might not be in Heaven but it was the logical place to start. Benny's current obsession to produce a musical version of *Paradise Lost* could have drawn him there for background and inspiration.

He moved cautiously into the white mist, his heart thumping in his ears. His hand clutched the medicine stone in his pocket. This amulet, now in its astral form, was the work of an Indian shaman and guaranteed protection against the evil ones, according to Eckert. He remembered the gaunt psychic's solemn warning: "These spirits are shape-shifters. They may come at you as hideous creatures or as friendly forms offering to help you. Trust no one!"

For a few moments nothing happened. The mist enveloped him completely, emitting a faint hum like a low-voltage electrical field. Then an ominous sound began in the distance, a staccato kind of crackling that resembled static. This could not be static from a cheap radio. Up here, so far as he knew, there were no radios. Suddenly, a shadow appeared in the near distance, moving toward him, growing larger each second. *Oh shit!*

The attack came with incredible speed. With the tremendous roar of a cataract, a gigantic squid burst from the mist, its suckered tentacles spread wide, its great horny beak agape to seize Roscoe. As the beast lunged at him, he managed to hold the medicine stone aloft. The creature shrieked with rage and veered off at the last second, leaving behind a sulfurous stench.

"Well done," a voice said.

Roscoe spun around, brandishing the stone.

The speaker was a ruddy-faced man with muttonchops who wore the domed hat and uniform of a turn-of-the-century policeman. On his back were large white wings that looked a little frayed and soiled.

9

"Azy now, lad. Azy does it. I'm here to help ya." Roscoe was not about to be fooled by a shape-shifter, however Irish he might seem. He held the medicine stone in front of him like a shield. "Begone, evil spirit," he said, trying to imitate the exorcists he had seen in old movies. This had no effect. The policeman was still there, smiling with amusement. It occurred to Roscoe that "begone" might be fancy English beyond the comprehension of a simple Irish policeman of the 1900s. So he tried "Scat!" "Beat it!" "Go away!" and finally, "Haul ass, Buster, or I'll kick you in the balls and shove your nightstick up your ass."

The policeman bent over with laughter. He obviously understood Roscoe's meaning. "That will be pretty hard to do, boyo," he said. He unzipped his fly and opened it wide. There was nothing but empty space where his genitals should be. He turned around and dropped his pants and spread his creamy buttocks. He had no anus, either.

Very strange, but strange things are to be expected in the etheric world. It struck him that perhaps he was being subjected to the bad cop-good cop routine; the squid being the "bad cop," who scared the shit out of him, and this one, the "good cop" who would offer beguiling friendship to gain his trust. But if the cop *were* one of the shape-shifters, why didn't the medicine stone ward him off?

A terrifying snarling and howling erupted all around him. The chilling sounds moved closer. *Evil ones gathering for the kill?* He could fend them off with the stone if they came at him one at a time, but if they swarmed from all directions. . . . The policeman looked amused. Had he summoned them here? Roscoe wondered. His throat tightened with fear. Should he trust the cop?

He did not get a chance to decide. The mist suddenly disgorged a writhing mass of beasts from all directions--a blur of bat-like wings, twisting serpentine bodies, crested reptilian heads with glowing red eyes. As he desperately reached for the medicine stone, he felt something pin both arms to his sides and lift him up. He was in the grasp of the policeman and they were flying upward. As they rose, the demons rushed around them, splitting the ether with furious screams, but keeping their distance.

The policeman taunted the frantic hoard with a haughty smile and a salute with his upraised middle finger.

"I love pissing them off. That's the beauty of being an escort."

"Don't piss them off too much! They seem to be moving closer."

"They can't harm me or anyone under my protection. Can't you see I'm an angel, a superior spirit. The wings should have tipped you off."

The demons slowly fell back and began to disappear into the mist below.

"I figured you might be one of the demons dressed to fool me," Roscoe said

The policeman shook his head in wonderment. "You're a piece of work, Duffy. I did everything I could to advertise myself as a good guy: the endearing Irish brogue, the uniform of a lawman, the wings of an angel--and you missed it all. The boss will get a big kick out of this--a big kick!"

There's the nub of it. Who's the Boss? Where are we going?

"Who's the boss and where are we going?"

"Sorry. Can't tell you."

New doubts seized Roscoe. Perhaps this really was an evil one after all! Maybe the stone didn't work on all demons. Maybe the attack was pure theatrics to scare him into the clutches of the policeman. Maybe that static *was* from cheap radios. After all, every radio transmission ever made is still traveling farther into the cosmos. Why wouldn't the evil ones have radios to monitor earthly life. Of course it would take time for radio broadcasts to reach this distant realm. By now "Ma Perkins" and "Just Plain Bill" of the 1940s could be coming in. Possibly even "The Shadow."

Who is the boss? Where are we going?

Chapter Two

The policeman carried Roscoe upward at such terrific speed they quickly left Chaos behind and entered a new dimension. He was aware of buildings and houses, but traveling at such high speed he only glimpsed them. He thought he made out cobblestone streets and trolley tracks and telephone poles connected by drooping strands of wire. Occasionally, he caught a whiff of horse shit. Then they were angling downward, toward a roof. Roscoe thought they would land on it feet-first but the policeman did not change their attitude. They were about to arrow into it head-first! Forgetting his body was immaterial, Roscoe screamed just as he was about to smash into the roof. But there was no impact. He and the policeman went through it with the ease of light passing through smoke. They drifted down through the building, passing barred windows and a row of empty jail cells. The cells had the distinct look of stage props.

When they reached the first floor, the policeman released him in front of a wide mahogany-paneled counter that rose above his head. A lighted globe atop an ornate wooden spindle beamed down on each end of it. Behind the counter a policeman dressed like Roscoe's escort talked on an upright telephone, holding the mouthpiece stem in one hand and the pestle-shaped ear piece in the other. This was a police station of the early 1900s.

"Wait here," the escort said. "Got to return these wings to Wardrobe."

"Those aren't real angel wings?"

"Just props. We've never needed wings to fly, but people expect angels to have wings, so we wear them when meeting newcomers. They feel reassured."

The angel walked off.

Roscoe looked around. The room was crowded with cops. At first, everything seemed normal except their button-down-the-front coats which reached almost to their knees; uniforms that were ugly and likely to split a seam in a tussle with a perp.

As he watched them, he gradually became aware of something odd. They seemed to have nothing to do. They chatted, or played cards on wooden benches, or dozed in chairs along the wall. A few were reading tabloid newspapers. They seemed to be waiting for something.

A buzzer sounded that jolted the policeman into action. They rushed to the counter, crowding themselves into a tight group. Each looked expectantly upward at the cop on the desk. He bent out of sight for a moment, then reappeared holding a small roulette wheel. He spun the wheel. It came to a stop. "Number 17. It's Murphy," he said. The cop named Murphy gave an exultant whoop amid murmurings of disappointment. The others returned to what they had been doing before the buzzer sounded. *What was that all about?*

He turned to ask his angel escort, who had rejoined him moments earlier, but the angel raised his chin and shook his head in a not-now gesture. He led Roscoe down a hallway to a door with **Chief** painted in black on its frosted glass panel. The angel knocked, then he and Roscoe passed directly through the closed door.

"Ah, you finally made it, Roscoe," said a large policeman sitting behind a worn oak desk at the far end of the room. His bulbous eyes crossed slightly so they appeared close to his nose. He wore a mustache cut like a small paint brush.

The nameplate on his desk read: **Chester Conklin, Chief of Police**. *How incredible! First the name for no reason, and now the man himself!*

"We thought you'd be here long before this, but you backed off the first time you reached the edge of Chaos," Conklin said. "Can't say I blame you, though. You couldn't have known Bruno here would be waiting to escort you."

Roscoe was struggling to make sense of this whole business.

"How did you know I was coming?"

Conklin leaned back in his chair. He steepled his fingers.

"We track all astral travelers who are policeman. We put a tag on them, so to speak, by linking my name with theirs..."

"So that's why your name came up whenever I thought of my own."

"Exactly. So wherever Roscoe Duffy goes in this infinite ether, the Chester Conklin name goes with him. Makes it easier for us to locate you, and it tells everyone else we have first recruitment rights."

"I don't understand...."

Slowly, patiently, Conklin gave Roscoe the Big Picture, which was indeed a little complicated. To begin with, Conklin said, imagine the pain of having nothing to do *eternally.* Life in Heaven would be unbearably boring if one did not have something to do.

"So every soul here is free to be and do whatever pleases him," Conklin said, "within certain Divine limits, of course. For example, some of the religious types want to sit at the right hand of God...others work at operational tasks, like showing newcomers around, publishing magazines, serving on committees, organizing entertainments or, like us, working in the Security Force.

"But as you might guess, there aren't enough jobs to go around. So those without real work create virtual domains appropriate for the work they would *like* to do. We have bankers, lawyers, firemen, soldiers, carpenters—souls in every occupation you can think of—working at virtual jobs in virtual settings that are realistic down to the smallest detail," Conklin said.

"We even have individuals who choose to be virtual Mafia dons," Bruno added. "A few of them really *were* Mafia dons. And why didn't they go to hell, you ask. Because they gave tons of money to the Church," he said with obvious distaste. "This rankles a lot of us, but whenever we complain, the higher-ups trot out the no-sinner-is-beyond-redemption excuse."

Conklin leaned forward in his chair as though speaking in confidence to Roscoe. "You'll also be surprised to know we have virtual prostitutes up here. Both the wannabes and the real professionals. You see, in the ultimate weighing of deeds, screwing doesn't count. The Old Man feels guilty about giving men a johnson with an irresistible will of its own. He feels his procreative design is the root of the problem, not their weaknesses."

"Another Divine concession that irks some of the righteous up here," Bruno said.

So you have sex up here!" Roscoe said.

"Virtual sex," Conklin replied.

"Which is still pretty good, from what I hear," Bruno said.

"And the Almighty doesn't mind?"

"He doesn't mind a bit. It's only the prudes who gripe about it," Bruno said.

Conklin continued with the Big Picture, adding detail after detail until Roscoe's ability to process the information onslaught began to fail. At length the police chief paused and raised his hands.

"Okay. Enough of that for now. I'm sure you have a lot of questions," he said.

After listening for so long, Roscoe was grateful for the chance to talk.

"Why is this a police force of the early 1900s?"

"Because that's when all of us on this force lived, so we fashioned a police unit of those times. It's familiar. Comfortable. We'd be unhappy having to learn all the modern stuff--computers, forensics, latent prints, DNA and so forth."

"You were never a real cop. How come you chose to be one here?"

"Always wanted to be one. I hated being in movies. I hated always being the stupid bad guy. Chaplin and that whole bunch

15

rubbed me the wrong way. Egomaniacs. Kissy, kissy, phoney Hollywood types."

"Is this a real police outfit or a virtual one?"

"Oh, we're real, all right. So are all the other police forces you'll run into up here--the ones from different eras. We're all sort of supernumeraries working for the Head of Security, Brad Stuckey. Colonel Brad Stuckey--a real tight ass."

"Your cells are empty. You don't seem to have caught many offenders."

"There aren't many offenders in Heaven. You can't hold spirit matter in a cell, anyway. The cells are just props to give this the look of a real police station. The only way to detain an offender is to swat him with a Detainer, a large racquet commonly called a 'sticky plate.' It is electrically charged to attract and hold his atoms. Then you just stack the racquet on a shelf somewhere until it is time to release the prisoner by reversing the electrical field of the plate," Conklin said.

Roscoe suddenly remembered the strange scene he had witnessed down the hall. What was that all about?

"Job sharing," Conklin said. "There isn't enough police work to go around--especially with other police units competing for assignments. So when a call comes in, we spin the roulette wheel to see who gets to answer it."

"Which brings us to the reason we've just begun to tag astral travelers who are cops," Bruno said.

"But I'm retired."

"Doesn't matter. You still plan to putz around with detective work, and that's where we come in," Conklin said. "We figure you might be able to throw some work our way. It would be a big morale booster. Some of the boys are thinking of quitting because there's so little to do. And the assignments Stuckey gives us are menial--like traffic control, domain disputes, grabbing wandering newcomers before they blunder into Chaos. This is not the kind of work we were hoping for."

"So can you help us?" Bruno said.

16

Roscoe beamed. What incredible luck! An entire police force at his disposal! Never mind that they were way behind the times.

"Absolutely," he said. "You can help me find Benny Spielmacher."

With a spectacular horizontal leap, Patriots wide receiver Boone Dixon caught the dying pass in his fingertips before slamming to earth in the end zone. As the stands erupted, Boone knelt and mumbled the hasty prayer of thanks that had been his lucky talisman throughout his football career.

"I wish they wouldn't do that," the Almighty said to Michael the Archangel. "Why do they think I help anyone in a sporting contest!"

God and Michael sat beside an oval viewing port in the golden floor of heaven, looking down on the game between the Buffalo Bills and the New England Patriots. Michael nodded in sad agreement. Mortals' ignorance about the Almighty was exasperating. Of course He didn't intervene in sporting events! The Old Man had been hooked on contests since they began. Dinosaur against dinosaur, gladiators, chariot races, marathons--eon after eon, as games were created, he followed them with passionate interest. Where's the fun in watching a contest if you're fixing it? No sir, when it came to contests, the Almighty was a laissez faire God who turned off his omniscience and foreknowledge. That is why He could bet Michael a little jasper or pearl on the outcomes. Michael suspected the Old Man enjoyed the way His wagering scandalized the white-robed Elect at His right hand, who perpetually and monotonously sang His praises.

With 10 seconds to go, the Bills were on the Patriot's 20 yard line, behind by a point. Fourth down. Kicker and holder moved into position for a field goal try. This was it! If the Bills kicked a field goal, Michael would win his bet with the Old Man. But Michael was not to see the crucial play. As the Buffalo linemen settled into their three-point stance, Jeremiah the Prophet stepped from the Host surrounding the heavenly throne and demanded the Archangel's attention

"Once again, I must protest," the old doomsayer whispered, beckoning Michael to accompany him out of the Almighty's earshot. Jeremiah was spokesman for the Pan Heaven Advisory Committee of 100. "We object to Him watching sports. It is beneath His exalted dignity to watch humans doing silly things with balls and sticks and bladders. But that is the least of it, Michael. When He turns off his omniscience and foreknowledge, He puts Heaven in jeopardy."

Michael frowned at the gaunt elder. Jeremiah had made this complaint so many times, Michael could almost recite it word for word. "He's been doing this for millennia and nothing has happened to Heaven, Jeremiah. What's to worry about?"

The prophet bristled at this curt reply. He didn't like this arrogant Archangel. Strictly speaking, God should have chosen His crony from the higher orders of angels--the Seraphim, Cherubim, Thrones, Dominions, Virtues, Powers or Principalities--or perhaps even the prophets! But he'd chosen a vulgar commoner. A mere Archangel. A member of the class almost at the bottom of the celestial hierarchy. And all because Himself wanted someone who could share his interest in sports!

"When He turns off His omniscience and foreknowledge, Satan and his agents plot His overthrow!"

"So what if they conspire, Jeremiah! They are powerless. As soon as he restores his omniscience he sees what's afoot and stops it."

"But they only plot when he's watching sports. When he turns his powers back on they grovel and slither about in Hell as though nothing has changed. Heed me well. Satan is conspiring with malcontents among us to mount a revolution. You're are such a blind fool, Michael."

Michael ignored the insult. Poor old Jeremiah. His gradual decline to a prophet of no consequence had made him bitter and vituperative. He had no evidence to back his allegation, only his "prophetic vision." Conspiracy? Revolt? Impossible! The archangel had unshakable faith in the Almighty's foreknowledge and omnipotence. He turned away without responding--effrontery which left Jeremiah twitching with anger--and returned to the oval viewing port. The Almighty smiled his smile of supreme radiance and held out his hand. "Patriots blocked the kick. Cross my palm with Jasper, please."

Colonel Bradford Stuckey, a proud son of The South, had the flat-ab physique of the Green Beret and CIA operative he had been in life. His high cheekbones and brush-cut hair spoke of stern idealism and steely resolve. He wore the sleeves of his camouflage fatigues folded up to regulation width above his biceps. Damned if he'd be seen in a gauzy pansy tunic!

Right now, he was engaged in his favorite activity: shooting. Swinging the shotgun smoothly, leading his target by just the right amount, he fired. The artificial cherub blew apart, showering down virtual feathers and bits of latex. It would be a damn sight better to shoot real cherubs, he thought bitterly. When he first arrived in Heaven, he had treated those fat little sybarites as his skeet-shooting targets. The pellets passed through their etheric bodies harmlessly, but startled the little crybabies into squealing and tumbling in uncontrollable loop-the-loops, a consequence that tickled Stuckey immensely. But now that pleasure was denied him. The cherubs had appealed to the Almighty and shooting them was now prohibited. Stuckey had to be satisfied with firing at artificial cherubs made by former Taiwanese shoe makers. Because of differences between eastern and western systems of measurement, however, they could not be relied upon to adhere strictly to cherub blueprints drawn up by Stuckey and one of his Army engineers.

"Last one, Colonel," Sergeant Lester Mooch called as he loaded the cherub-launching device.

"Pull!" Stuckey barked.

The launched cherub pinwheeled and slid into an erratic dive, the result of one wing being larger than the other. Stuckey quickly fired one barrel, then the next, and missed both times. He was so absorbed in cursing Taiwanese workmanship he didn't hear the velvety sound of cherub wings behind him until it was too late. Three of the vengeful little creatures hit him squarely with an exploding barrage of methane-filled souvenir balloons from Hell that left him gagging.

Stuckey hurled his shotgun after the departing cherubs, screaming vows to be revenged in the most savage terms.

Sergeant Mooch waited until Stuckey's wrath spent itself, then said: "Time to be going, Colonel. Here's your camo." Mooch helped him into a white burnoose, grunting sympathetically as Stuckey grumbled about wearing "goddamn towelhead rags." Stuckey was equally unhappy when Mooch pressed a sticky black beard onto his face. But the disguise was effective. In the flowing burnoose with its hood shadowing his bearded face, Stuckey looked like a holy ascetic just back from fasting in the desert.

Mooch then changed into his disguise; a multi-colored jester's outfit with sawtooth collar piece and a droopy pointed hat tipped with a bell by Gucci. Mooch liked to dress up in saucy clothes. His one regret about joining the Army was that he no longer dared to wear his jester's costume to parties.

It took Stuckey and his sergeant only minutes to teleport themselves to the Central Administration Building in the center of Heaven's capitol, the Golden City. They strolled casually through its white-marbled lobby, attracting no curious glances from passers by, most of whom were members of the Heavenly Administrative Staff. Stuckey and Mooch pretended to chat and not to notice they had paused in front of an elevator marked "For Use By Executive Staff Only." The Colonel waited until they were alone, then stepped with Mooch through the elevator doors. Had he been on official business as Head of Security, Brad Stuckey would not have cared who saw him enter the elevator to Hell. He would have filed a post-visit report which legitimized his trip. But this was not a legitimate trip and there would be no report to account for it.

"How are we doing for time?' he asked.

Mooch looked at his watch. "Should still be the first quarter.

Last I heard, Cleveland was leading Detroit by a field goal."

Stuckey dismissed the score with an exasperated swipe of his hand. He had more important things to think about.

The elevator carried them swiftly down through Chaos. Stuckey could have made the trip without the elevator. An amulet on a chain around his neck--an amulet worn only by high officials-- protected him and any one he brought along, but the elevator was faster. Time was critical.

Hell had changed over the last 500 years. The change began when the Heavenly Oversight Committee finally came to the view that Hell's brutish and ugly nature did not reflect favorably on its benevolent creator; and so, little by little, conditions in Hell had been mitigated. Rivers of molten lava had been replaced by rivers of virtual sewage sludge. The ubiquitous flames that once filled the region's air with a stinky haze were now clean-burning flames fueled by methane gas-eaters. These devices worked benignly with one exception. The collegiate pranksters on the Heavenly Oversight Committee had designed them to ignite the passed gas of anyone close to them. Thus an individual who thought he was discretely breaking wind was startled and mortified by emitting instead an explosive flash of blue flame.

The damned no longer writhed in perpetual torment: they suffered in daily shifts of 8 hours on, 16 hours off. Other concessions gave each individual the right to 3 hours of air conditioning per day, a college education, and virtual sex.

Satan's palace, Pandemonium, sat on Hell's highest hill overlooking the flame-licked expanse that stretched to the horizon and seethed with wailing souls more numerous than all the grains of sand in the world.

The original Pandemonium was a gothic castle, but as eons rolled by it underwent modifications that turned it into an architectural mishmash: a little Greco-Roman here, some Bauhaus there, a bit of early Rococo in the architraves, and in the fissured walls dark with dripping moss, a large dose of House of Usher. The forlorn aspect of the Palace was accented by weeping willow trees that trailed their lugubrious branches in a scummy green moat. The upper portion of Pandemonium presented a confusion of Disneyworld towers and turrets, cleverly foreshortened to deceive the eye and signify (the Oversight Committee believed) the deceitfulness to be found within Satan's palace.

The latest modification, designed by Rube Goldberg, had changed the front entrance. Reserved strictly for the arriving damned (the *nuevos*), the front entrance was a geodesic dome with a hidden trap door. A few steps into the dome put the visitor over the door, which suddenly gave way, dropping the startled soul into a bumper car. A giant vacuum cleaner sucked the bumper car up an all-glass elevator shaft and spit it into a downward spiraling tunnel, at the end of which the dizzy visitor collided with a huge gong. The vibrations of the gong teased a thread loop off a trigger that released a hammer, which struck a button that lighted a sign at the reception desk: *Incoming*. Thus alerted, the desk clerk ran to the mouth of the chute through which the arriving visitor, now decanted from the bumper car, was traveling at rocket speed. The clerk's job was to catch the visitor as he shot out the chute. Feeling it quite proper to have a little fun at the expense of the damned, the Oversight Committee manned the reception desk with uncoordinated individuals who sometimes missed the catch, in which case the visitor arrowed head-first into a giant archery target.

Those who suffered this novel entrance protested it was humiliating. They demanded to know the reason for it, but they were, after all, the damned, with no right to demand anything. Initial investigations by a rather bored Grievance Committee lasted a century but turned up no logical reason for it. Another committee was appointed to continue the investigation. That committee, now celebrating its second century, was still formulating its report.

A handsome young man in a gray Armani suit met Colonel

Stuckey and Mooch as they emerged from the elevator in a mahogany paneled lobby of Pandemonium. He had the condescending manner of an assistant to an important man, making inane small talk as though he were performing a task beneath his dignity. The young man led them down the pillared gallery of an inner courtyard to the Grand Council Room. He pointed to their designated seats among five individuals clustered at the far end of an immense black marble table.

Stuckey had been here once before, but the room still dazzled him. The vaulted ceiling was worthy of a Renaissance palace, with gilt coffered paintings of muscular young men entreating voluptuous women in gauzy peignoirs that revealed their tiny pink nipples. The women were mostly in postures in incipient flight but their faces, flushed with yearning, were turned toward the men. They reminded Stuckey of painful experiences with girls in his teenage years: so near and yet so far.

Lining the walls were huge murals swirling with gold astrological symbols against a powder blue background. The mammoth double doors at each end of the hall were painted in glistening red lacquer with black trim. Over either end of the table a grand tiered chandelier glittered with thousands of crystal pendants. Exuberant flames danced in torches positioned at regular intervals along the walls.

Lucifer entered through an ornately carved door behind the red velvet throne at the head of the table. He did not have horns and a tail, or a red cape, or a triton. He wore shiny black loafers, dark pants, and a black turtleneck sweater. Erect and deliberate in his movements, he seated himself with regal dignity and gestured to servants to close the hall doors and leave. He was remarkably handsome. Stuckey had expected him to have the bestial features of a gargoyle or a face hideous with the ravages of foul diseases. On the contrary, Satan looked like a middle-age fashion model. Slim and just above average height. The face perfectly proportioned. Slightly protruding brow line, high intelligent forehead, well defined cheekbones that set off the flat planes of the lower face. His full head

23

of gleaming black hair, which he combed straight back, receded slightly on either side of the forelock. A neatly trimmed beard and mustache added a touch of sexy maturity.

It seemed incredible to Stuckey that a being this elegant could be the reviled ruler of Hell. Nor did Satan seem sufficiently mighty and awful to lead a plot to overthrow God. But such was the case.

"Thank you for being so prompt, gentlemen. The second half is about to begin, so we must go directly to the business at hand," he said.

Of the five others at the table, Stuckey knew the identity of only one: Shapiro, Satan's lieutenant and public relations director. The other four were disguised.

The Devil listened intently as each gave a brief report on the progress of his part in the plot. There were some problems to overcome: finding enough operatives who could be trusted, laying the political groundwork for the coup, concealing the construction of certain equipment. First and foremost, at the moment, were concerns about security. There had been a breach, an accidental one it appeared, but one that could not be ignored. Security was Stuckey's responsibility.

"You are sure this individual found our secret site by accident?" Lucifer asked Stuckey.

"Absolutely. He was one of those damned astral travelers who show up now and then. He was being a tourist, visiting sites willy-nilly, and he happened to pick this site number at random. He was only there a few minutes before we picked him up. I'm sure he hadn't the slightest idea what he was seeing."

"You have neutralized him?"

"Oh, yes. There is not even a 'body' to be found," Stuckey said, smiling at the thought of his clever handiwork.

"But now there is a second one," said the one disguised as a beggar.

"Yes, we know. That may be a coincidence. But we'll find out and take appropriate action."

The meeting turned to other concerns, the last of which was a secret password by which they might identify themselves to each other and their allies. No one suggestion won unanimous approval, so they compromised by composing a password of a few letters from each of the suggestions. The result was: *Farsididdyfasgatagee*. They congratulated themselves that it was democratic, memorable, and so meaningless it could not reveal their plot.

"Yeah, but how you gonna work that into a conversation?" Mooch. whispered to Stuckey. The Colonel was about to bring this to the attention of the group when Lucifer adjourned the meeting. The fourth quarter was almost over. They had to disband and resume their innocent or tormented ways before the Almighty turned his Omniscience back on.

"Spielmacher. Sure, I remember Spielmacher," Conklin said. "Short guy. Bald on top. Right?"

Duffy nodded.

"What a coincidence. I escort him, then you," Bruno said. "If you two had better timing, I could have brought you both here at the same time and then you wouldn't have to go looking for him...but then we wouldn't have any detecting to do, would we?"

"So you don't know where he is?"

"Sorry. We don't," Conklin said. "We made the same pitch to him that we made to you. He wasn't interested. Said he was through being a detective. He had other plans. So we removed the 'tag' and he went on his way. That's the last time we saw him."

"I don't suppose you know what those plans were."

"To be honest, I wasn't paying that much attention. He did mumble something, though. Did you catch it Bruno?"

"I only heard part of it, and that didn't make sense. It was something about trying to break his leg. A little off, is he? "

Roscoe shrugged and tilted his head in a gesture that sandwiched the possible meaning "I don't know" with "It's nothing, just a small eccentricity." He had the feeling he knew what the leg business meant but couldn't yet put his finger on it.

Conklin pushed his chair back and swung his feet up on the desk. "Okay. You're the detective. What do we do now?"

Roscoe felt a prickly surge of excitement. He had always wanted to be in charge. It occurred to him he ought to have a hallmark. Nero Wolf had his orchids, Spenser his reps and recipes, Columbo his cigar. The only possibility Roscoe could come up with at the moment was a toothpick. Maybe roll it from one side of his mouth the other? Would this be a clever signature habit? But once again indecisiveness assailed him. Was a toothpick manly enough? Was it simply too crude? Was it laughable? He decided to put the toothpick decision on hold.

"Put out an APB. Maybe someone reported a bewildered traveler. Not likely, but might as well cover all the bases," Roscoe said.

"Myrtle will love that," Bruno said.

Conklin explained: "He's being sarcastic. Myrtle's the sole operator of our central telephone service. She will have a fit when we tell her to contact all those other police units. They all have different telephone technologies. We'd probably be better off with carrier pigeons--and more secure."

Be patient, Roscoe told himself. Half a loaf is better than none. The APB would at least set these cops in motion.

"For now, get every man out there asking questions."

"Oof! You know how big Heaven is? We could spend two eternities interrogating just a few people at the countless sites. We need some kind of lead. Some direction to go in," Conklin said.

"Might be a good idea for Roscoe and me to start at the Eye in the Sky," Bruno said. " Maybe they tracked him for a little while after he got here. They've been doing that more often since Stuckey took over Security," Bruno said.

Conklin agreed that was a good idea. Meanwhile, he would send the men out.

The Eye in the Sky Bureau (*EITSB*)was in the largest building complex in Heaven. Inspired by the surveillance system at a gambling casino, it tracked the lives of people on earth, recording their good deeds and bad deeds. Originally, this was St. Peter's job, but as the world population grew, surveillance and the judgment process became too great for him, so *EITSB* was created.

At the reception desk, Bruno got directions to the department that might have followed Benny. He and Roscoe set out with a map, traveling down long corridors, branching off into other corridors, rising a level, descending two floors, moving from one building to another. As they passed open office doors, Roscoe saw white-robed individuals sitting on stools around small tables. Each observer was equipped with a downward-pointing telescope that penetrated the floor. Some of the watchers were peering intently into their scopes; others were writing things in notebooks. He flushed with shame at the thought that someone had seen and recorded things he had done that he now wished he hadn't done.

"Here we are," Bruno said. He had pulled up in front of a door marked "S Department." They entered a small reception room lined with tubular plastic chairs and round tables layered with magazines printed in Heaven. "Herald Angels Recount Five Biggest Announcements," read a headline on one. "Pagan Gods Hold Thunderbolt Tournament," read another. "Cronos Eats Another Child," blared a third. Yet another, "Preparations Underway for Annual Masque," especially intrigued Roscoe. He didn't know what a masque was, but it sounded something like a Mardi Gras.

At the rear was a desk with a secretary, and behind her, an office door marked "Manager."

"Oh, it's way cool to see you, gentlemen," the secretary said in high nasal tones. She was a pretty blond with frizzy hair and harlequin eyeglass frames. She chewed open-mouthed on a wad of bubblegum. "You're almost the first people to come here in a week. It is *so* not fun to sit here with nothing to do!" She followed this with a rapid series of bubblegum snaps that left a tiny smear of pink gum on her upper lip. Roscoe felt sorry for her. In life she had been a dimwit child of the supermarket magazine culture. Death had not improved her. "I hope you have an interesting request," she said with a coquettish flutter of her eyelashes.

Roscoe tried to think of snappy comeback, the kind Spenser would make. He couldn't think of one.

"My request is a hard one, sweetheart, but it may not be the one you had in mind," Bruno said with a lecherous wink. The girl giggled.

Amazing that an angel with no genitals can whip off a risqué quip like that!

The door to the manager's office opened. The secretary straightened in her chair and put on a serious face. "What do these gentlemen want, Darlene," the manager said. He was short and tubby, a human beach ball. He held his trousers well above his bulging stomach with a pair of wide blue suspenders. His pudgy arms dangled slightly away from his sides because the armpits of his suit jacket were too tight.

"We'd like to talk to the watcher who has been covering Benjamin Spielmacher," Roscoe said.

The manager's eyes narrowed for a moment in what could have been annoyance or alarm.

"That is not permitted."

"This is official police business," Bruno said.

"There is a new regulation. No one can speak to a watcher unless he is cleared by Colonel Stuckey. And to be cleared by the Colonel you have to submit the proper paperwork...."

Darlene frowned and seemed about to speak. Her boss shot her a tight-lipped glance which cut her off.

"Unfortunately, we happen to be out of the correct forms at the moment. Come back in a month and we may have them, if the Supplies Unit gets around to it."

Darlene apparently forgot the silent warning of moments before and started to speak: "But Mr.Cudworthy, I don't...."

Cudworthy exploded. This gum-chewing airhead in rhinestone glasses was more than he could bear, especially now.

"Shut up, you nit-wit!" he said. Tomorrow he would insist that Personnel replace her.

He tugged vigorously at his suit jacket as though his outburst had caused it to slip uncomfortably out of place.

"Goodbye, gentlemen. I have to attend a meeting."

With that he waddled through the front door.

Darlene began to cry. "He's so mean to me," she sobbed. "In Heaven we're always supposed to tell the truth, isn't that so?"

Roscoe put his arm around her. "Absolutely, sweetheart. Nothing but the truth." He gave her his handkerchief to blot her tears.

"But every time I tell him the truth, he gets mad at me... I tell him his breath is bad, he gets mad...I tell him he's too fat, he gets mad...I tell him he farts so loud in his office people can hear him--he gets mad. And he was furious when I told him he'd never get laid with that huge belly of his."

Roscoe consoled her with a light finger rub across her shoulders. He leaned close to her ear and whispered: "And what truth were you about to speak when he told you to shut up?"

"I won't get in trouble if I tell you?"

"You have my word. After all, you are simply telling the truth."

And the truth that came from Darlene was that there was no new regulation requiring investigators to get Colonel Stuckey's approval. Not that she knew of. Stuckey had been here just yesterday and spent an hour in Cudworthy's office. If the Colonel had established the regulation Cudworthy claimed he had, she would be the first to hear of it.

With gentle prompting from Roscoe, Darlene saw the implication of what she had said. There was no reason why the two detectives could not talk to the watcher of Benny Spielmacher. She went to her Rolodex. The person they should see was Rose Trautman in Section D, Corridor F, Room 7, Table 3, Telescope 8.

As for Roger Cudworthy, after leaving the three in his reception room he slipped into an empty office down the hall and closed the door. Then he picked up the telephone.

Rose Trautman was not beautiful. Her black hair hung straight down, cut in a bang across her forehead and clipped to a curtain edge at shoulder level. The striking feature of her face was not her eyes, which were brown and quite ordinary, but a short turtle nose turned up so sharply one stared almost directly into her nostrils. There was a hint of too much testosterone in the black eyebrows that came together almost seamlessly just above her nose, and her upper lip bore a large a brown mole with several bristles. The rest of her body was concealed beneath her white robe, but it was apparent that she was thin and quite flat-chested.

Yet to Roscoe, the total effect of her odd features was an exotic kind of beauty that aroused him. It was the kind of beauty he saw in Myrna Klotksy, his first crush, when they were in junior high school; but with Myrna that beauty lasted only for a youthful moment. When she reached high school, she began the transformation into a fat, coarse-featured woman who would eventually marry a butcher.

But in Rose, who was dead, the exotic beauty he saw was fixed forever. Roscoe found it difficult to concentrate on questioning her. His eyes wandered hungrily from her lips, to her small ear, to the dark orbs that were her nostrils. He felt a rush of sexual excitement he hadn't felt in a long time.

They had moved away from her colleagues, into an empty staff lounge.

"You understand I can't reveal anything I observed about him before he got here," she said. "That is against the rules."

"We just want to know if you tracked him after he got here," Bruno said.

She looked a little puzzled. "Well, I did. We don't normally track people after they get here, but Colonel Stuckey has ordered us to track any newcomers who wander about. Benny was one of those. But it's all in the report I gave Stuckey. You could get it from him. Why come to me?"

"To be honest, he doesn't like to share information, especially not with peons like us," Roscoe said. "It is easier to get it from you, and maybe even help you remember a few more details that might help us."

She inclined her head to one side, considering this. Her eyes narrowed and moved to one side as though she found something troubling. Then she straightened up.

"Okay. But there's not that much I can tell you. After he left your police station he wandered about a bit. Just seemed curious. He visited the *Plains of Recreation,* then *Eccentrics Corner.* From there he went to the *Pasture of the Pagan Gods and Heroes* and finally to *Showtime in Heaven."*

"Why 'finally' to *Showtime in Heaven* ? " Roscoe asked.

"Because after he left there I lost him. The surveillance tape ran out and by the time I got a new one in, he had gone and I couldn't locate him."

"You have Benny on film?"

"Oh, yes. See, each watcher tracks and films three people. Since you can only *watch* one at a time as you film him, the other cameras continue to record the lives of the other two."

Bruno explained: "This way there's a complete film of each person's life as backup for the written summary the watcher submits when you die."

"Can we see the tape of Benny at *Showtime in Heaven?*" Roscoe said.

She lowered her eyes. "I gave it to Colonel Stuckey."

"Can you recall what was on the *Showtime* tape?"

"Sorry, no. I was watching one of my other people when Benny was there. I didn't look at his tape before I gave it to Stuckey."

"Damn!"

Rose frowned, something turning in her mind. Then she said.

"I'm sorry, too, that I gave him the tape. I don't know why, but I don't trust him."

She looked Roscoe straight in the eye for a long second and he sensed she was on his side. Then she smiled at him in a way that he felt was definitely intimate and inviting. He almost wanted to forget about searching for Benny.

But it was time to leave. "Don't tell Cudworthy we talked to you," was all he could think of to say.

As they were leaving *EITSB*, Roscoe said to Bruno: "By the way, Benny's visit to *Showtime* explains his 'broken leg' remark. 'Break a leg' is a show business term meaning 'good luck.' It was his offhand way of saying he was going to check out the theatrical possibilities up here."

Bruno was impressed. "I guess you're not so dumb after all."

Sergeant Mooch and Stuckey had viewed Benny's tape to see if they could learn anything more about the traveler they had already neutralized. They found nothing useful. But now, with his boss out of the office, Mooch ran it again.

There was the short, pudgy figure of Benny in his blue nylon warm up jacket and ridiculous plaid pants walking through the arched gate of the *Showtime in Heaven* lot. Benny paused several times to watch actors in costume pass by. He apparently saw some deceased stars he admired, because on two occasions he uttered an exuberant "yes" and started toward them, but they disappeared into doorways before he could catch them.

Mooch wasn't interested in Benny's wanderings among the studio buildings. He fast-forwarded to the part he really wanted to see, which was Benny's conversation with Lance Petard, the head of *Showtime in Heaven* productions. Petard was the reason Mooch was rerunning the tape. Petard caused delicious shivers to tickle the sergeant's scrotum.

Lance Petard was hardly the military type. A slight figure in form-fitting beige slacks and a white silk shirt open almost to his navel, he walked like a female model, one foot crossing over the other as he advanced, so that his hips swayed and his tight buns smooched each other in a tantalizing way. Mooch especially loved the way Petard was given to exaggerated facial expressions and dramatic movements of his head and hands, even when he was saying the most ordinary things.

"So here's the thing," Benny was saying. "We make a musical of *Paradise Lost*. Is that perfect or what! Where could you find a better story for the audience up here! And we don't have to include a lot of the boring stuff, like the fancy poetry you can't understand, and the lists of old timers with funny names you couldn't care less about."

Lance pressed his delicate hands together and hugged them to his chin. "Oh, that is absolutely *divine*. Imagine the *thunder* and *lightning*...oh yes!...and imagine thousands angels with flaming swords doing dance extravaganzas up and down a white staircase with a hundred steps...eat your *heart* out Busby Berkeley!"

"And Satan in Hell," Benny said, "Can you picture him in a red cape and a goofy mask belting out a big song like that guy in *Phantom of the Opera*...and bleachers full of the damned in rags, waving tattered flags back and forth, singing about revolution and freedom. Can you picture that, or what!"

"How *absolutely* de-lish-ous!"

"Tell you who I see as God," Benny said. "Lionel Barrymore ...without the Dr. Kildare wheelchair, of course. What do you think?"

"Wonderful concept, dear boy. But Lionel can't *sing*."

"No problem. We'll have him lip synch to Paul Robeson's voice."

"And Eve. Who do you see as Eve? Perhaps someone throaty and butchy like Marlene Dietrich...."

"Hell, no. We need big tits and super sexiness, like Marilyn Monroe or Jane Mansfield. You gotta make the audience understand that Eve was such a hotsky totsky Adam's pecker made him do what God told him not to do. He couldn't help himself."

"Of course, yes."

"And she also has to be blond," Benny continued, "because the audience has to think, *of course,* only a dumb blond would fall

33

for that bullshit from the snake. But we still make her sympathetic with a big song...something along the lines of 'Why was I blond? Why am I living?'...and so forth. She's never gonna get the answer, of course--because then she wouldn't be a dumb blond--but the audience feels for her. Are you with me, Lance baby?"

Petard clapped his hands in delight. Mooch loved the way he did that.

Benny was on a roll. "Okay, now here's the deal with Adam. He's gotta be a sorry schmuck. Here he is ruined by his pecker, is saddled with a dumb blond for a mate, and is forced to go to work. We know how down he feels because he sings country western songs about trains and prisons and cheating women. Never mind the songs have nothing to with his situation--the audience will get the idea. And we drive his wretchedness home by having him played by an actor whose face is his soul. Who would you pick?"

"How about Lon Cheney Jr., the guy who kept turning into a werewolf...talk about a *sad* face. He would be fab-u-lous..."

"Right on, babe. And then we'll..."

"Mooch, turn that thing off. We've got work to do." Mooch had not heard the Colonel enter the office. Stuckey dropped into his desk chair with a grunt. He looked out the window for a moment, thinking, drumming his fingers on his khaki desk blotter.

"This new traveler is a Roscoe Duffy," he said at last. "He's here to find Benny Spielmacher. Conklin doesn't know enough that would help him. But Duffy just went to EITSB looking for leads. Cudworthy put him off," Stuckey said.

"So he doesn't have much to go on."

"Not yet, but I don't want him nosing around. Neutralize him. You'll have to catch him when he's not protected by that angel from Conklin's outfit."

"Okay, Colonel, but there's some bad news. Professor MacLaren has disappeared. Taken off. We haven't found him yet."

"Shit!"

"Maybe we should concentrate on finding the professor before we grab Duffy."

"Hell, no. Get them both. We'll catch the professor. I'll make that little Scots prick wish he never crossed me!"

Satan's Lieutenant and Public Relations Director, Max Shapiro, rested an elbow on the corner of the black marble table in the Grand Council Room. He was alone with Satan, who sat on his red velvet throne. As Shapiro spoke, his free hand made small circles in the air as though it were a flywheel that kept his thoughts flowing and made them comprehensible.

"Okay, so we assume the coup succeeds," Shapiro said. "That's only half the battle. Then you got to persuade everybody else to go along with you as kingpin. That won't be easy."

"So where do we begin?"

"First off, you don't want to be called Satan anymore, or the Devil, or even Lucifer. Those names will never lose their evil connotations. So when you begin your first address after the coup, you open your arms to them and say as humbly as you can, "Please, my friends, just call me Bob."

"That's it? No last name? Just Bob?"

"Just Bob. You don't want to give them a last name, because no matter what it is, it can be twisted and uttered in scorn. But not so with "Bob." It's spelled the same way backwards and forwards, and no matter how you try to change the accent or pronunciation, it comes out the same. I mean if someone said "Bob" derisively, it would sound pretty much like "Bob" spoken with any other sentiment."

"I don't quite see the point of this."

"Ratings. You've got to maintain high ratings. If the pollsters can't tell what people mean when they say "Bob," they can never come in with negative numbers that stick. One of our talking heads will say, yes, but the pronunciations you count as negatives we count as positives."

"This is getting pretty devious, even for the Devil's

lieutenant."

"Look, you know even better than I that it's crucial to maintain popular support, or at least the appearance of it. It is lack of popular support that's going to topple this Almighty. He has pissed off too many constituencies, and his bad ratings are persuading even those not among the pissed that something is wrong and it's time for a change."

This indeed was the situation emboldening Satan to mount a second rebellion. Individual malcontents from disaffected groups had sounded him out on the possibility of a coup and he had solemnly sworn to lead them and to win! He had means they didn't have--the battle hardened legions of the fallen angels, plus unlimited reserves of the damned who could be drafted whether they liked it or not. Given assistance in key areas by the traitors in Heaven, he could infiltrate his forces and carry the day! There were problems yet to solve, but the campaign had every prospect of success. What worried Lucifer was the aftermath, when he ascended to the Throne of Heaven. He was joining forces with three malcontent factions, and keeping them happy would be difficult.

One faction was the pagan gods. Not all of them, of course. Some were content to reside in the far corner of Heaven reserved for them, drinking ambrosia; stealing each others' wives; fathering half-serpents and ogres; working enchantments on enemies, relatives and former friends. A few continued to revel in perversity or decadence. Cronus still ate one of his children now and then, only to vomit it up later on. Bacchus remained the center of colossal orgies of wine, women and song. Mercury, for all his other praiseworthy habits, had grown fonder of thieving. A handful of gods still delighted in metamorphosing into swans and other animals and raping mortal women to see what they could clone. The results of these unions were a mixed bag. The violated women gave birth to prodigies of beauty, wisdom and athletic prowess just as often as they did tyrants, madmen and deadly aquatic mutants. Among notable offspring of god-human couplings in recent years were, on the positive side, a .325 major leaguer hitter and two All-Pro wide receivers, and on the negative side, several rock musicians who jumped like kangaroos as they played; the inventor of telemarketing; and a thimblewit who became President of United States. Rightly or wrongly, many disappointing results of the couplings were thought to be the work of the toothless god, Dentus, who was besotted with redneck women.

But other pagan gods were disgruntled with their lot. The conspirator disguised as a beggar put their case to Lucifer:

"We once were the mighty rulers of the earth, the sea, the air and the heavens. Men dedicated groves and temples and altars to us, and worshipped us with sacrifices and prayers. And look at us now! Our former powers have been taken from us. We are shunned by the mainstream residents of Heaven and made to live in a distant place among goats in cold mountain tops! We are viewed as savages with only enough wit to carouse, intrigue against each other, and play with lightening bolts!"

"What specifically do you want to gain by revolting?" Lucifer said. Best to come to the point directly, he thought, or this rustic would bend his ear for hours.

"Revenge upon the Almighty for stealing our powers and keeping us isolated in the boondocks! And majesty--a return to our former majesty. We want to show ourselves to men, so they will once again believe in us, and dedicate altars and temples to us, and offer up sacrifices of goats and sheep and the occasional virgin."

Lucifer felt a small burble of heartburn at the thought of trying to keep these bumpkins happy. But he needed their help in the coup. He stroked his pointed beard, as though earnestly pondering the beggar's proposition.

At length he said: "I shouldn't set my heart on sacrifices of virgins. They're an endangered species. Sacrifice one of those, and the Department of Environmental Protection would have your priest's ass in a wringer. And goats and sheep are doubtful. The penalties for wantonly killing animals are worse than those for bilking your company's investors of millions."

"Then what's the best we could hope for?"

"Maybe a little chicken blood."

The beggar looked glum. "But at least in a place of splendid marble monuments and temple-like memorials?" he said with faint hope in his voice. "Like Washington, D.C.?"

Satan shook his head. "More likely a storefront church in the Bronx, or maybe South Central Los Angeles."

The beggar's shoulders sagged. "My associates won't like this." He shook his head woefully. "This could be very, very bad." What he meant was the greater gods were notoriously irascible and capricious; they might respond to this bad news by changing him into serpent, or chaining him to a rock so an eagle could peck out pieces of his liver every day forever.

Lucifer, however, took the beggar's distress as weakening resolve to remain in the conspiracy.

"Cheer up," he said. "We'll find some way to make you gods glorious again."

As he said this, he had no idea what that way might be. But then a small thought took root in the back of his mind. Maybe he could give them dominion over the Panama Canal. Nobody gave a shit about that anymore.

A second faction, the one Satan liked least, was what he privately called the Army of the Addled Righteous. They were a secret brotherhood of malcontents from the fundamentalist ranks of all the world's religions. The two representatives who first approached Satan happened to be Americans.

"It's absolutely intolerable the way He is slacking off!" said the heavyset one in the blue silk suit and vest. His abundant brown hair, glistening with gel, rose up like a cresting wave and flowed back slickly over the top and sides of his head. A black silk eye mask hid his identity.

"His policies up here make a mockery of our ministries. Of the sinning we tried to prevent. Of the hellfire sermons, the shouting, the jumping, the speaking in tongues, the snake handling...all the ways we preachers tried to keep men from falling into your clutches. All of it, mocked! Made to seem ridiculous!"

"Amen, brother," said his cohort. He was a small man in a black suit, too thin to fill his collar and cuffs. He carried a bible. A black paper eye mask hid his identity.

"We threatened our flocks with damnation for committing sins of the flesh. We wrestled mightily with those temptations ourselves, mortifying our bodies, denying ourselves all pleasures of the world, getting arthritis from hours of prayer on cold wooden kneelers. For what?"

"Say on brother. Say on!"

"He winks at fornication. It is rampant up here and even carried on in public! Adultery is not punished, nor is masturbation. This should not be!"

"Amen."

"There are prostitutes walking the streets of Heaven. Impossible! And money, money, money. Mammon reigns. There are murderers and thieves and despots up here because they bought their way in."

"Amen."

"This God of the New Testament has betrayed us. He has broken his promise to punish the wicked and reward the virtuous. And every day He degrades Heaven further by making more concessions to the whiners and demanders of 'rights.' Now we have a place in Heaven for pets and endangered species! We have game shows! And the latest insanity, thanks to the whining of the motorheads, is a Celestial Automobile Junkyard. Now even dead vehicles share the rewards of Heaven with the righteous!"

"I hear what you're saying," Lucifer said, utterly bored.

He continued:"I have not prayed for guidance, because He would *never* advise me to *replace* Him. But I have searched my heart and decided that is exactly what must be done. And *you,* sir, are the one to replace Him!"

This pleased Lucifer immensely. Yet he could not ignore the tremendous irony of churchmen wanting to replace God with the Devil.

"I am flattered, sir. But you can understand my wonder at

your decision to make me God's replacement. How do you and your colleagues justify this extraordinary change in your regard for me?"

It will indeed be a painful turnabout to swing foursquare behind you, the preacher said; but he and his fellow conspirators were following precedents in religious history, wherein otherwise objectionable acts by religious leaders were condoned as matters of Holy Expediency.

"And so we put the case thus: Provided you will do what we ask, we *must* support you, Lucifer, because you are our *only* hope of sending the wicked in Heaven to Hell. By supporting you, beast though you have been, we also right a great wrong. The sinners in Heaven, rightfully yours, were stolen from you. As the ruler still of Hell, you will reclaim them and hurl them into the fiery pit they should have been sent to in the first place. And as the new ruler of Heaven, who has restored the old rules of sin and punishment, you are just, and we can only applaud the fairness of your doing this. You will also rescind all those stupid concessions the Almighty has made to the spoiled newcomers in recent years."

"And don't forget to replenish the virgins in Paradise. Some of the Muslim martyrs are complaining they are not getting all they were promised," squeaked the Amen-sayer.

"Do you accept our terms?"

Lucifer saw the Preacher's case was clever, but not without a contradiction.

"I assume you will continue to denounce Satan," he said.

"Absolutely. With renewed dedication," the Preacher answered.

"And still praise God...."

"Most assuredly."

"Yea verily," chirped the Amen-sayer.

"Then you will wind up denouncing and praising the same person," Lucifer said. "A problem?"

"Oh that." The preacher chuckled. "No problem at all. We do the aspect thing so popular in Eastern religions. At the highest spiritual level, opposites are merely aspects of a single entity--your yin-yang concept. So it is that God and the Devil are opposing aspects of a single deity. Thus you can praise God without praising Satan, and denounce Satan without denouncing God. No problem at all!"

A rather simple-minded resolution of a paradox, Satan thought, but one that would satisfy the vast majority of men. It struck him anew that religious pontificators like this preacher came uncomfortably close to being his equal in sophistry and deception. He wasn't sure, either, that he liked the idea of being praised one minute and denounced the next. Among other things, it would make it hard to decide what to wear each day--something splendiferous with godlike refulgence, or some kind of Elton John costume so outrageous it cried out to be reviled.

Nevertheless, Lucifer shook the preacher's hand.

"I accept your terms."

"Thank God," the preacher said.

"Let's hope He didn't hear you say that," piped the frail man in black.

Anger did not motivate all the conspirators. A third faction, a group within the Nation of Elders, were fearful the Almighty was losing his grip in ways that could be catastrophic.

The old man speaking for the Elder faction smelled of frankincense and myrrh. He wore a robe of coarse brown fabric and a multicolored headpiece made of three cloth tubes coiled one upon the other. The lower half of his face was hidden by a white scarf. He and Lucifer sat on one of Pandemonium's balconies that commanded a panoramic view of the flickering fires of Hell.

Lucifer poured tea into a glass for the old man.

"Sugar?"

"No."

"Did you have a pleasant trip down here?"

"The elevator ride gave me gas. I'm afraid my flatulence startled the young man who led me here."

"You mean, of course, when blue flames shot out your ass. Unfortunate. It's those damned methane eaters. You must have

41

stood too close to one. I hope you didn't singe your robe. Let's have a look."

The old man stood and turned around. There was a plate-size black spot on the fabric covering his buttocks.

"Oh well, a virtual washing will take care of that," Lucifer said. The old man sat down. He gazed into his glass of tea for several moments. He began to speak slowly, not lifting his eyes from the glass.

"This is very difficult for us to do. Most of us have been with Him almost from the beginning. We have been his prophets, his exemplars, his steadfast messengers. I myself knew Him when he was a burning bush."

Satan poured more tea into the Elder's glass.

"I never thought it possible He would age, but He has. He is getting forgetful and irascible. The other day He asked whether Abraham had sacrificed Isaac as He had commanded. When we told Him he'd canceled that order thousands of years ago, he got angry and said he'd never canceled the order. Another time he started fuming about something or other taking place on earth and threatened to wipe out humanity with a huge flood. When we told him he'd already done that, He stamped his foot his so hard He put a crack in Heaven's Mount Olympus. 'Don't you pissants tell me what I have done and haven't done!' He roared.

"More than once we have kept him from repeating punishments He's already inflicted on mortals. Plagues, boils, the pillar of salt. You should have heard Him rage when we told him he'd already done the locust thing.

'Did not!' he bellowed.

'Did so!' we insisted.

'Did not!'

'Did so!' The dangerous thing is that almost all of his punishments are outdated and won't work anymore. Mortals now have weather forecasting, flood controls, antibiotics, fire departments, hybrid seeds and insecticides. If he tries to impose the old punishments and sees they won't work, His colossal anger could lead Him to devise new, more terrible punishments that could threaten even us. He's becoming more unpredictable every day. It is not inconceivable that if he spins out of control he might accidentally blow up Heaven."

"That is certainly a new Big Bang theory!" Lucifer said. He waited for the laugh he thought this would evoke.

But the old man did not find this amusing.

"He forgets names and does what Babe Ruth used to do. Calls everybody 'Kid.' This can be confusing. 'Hey, kid,' He said to a group of us the other day. 'Lord?' I said, thinking he was addressing me. "No, kid, I mean the kid behind you.'

'Here, Lord.'

'No, no, The kid *beside* you.'

'You mean me, Lord?'

'NO. The kid on the *other* side.' By the time he connected with the right 'kid' he forgot what he wanted to say."

The Elder went on to lament additional evidence of the Almighty's decline. He sometimes forgets a responsibility, like bringing the Sun up every morning, which means a bitchy Pagan god has to be cajoled into carrying it across the sky in a golden chariot. He screws up easy assignments, as when He afflicted everyone in a small town with gallstones when he was supposed to produce a brief shower of hailstones. He gets miracles wrong. A man with a shriveled hand prayed to have both of his hands look alike. Instead of making the shriveled hand like the man's normal hand, he made the normal one look like the shriveled one. Another time, He shortened the left arm of a girl with a short left leg, tilting her proportionately instead of curing her.

Satan listened patiently until the Elder finished, then smiled his best smile of sympathetic understanding.

"And you want me to replace him...."

"Not necessarily. He has to be removed before he can do great harm to Heaven and Earth. And you are the only one with the forces and the wiles to do it. But once that is done we must hold an election. You will have to run against other nominees. The unprecedented opportunity for you, the Devil, to run for God's seat is your reward for overthrowing him, and if you win...we will all accept you."

"Would I have any chance of winning?"

"A chance, yes. You would be the hero of the hour to the victorious forces. That would certainly help. But... frankly, your reputation will be a detriment."

"Then this is what I want you to do for me." Satan reached into his jacket pocket and withdrew a pamphlet entitled *The True History of Satan: The Never-Before-Told Story of His Innocence and Wrongful Damnation.*

"Read this and make up your own mind. Then circulate it among your fellow conspirators. Do that, and I will accept your terms."

The old man nodded and slipped the pamphlet between his robe and the bare skin of his chest, where it would soon smell of frankincense, myrrh and body odor.

The two shook hands and Satan led the Elder to the elevator. He took his leave as quickly as courtesy allowed, fearing the old man's anxiety over another elevator ride might trigger more fiery flatulence.

Chapter Three

The neighborhood surrounding *Showtime in Heaven* replicated the affluent residential areas of Hollywood. Tall palm trees trimmed to their tops lined the avenues. Villas in white stucco or adobe sat back a uniform distance from the road, some fronted by a circular gravel driveway, others by a small courtyard framed by low, vine-covered walls. Mexican gardeners in tan shirts and brown pants watered succulents and pruned shrubbery with red, saucer-size blooms. BMWs, Cadillacs, Jaguars and Porsches gleamed importantly in driveways, along with the occasional vintage Rolls Royce or MG.

Situating the *Showtime in Heaven* studios in the midst of this upscale residential neighborhood was historically incorrect, but the movie crowd now living here had done that to rescue the studios from an adjacent domain now ruled by Hell's Angels (who had made significant donations of teddy bears to children's hospitals).

As he and Bruno made their way to the *Showtime* studios, Roscoe admired the houses. Death is truly a blessing, he thought, if you can live in one of these luxurious houses and have a swimming pool, a gardener, and a fancy car.

"That's Jack Benny's house," Bruno said, pointing to a modest stucco villa. "And over there is Loretta Young's. Three houses down, on the right, is George Burns's."

"Really! You mean I could go up and knock on their doors and meet them? Benny will love this."

"Oh, you won't find them in those houses. So many people want to live in this neighborhood, you only get to live in a house for two months. Then someone else moves in. The only reason a house is identified as that of Jack Benny or Burns or any other movie idol is because it was identified as such on star maps."

"So this whole layout is authentic and not authentic," Roscoe said.

"Exactly," Bruno said. "Pure Hollywood."

At the end of the avenue they came to a scaled down *Arc de Triumph* that was the gate to the *Showtime* lot. As the guard was giving them directions to Lance Petard's office, Clark Gable drove his Stutz Bearcat through the gate, waving to the guard as he did so.

"That's my kind of car," Bruno said.

"I don't get it," Roscoe said. "Up here people teleport themselves around. Why drive a car? It's so slow."

"You forget where you are. This is the Hollywood movie types want, where glamour, style and a show of wealth still count. Wouldn't be half as much fun otherwise."

Lance Petard's outer office was a symphony of walnut paneling and tubular art deco chairs and ottomans. A large glass-fronted case displayed his awards from the Heavenly Academy of Arts and Sciences. The framed ones were signed by well-known Popes and Prophets. Each of the trophies bore a huge gilded lily surrounded at its base by adoring nymphs.

A slim male secretary literally stuck his head through the heavy carved door to Petard's office to announce their arrival. He then withdrew his head, tilting it up and a little sideways, and widened his eyes theatrically as if to say, "Your very important moment has arrived." Roscoe and Bruno walked through the door.

Petard sat behind a curved walnut desk paneled on the front and sides in green leather trimmed with ornate brass studs. The curved window behind him offered a view of the studio buildings and a glimpse of the palm trees and villas beyond. The detective and Bruno sat facing Petard in chairs upholstered in faux leopard skin.

Petard was leaning forward, his slim fingers rolling and unrolling a small piece of paper that might have been a candy wrapper.

"Yes, we had a wonderful chat. Benny has some absolutely *incredible* ideas for a musical version of *Paradise Lost,*" Petard said. "I told him I would seriously consider producing it *after* we put on the Annual Masque."

"What's that?" Roscoe asked.

Petard's eyes flinched, as though offended by Roscoe's ignorance, but he quickly smiled as though presented with a most interesting question that he was happy to answer.

"It's a kind of entertainment that was popular at the English Court in the 16th and 17th centuries. A masque is a costume spectacle with singing and dancing and dumb shows featuring masked actors who play the parts of deities and lesser creatures of the forest and sea. The Almighty and His court simply *love* this kind of pageantry. It brings back memories for them."

"Sounds interesting," Roscoe lied.

"I saw one a long time ago," Bruno said in a neutral tone.

"We can't *wait* to put it on. Our theme is the sea. What a spectacle! We see Poseiden, just after he is coughed up by Cronus, who swallowed him years before. The scene shifts to his palace in the depths of the Aegean. Simply *dazzling. . .* then he appears in his glory, his head *crowned* with sea shells and aquatic plants, riding in a chariot pulled through the water by sea horses, and attended by the hundreds of river gods and the 3000 sea nymphs he created. We see him fighting *horrible* sea monsters with his triton, and making *such tremendous* raging storms, and striking the ground with his triton to make an earthquake...."

"Fascinating," Roscoe said.

"Yes, well, I won't go on, except to say there's much more. And the finale is the *spectacle* of spectacles. The entire ensemble—a cast of thousands—emerges from the sea, rank by rank, and kneels before the Almighty. And here we have added a little *modern twist* that is de-lici-ous!"

"Oh?" said Roscoe, scratching his ear and wondering why a bright red African rug was on the wall and not on the floor.

"Picture this. The mermen aren't the scaly, slimy things they normally are. They walk out of the sea wearing *black wet suits* and *air tanks!*"

Petard waited for some kind of *bravo!* in their reactions, but the two merely sat there. After several awkward moments of silence, Bruno said:

"So, about Benny."

Before Petard could answer, a young man walked through the closed door. He looked to be in his late twenties, short and heavily muscled. He wore a black tee shirt. His dark hair was buzzed to the skin around the sides, so that the longer hair on top perched there like a piece of turf. A slim silver ring hung from one nostril and a round silver stud pierced his tongue.

"Sorry I'm late," he said. Roscoe sensed there was more aggression in his manner than apology.

"Gentlemen, this is my assistant, Fremont Taylor. I thought it might be helpful if he sat in our discussion." Petard introduced Roscoe and Bruno. Taylor noticed Bruno giving him an odd look and he responded with a cold, challenging stare.

"I really can't tell you any more about your friend, Mr. Duffy," Petard said. "We finished our chat and agreed to meet again at some point after the Masque. Then Benny expressed a desire to see the sights in Heaven and I asked Fremont to give him a short tour. I never saw him after that."

Roscoe turned to Fremont. "Where did you take Benny?"

Fremont paused a beat, making them wait on *him*. Roscoe had seen this kind of street arrogance before.

"Nowhere. We stopped in my office while I made a phone call. It was private, so I turned my back to him as he sat in front of my desk. When I turned around he was gone."

"Just like that?"

"Just like that!"

Roscoe noticed that Petard was compulsively shredding the

little piece of paper he had been rolling between his fingers.

"No word of goodbye?"

"None."

"There, you see, gentlemen, we can't give you much help," Petard said.

"When you two finished your chat, did Benny mention any sites in particular he'd like to see?"

"No, he really didn't know what there *was* to see. He did express a desire to watch us put the Masque together, and I said that perhaps I could arrange for him to visit some of the sites where rehearsals or prop fabrication was going on, but we left it at that," Petard said.

Then he rose and walked around his desk toward them, extending his hand and smiling.

"Anything else?" he said, shaking Roscoe's hand. It was obvious he didn't expect there to be anything else. Bruno handed him a card with his number on it.

"If he does happen to come back here, I will call you immediately. He could well be just wandering about, you know. There's lots to see."

"We would appreciate that," Roscoe said.

Then the two detectives left.

"I've seen that Taylor before somewhere," Bruno said once they were back on the street. "I think he was involved in something we were investigating, but I can't remember what it was."

"He's an arrogant little bastard. He seemed to make Petard nervous."

"I think they're hiding something," Bruno said.

"I get that feeling, too. But it could be just something having to do with them and not Benny. Needs looking into, though."

"Right. I'll call Conklin to see if he can fill us in on Taylor."

"I'll wait for you over there," Roscoe said, pointing to a bench in front of a line of tall shrubs.

It was a beautiful California day in Heaven. Sunny and

49

mild with just a hint of a breeze. Roscoe watched the leisurely progress of luxury cars and limousines. Occasionally a battered pickup with Mexican laborers went by. In the driveway on the opposite side of the street, a woman unloaded several department store shopping bags from her Jaguar. Sleek and tanned, she wore a peach blazer over a frilly white blouse and a light blue skirt. She struck Roscoe as a movie executive's wife who probably had a personal trainer and unlimited credit on Rodeo Drive.

Roscoe noticed with no great interest that his view up the avenue was now partially blocked by a stationary man, a few feet away, in a black leather jacket and blue jeans. He stood with his back to Roscoe, holding something in front of him that was hidden by his body. Then he reached one hand into a jacket pocket and pulled out a ski mask, which he pulled over his head with a short, swift movement.

This ominous behavior startled Roscoe into full alertness just as the masked man turned and walked deliberately toward him. He was holding what looked like a huge tennis racquet. He swung it slowly back and forth as he advanced, then raised it above his shoulder in a striking position as he suddenly rushed at Roscoe. The detective instinctively sprung up and ducked to his right, just dodging the swipe intended for him. The man came at him again, swinging the racquet thing with greater speed, but missing as Roscoe ducked beneath the blow.

"Hey! Hey! Hey!' Roscoe shouted. It was all he could manage to say as he kept ducking away from the intended blows. Although he was fully occupied in avoiding the relentless racquet, a corner of his mind remained outside the situation, insisting his body was immaterial, and that a blow from a giant tennis racquet would pass harmlessly through him. But his instinct told him to keep dodging. Obviously, this wild man thought his implement could do Roscoe some kind of harm!

He could not keep this up much longer. Sooner or later he'd get hit. Then he saw a flash of movement in the bushes behind the attacker. A short man darted forward with a tubular thing in his hand. When he got within a foot of the assailant's back, he pushed a handle on the tube producing a mist that all but enveloped the man and his racquet. Roscoe could scarcely believe what happened next. The assailant began to shrink. He dropped to his knees and leaned forward on his hands. Then he suddenly became a thing with small hooves and four legs. The terrible assailant of moments before was now a sheep.

Roscoe was speechless.

"Ach, yeh were a wee bit lucky I was hiding behind thet bush," the small man said. The tubular thing he used to spray the assailant was an insecticide gun, which he continued to grasp. Roscoe's stomach tightened. Was this strange little man lusting for another victim? He stumbled backward, ready to run for his life.

"Noo, noo, ye've got the wrong idea. I've noo intention uh harmin yeh," the small man said. "I'm on yer side, though ahm sure thet's as gret a surprise to yeh as it is to mey."

He dropped the sprayer to the ground. The small man was ruddy faced and bald on top, with a wispy white fringe below. The end of his nose was bulbous and bumpy like a piece of cauliflower. He wore a white lab coat that reached to his shoe tops.

"My side?"

The man pointed to the sheep. "This former person works for Colonel Stuckey, who's tryin' to catch me. Somebody must have spotted me in this area. This goon was lookin' aboot fer me--and almost found me hidin' behind that shrub--when yeh took his fancy. Thet means yeh and I ur on the same side. He meant tuh harm both of us. What's yer name?"

"Roscoe Duffy."

"Doon't ring a bell. Mine is Angus MacLaren. Doctor Angus MacLaren. I'm a professor of biology."

The sheep brushed against MacLaren's leg. He nudged it away roughly. Out on the sidewalk passers by were pausing to stare at the sheep in a black leather jacket and jeans. The little Scot carefully picked up the giant racquet, which gave off an almost imperceptible hum. He pushed a button on the handle and the humming stopped.

"This is a policeman's tool. A Detainer, commonly called a 'sticky plate.' If he'd hit yeh with it, yeh would've stuck tuh it like filins tuh a magnet."

Ah yes, the tool Conklin had described.

Bruno appeared on the sidewalk and walked quickly across the grass toward them.

He frowned at MacLaren. "How did you get that? Only police are allowed to carry them, and only when authorized to do so. Unless you've got a good story, my man, I am going to have to take you in!"

"Hold on, Bruno. You won't believe what just happened."

The three of them walked away from the sheep, which by now had attracted a small crowd. A police siren whooped in the distance. Bruno carried the "sticky plate." The professor carried the insecticide gun. Bruno listened in astonishment to Roscoe's account, then asked the question Roscoe was burning to ask.

"Where did you get that stuff you sprayed on him? I've never heard of anything like it."

MacLaren stopped in front of a bench and sat down.

"Well, I was intuh clonin' sheep and quite by accident I came up with this substance thet turns *human souls* intuh sheep. It was very excitin', of course, a true scientific breckthrough, buh I had tuh keep it a secret. I knew it would no be permitted up here. Not with so many anti-science fundamentalists havin' such a big say aboot policy. They wouldn't understand I was no interested in turnin' people intuh sheep, buh in learnin' how thet could happen. It was basic research thet would someday, somehow, be of gret benefit in advancin' our ability tuh improve our lot."

"But very dangerous," Roscoe said, "if the wrong people could turn individuals into sheep."

"Aye...and ahm very soory to say thet is whut happened. I was tryin' tuh develop a serum thet would undo the transformation. My assistant, Willem, voluntarily underwent the change intuh a sheep so thet I might test the serum. I was certain it would work... buh, ach, it didn't."

He paused at gazed into the distance. Roscoe saw tears brimming in the professor's eyes.

"He remained a sheep...After a while his friends reported him missin'...There was an investigation...Colonel Stuckey pressured me intuh revealin' what had happened...he promised to keep everythin' secret, and said I would be allowed tuh continue lookin' for an antidote *provided* I would do what he asked...I was desperate tuh find an antidote and bring poor Willem back, so I agreed."

"I knew that bastard was no good!" Bruno said.

"What did you do for him?" Roscoe asked.

The professor drew back, grimacing with the pain that question caused.

"Besides Willem, I turned two people intuh sheep," he said at last. "I did no want tuh do it, believe me. I was told they wur dangerous individuals. Thet this was the most humane way tuh deal with them. I tried tuh make myself believe this, buh I no could do it. After I did the second one, I knew I could no do this any moor. The second person was no even a permanent resident here. Just some astral traveler who kept sayin' he hadn't done anythin'...I believed the poor guy, buh Stuckey's man was right there and I did no dare *not* do it."

Bruno clapped his hands and beamed at Roscoe.

"Did this traveler wear a blue nylon jacket and plaid pants?' Roscoe asked.

"Aye, he did."

Benny!

"And where are these sheep?"

"I di na know. Stuckey's man took each away, includin' my assistant. He's their hostage and they figured thet would be an additional reason Ahd go on workin' for them...buh I bolted anyhow. Now thet I have the antidote, I'll find Willem myself...if they do no catch me first."

"They can't touch you as long as you're with me," Bruno said.

53

MacLaren leaned back and rested both arms along the top of the bench. The tension drained from his expression.

"If one of Stuckey's men wur to catch me, it would no be pleasant. Ahd be stuck to the Detainer and stored someplace. They'd release me long enough tuh turn more souls intuh sheep, then *swat*, back Ahd go ontuh the Detainer."

"I wonder what would have happened if Stuckey's man had caught me on the 'sticky plate'?"

"Whatever yer doin', Stuckey doesn't like it. He's an evil man. Unless yeh can be useful tuh him, Ahd say he'd probably get rid of yeh permanently by throwin' yeh over the wall."

"Wall?" Roscoe said.

"The wall around Heaven," MacLaren answered. "If yeh wur stuck to the Detainer, he would extend it over the wall, reverse the field holdin' yeh, and fling yeh intuh Chaos."

Roscoe's stomach churned at the thought of that place.

"That's pretty risky. If he got caught doing that he would be sent straight to Hell," Bruno said.

"True. Buh apparently Stuckey's men have already gotten away with it several times. His man got tuh talkin' once and said as much, buh he complained aboot the risk. He preferred turnin' individuals intuh sheep because it was as effective as throwin' them over the wall, and just aboot risk-free."

"Can't we stop this maniac by reporting all this? Who's his superior?" Roscoe asked.

"Michael the Archangel. But we don't have any proof to back charges against him. The hierarchy are sticklers for proof," Bruno said.

"We've got the professor here."

"Stuckey would simply call him a crackpot and deny everything. Without more evidence to support our charge, Michael would have to believe Stuckey,"

"What if we take direct action," Roscoe said. "Swat him with the Detainer and dump *him* over the wall."

"Won't work if we try it. Higher ups like Stuckey have an

immunity to the 'sticky plate' when it is used against them by any one other than their superiors," Bruno said.

Roscoe turned to the Professor. "Would that immunity protect him against being turned into a sheep?"

"I di na know. I no have tried it on any one in the hierarchy."

"Bruno could protect us as we tried to do it...if it failed, we'd still be safe."

Bruno shook his head and sighed. "Nope. Sorry. I am strictly forbidden to harm anyone, nor do I have the power to protect anyone who is attempting to inflict harm, as you would be. So you would be on your own. But this is not the time to even consider that. We've got to keep Stuckey in play for now. He may be our only hope of finding Benny."

"Aye, Stuckey knows where the sheep ur, buh the one who took them from me must know, too. He'd be easier tuh get tuh than Stuckey."

The professor described the man. Roscoe and Bruno looked at each other, sharing the same thought.

Roscoe nodded. "Sounds like Fremont Taylor."

"No surprise he's hooked up with Stuckey. I was right about him. We were sure he was involved in smuggling chemicals of some sort but we never got to prove it. Word came down from Stuckey that the matter had been resolved and we were to close the investigation."

"Why smuggle chemicals into Heaven?" Roscoe asked.

"During the First War in Heaven Satan used saltpeter to make gunpowder. It was an experiment that failed, of course. The cannon balls and grapeshot flew harmlessly through the etheric bodies of God's armies, but it did momentarily discombobulate them. So after the War, He banned salt peter in Heaven. That edict caused a lot of bickering among the Elders. The issue was if you ban one chemical, shouldn't you also ban others, but they couldn't agree on what those others should be. The Almighty got tired of listening to them argue so, just to shut them up, He banned the importation of all chemicals, but there's still demand for certain ones. Some women are addicted to wearing perfume, so they buy the smuggled ingredients and make bath tub perfume... or they mix up favorite hair potions and dyes. Some of the theatrical people buy chemicals they need to make powders and pigments for makeup...things like that.

"So long as the chemicals are harmless," Bruno continued, the authorities look the other way. But we got word that Fremont was bringing in chemicals that were dangerous. Thanks to Stuckey, we never got to learn what they were."

"Where do the chemicals come from?"

The Professor answered. "From Hell. Over the millenia, the effluvium of Hell's noxious vapors and the sulferous constituents of its molten rivers have seeped intuh the substrate tuh produce minerals and compounds yuh need to make almost any chemical. That's how Satan came by the salt peter."

Roscoe said. "But here's what I don't get. You don't need money up here, so where's the profit in smuggling?"

"Popularity, cachet and above all, favors," Bruno said. "Not a few of the hierarchy got their positions through favors they earned as smugglers. It's considered a benign kind of social climbing, so long as the smuggled materials are not harmful."

In the distance a policeman had put a leash on the sheep and was leading it to a van.

"I could have Conklin send the men out looking for Taylor. They would love to be hunting for somebody," Bruno said.

"Go ahead. But unless they're lucky, that will take a lot of time. I may have a better idea," Roscoe said.

It had been a trying day for Lance Petard. The corps de ballet that would dance the parts of nymphs and river gods were just not following his choreography. They were doing jetes whenever they felt like it, and one male river god had brazenly performed a somersault instead of the lift that was called for. Lance could only interpret all this as spiteful defiance, though why he deserved this, Lord only knows. What was he doing wrong? Not enough dear-and-darling cajoling? And if this were not enough, the afternoon brought that most *worrisome* interview with those detectives, and that cretin, Fremont, staring at him, silently threatening him, as though he had given something away.

He needed relief. He needed exhilaration. He deserved it! He checked the doors of his villa to make sure they were locked. His white poodle, Fluffy, followed him, yipping to be picked up and coddled. Petard scooped up Fluffy and took her to the kitchen, where he snapped a leash on the dog's collar and secured the leash to an eye bolt next to the animal's water bowl. He walked to a door at the far end of the kitchen and opened it, releasing the pent-up odors of wood shavings and animal shit. Inside this specially constructed alcove were bags of feed pellets and wire cages containing a dozen rabbits. He reached into one cage and withdrew a brown rabbit, holding the trembling creature by the ears with one hand while cradling it with the other. He closed the door and carried the animal to the sink.

"Close your eyes, Fluffy," he said.

Fluffy seldom obeyed commands, but he always obeyed this one by draping both paws over his eyes.

Petard held the rabbit over the sink, lest it suddenly shit, and snapped its neck with quick twist of his hand. How Taylor managed to smuggle these live rabbits into Heaven was beyond Petard. He knew certain big names had entered heaven bodily, but he never heard of rabbits being accorded that honor. It was wisest not to ask.

He carried the dead rabbit to the rear of the villa and unlocked an ornately carved mahogany door. As he pulled the door open the air trembled with a sudden deep roar and a flash of light from somewhere below. With mounting excitement, he flicked on the light over a long descending staircase and carefully made his way down. At the bottom he turned right around a corner and walked several steps to within thirty feet of a dark pit surrounded by a waist-high cement wall. He could hear the thing hissing, anticipating what was to follow. In the dim light, Petard turned his back to the pit. Then he took a hand mirror from his pocket and raised it shoulder high so he could see behind him as he walked slowly backwards toward the low cement wall.

The thing sensed his approach, and when Petard stopped fifteen feet from the wall, the giant serpent rose up with a shattering roar, lifting its green crested head just above the level of the wall. The terrifying sound and sight of this huge scaly creature brought a thrill to Petard's loins. He shivered in ecstasy as he looked into its large red eyes in the mirror, knowing their lethal glance could dissolve his atoms unless he avoided direct eye contact and kept the mirror angled to reflect that glance back toward the serpent.

Petard felt himself nearing orgasm. At the penultimate moment he flung the dead rabbit over his shoulder into the pit. The serpent head darted higher, following the rabbit's trajectory, then released a blast of fire from its nostrils that caught the rabbit in mid-air, charring it black just before the serpent swallowed it.

Petard's semen flooded his silk boxer shorts. Virtual sex with even the handsomest boy could not compare with this. It was illegal and dangerous, and he was paying a high price for it, but there was absolutely nothing better than having sex with a pet Basilisk.

Roscoe and Maclaren made their way to *EITSB*. Bruno had decided to update Conklin on Fremont Taylor and agreed to meet them in two hours in front of *EITSB*.

The detective and the Professor hurried past the closed door of Cudworthy's office and proceeded to Section D, Corridor F, Room 7 and Table 3. Rose Trautman was bent over her telescope, oblivious of their presence. There were two other watchers at Rose's table. One, a man, looked up from his telescope just long enough to see who had come in, then returned to watching his subject. The other was a red headed woman who watched Roscoe and Rose with the silent, unabashed curiosity of a gossip.

"Hello, Rose," Duffy said.

She looked up, momentarily startled. She smiled warmly. *She likes me.* He was flustered.

"We're back," he said, feeling foolish.

"Yes, I can see that," she said, easing his embarrassment,

making it sound like the punch line in some comic dialogue they had planned together. Then a worried look crossed her face. He wanted to draw her close, but instead nodded his head in the direction of the staff lounge. The red haired woman watched with disappointment as this interesting pair and the little man moved out of sight.

In the empty staff lounge, Duffy introduced MacLaren.

"You're a friend of Benny's, too?" she asked.

"Never met the man. Ahm lookin' fer a fellah thets probably with him. Roscoe though yeh might be able tuh help us."

Duffy told her everything that had happened since he last saw her. Her expression became grim. She shook her head in amazement as he spoke.

"So your intuition was right. Stuckey's a very bad guy," he concluded. "Now we need you to find this Fremont Taylor and follow him. He will lead us to the sheep."

Rose said nothing. She looked past him, nervously rubbing her wrists, apparently unaware she was doing so. "Of course I'll do it, Roscoe, but it will be difficult," she said. "Somehow Cudworthy learned I talked to you. He threatened to fire me if I ever speak to you again. It isn't safe for you to meet me here."

"He couldn't have seen us come in. His door was closed."

"That doesn't matter. He pops in here without warning to check that I am following the people I am supposed to follow."

"Thet will make it risky tuh follow Fremont."

Rose shook her head. "Minor risk. He only checks the tapes. As long as I don't record Fremont, there's no evidence of what I'm doing. And if he ever demands to look through the telescope I can manage to 'accidentally' nudge it onto another subject before he looks. No, the real risk is being seen with you."

"What do you suggest?"

Rose thought a moment. "There's a virtual nightclub in Hollywood called *Morph's* that caters to gays and cross-dressers. I'll come as a man. Mustache, top hat and tails, and just in case somebody else is wearing that getup, I'll carry a riding crop. You don't need to dress up. If anyone is following you, they will think you're simply talking to one of 'those' people."

Roscoe felt a tick of anxiety. Was there something in her nature that led her to choose *that* nightclub and *that* disguise. *A riding crop!* Might he be terribly wrong about Rose Trautman?

"Tomorrow night at ten?" she asked. There was an unmistakable tenderness in her smile.

"You got it," he said, chiding himself for even considering that he could be wrong about Rose Trautman.

Bruno was waiting as they emerged from *EITSB*. Roscoe brought him up to date.

The angel was pleased. He was also concerned. As the three walked away from *EITSB*, he kept glancing about, scanning bystanders and the pedestrian traffic. "Stick close to me," he said. "Stuckey's got every cop and informer looking for you two."

"I can take care of myself," the Professor said, annoyed at the thought of his movements being restricted.

"Maybe yes, maybe no," Bruno replied. "But I'll tell you this. If you leave my protection, you'll miss out on the finest haggis in Heaven."

"What are yeh tellin me? Haggis?"

"Tonight, and every Wednesday night, is Haggis night at the station house. But it's only for the guys in the precinct and their guests."

The professor laughed. "Ach, yer uh crafty one, Bruno. I can refuse any bribe except haggis! Lead on!"

Engaged in conversation, they headed for the police station. After they passed a particularly deep doorway a man stepped out onto the sidewalk and followed them at a distance.

Chapter Four

The Goodfellows Social Club occupied a two-story brick building in the Brooklyn section of Golden City. It stood on a corner amid narrow streets dominated by mom-and-pop stores and restaurants catering to the neighborhood's Italian and Jewish residents. Its architecture was traditional Mafia, with windows on the second floor but none on the first. The solid brick walls of the first floor were meant to block views of what went on inside and thwart listening devices that read conversations in the vibrations of window glass.

Inside, Fremont Taylor strode past the bar where a heavyset member in a Hawaiian shirt was drinking espresso and carving the club's initials into the heads of virtual bullets. A half dozen other Goodfellows cursed as they slapped down cards at a round, felt-covered table. Taylor slid into a semi-circular red banquette across from Salvatore Punchinello (Sally Punch), head of one of Golden City's virtual crime families.

A fat man with glistening black hair that lined up in rows of small twisted curls, Sally Punch greedily stoked his mouth with virtual spaghetti and meatballs from a large platter. The napkin under his chin was permanently pre-stained with red meat sauce as part of the virtual meal. On the wall directly over his head hung a large oil painting of Al Capone.

"You didn't play fuckin' square with me, Taylor." Punchinello spoke with a mouth full of food, spraying tiny pieces of spaghetti and meat in Taylor's direction. "I don't like it when somebody thinks I'm fuckin' stupid," he said. "You hear me what I'm tellin' you?"

This was the hackneyed all-purpose opening statement of a Mafia don on the prod. Punchinello had committed it to memory with considerable difficulty.

Taylor spread his hands in the manner of a man dumbfounded by a false accusation.

"You lost me, Sally. I thought we had a good deal. You hide the sheep for us, and Stuckey doesn't reveal you never were a real mafioso."

Punchinello closed his eyes and tilted his head as if wrestling with his patience. He slammed his fist on the table.

"Those *ain't* regular sheep!"

"They're sheep. That's all you need to know, Sally"

"I don't give a shit what they really are, you dickhead. That's your business. What I'm sayin' is they don't eat like regular sheep and that has become an expensive problem. I try feeding them grass. They won't eat it. I try hay. They won't eat it. I even tried clover—no deal."

"So what do you feed them?"

"I got them to eat spaghetti and meatballs. But then, after a week, they wouldn't eat no more of that. So I tried chicken cacciatore. That worked--for a week. Now I have to feed them something new each week and their food gets more expensive with every change."

"Really!"

"Now they're eating veal piccata. Only it has to be *real* veal piccata. You know what it cost me to smuggle that in!"

"No idea."

"I had to promise the butchers' union I'd be in their Marco Polo Day parade. Can you imagine! I used to have them by the balls. Now they can tell me what to do!"

"That's not so bad, Sally. So you walk in a parade. No big deal."

"You ain't heard all of it. I don't walk in the parade. I ride on a float dressed in a spangly Marco Polo suit with a hat that looks like a woman's beret. That's bad enough, but worse, I got to stand in a pile of cooked spaghetti to commemorate his bringing spaghetti from China."

Fremont laughed.

Sally Punch flushed with anger. "That's just it, you dickhead. Everybody's gonna laugh at me. A mafioso who makes a fool of himself loses respect. Then where will I be? Up here I can't kill nobody. I can't break their kneecaps. I can't beat them to a pulp. The only way I can make people do what I want is to be menacing. You can't menace if people are laughing at you. Take your weird fuckin' sheep back. *You* feed 'em."

"Can't do that, Sally."

"Then I'll just set the bastards loose!"

"No you won't, you dumb shit. If you do, you know Stuckey will tell everyone you were simply a barber and never a mafioso. Just a pathetic wannabe. Then you'll have absolutely *no* credibility."

The hard glitter faded from Punchinello's eyes. His eyebrows gathered in a peak above his nose as though he were about to weep.

"Listen, you gotta do *something* to help me," he pleaded. "Maybe *you* get the food and bring it here. Then I don't have to do no more favors that make me look like a fool."

Fremont knew Sally would not dare cross Stuckey, no matter what, but it wouldn't hurt to pacify the sorry fuck with a lie.

"I'll see what I can do," he said.

If this had been an ordinary neutralization he would not be having this stupid problem with Sally Punch. Fremont would simply have released the three animals into the general sheep population in the verdant valleys of *Poesy* Land. But doing so meant no one would ever be able to pick them out from a thousand other sheep. And Stuckey definitely needed to keep these three identifiable--more or less. Right now, you couldn't tell who was who among the three, but

63

once they caught up with the professor it would only take three reverse transformations to identify each of them

Fremont left the Club feeling good about himself. He had handled Sally Punch like a pro. This would impress Stuckey and maybe win back points Fremont had lost for being careless with Benny. It pained him to recall that telephone conversation he'd had with his back to Benny. He had mentioned to Mooch that site 321 was "just about ready for show time" and that must have been what drew Spielmacher to the secret location. Stuckey had torn him a new asshole for that blunder. But now Fremont felt better. Things were back on track. "Alriiight!" he said to no one, exuberantly pumping his fist in the air.

"My sentiments exactly," Rose Trautman murmured as she peered through her telescope.

Roscoe arrived fifteen minutes early at *Morph's*. He wanted time to get the feel of things and blend in with the crowd lest any of Stuckey's many eyes pick him out as someone out of place who ought to be interrogated. If one of the Colonel's people did come after him, he was completely defenseless. Bruno was not with him. The angel had vigorously objected to Roscoe's coming here by himself, but Duffy overruled him. He wanted to be alone with Rose. He had, for a change, taken charge of a situation, and it felt good. To placate Bruno, however, he reluctantly agreed to wear a ridiculous disguise. The outfit was the only female attire available in the station house's wardrobe department. Even with Roscoe's too-large body forcing gaps in the seams, the costume transformed the detective into a dowager of the 1900s: pinched-in waist and flaring hips under a voluminous floor length dress. This was augmented by a modest bustle, a pleated white shirt with full sleeves, and puffy shoulder seams. The hair of the wig swept upward over a bun and disappeared beneath a wide-brimmed hat topped by a flurry of small blue feathers. His face was a somewhat forbidding portrait in lipstick, rouge, scented powder, blue eye shadow and mascara. A parasol completed his ensemble. Most of the other gay or cross-dressing men seemed to find nothing incongruous about a six-foot slumping dowager with thick forearms, hairy hands, no boobs to speak of, and a dress that was obviously too small. Among some of the cross-dressing men who took pains to look beautiful and stylish, he was scorned as a sissymiss with absolutely horrid taste. But there were others in the crowd who eyed him with desire.

The corset made it especially difficult to breathe and he had trouble moving in the heavy drapery of the skirt, which he kept stepping on. Roscoe felt sure his embarrassment was flashing like a red beacon. He took a seat at the bar. The bartender, a hefty blond in a ball gown, fluttered his eyes seductively as he served Roscoe a virtual scotch and water. As the bartender moved away, he looked over his shoulder to see whether his flirtation had had any effect. Roscoe nervously avoided his glance.

"My, my, you're a *big* sissymiss, aren't you. And you're so *strong,* too." The speaker wore a French maid's costume accurate in every detail. He had slipped into the seat next to Roscoe. It amazed the detective that a man could be such a good-looking woman. Trim figure. Shapely breasts. Slender legs in gartered black stockings. Even with a Dick Tracy chin and long Roman nose, the heavily made up face was strangely attractive.

The maid squeezed his thigh and moved her face close to his. "I bet a big strong brute like you could give me a very good spanking. I hope you like to spank poor, helpless little maids like me. Do you, darling?"

"Sorry, that's not my thing." He moved back a little and gently lifted the man's hand from his knee.

"I think you're just playing hard to get, darling. You're definitely the domineering type. Why do you look so uncomfortable? Oh, I get it. This is your first time out and it's a little frightening."

Me, the domineering type? "Yes, you're right, this is my first time out. I'm waiting for a friend."

The maid drew back, her eyes frankly caressing Roscoe from head to toe "What a pity! Well, if your friend doesn't show, I'll be *happy* to fill in for him." She laughed and walked away.

On the club's stage a drag queen in black net stockings and a pink tutu strutted and postured seductively as she sang "I Want To Be Loved By You, Alo-*oh*-own, Boop-boop-de-do." She bent over with each "boop-boop-de-do" and waggled her butt at the audience. This drew whistles, applause and shouts of encouragement. Roscoe found it disconcerting to watch a brawny male in the starched petticoats and full skirt of a 1940s bobbysoxer whistling with two fingers in his mouth. The variety of female outfits lent a surreal, time-travel quality to the busy scene. The calf-brushing skirts and cashmere sweaters of the '50s. The thigh-high minis of the late sixties. Some patrons dressed in the strapped overalls or earthy smocks of the Woodstock generation. There were prom dresses, naughty French peignoirs, a Swiss milkmaid costume, a nurse's outfit. Roscoe wondered what led each patron to choose his particular outfit. Was there a message in the choice? He did not like to ponder what message some of the patrons were reading into his getup.

At the front door a sudden burst of applause greeted the entrance of a dazzling figure. It was Rose in a white top hat, white vest and tails, white pants and matching shoes. She wore a ringmaster's curleycue mustache. The riding crop was the more conspicuous by being black. She walked in his direction, smiling briefly at those who nodded appreciatively at her outfit. When she was almost in front of him he smiled and started to speak, but she walked right past him without a glance and settled into an empty space at the end of the bar. Roscoe moved to her side and nudged her with his bustle.

"Hey there, good looking. Can I buy you a drink?" he said.

Rose gave him an annoyed look. "No thanks, I'm waiting for someone."

"Rose, it's me. Roscoe."

She was startled. "Oh my god, I never would have known. I didn't expect you to wear a disguise." She laughed. "It's absolutely terrible!"

"Well, if you didn't recognize me, I guess Stuckey's men won't either."

She ordered a Drambuie. He had another scotch and water.

"Fremont went to the Goodfellow's Club in Brooklyn. I could see the sheep in a fenced-in area behind the club. It's their bocce court. The members are grumbling about the 'sticky plates' used to keep the sheep confined."

"The sheep are stuck to these devices?"

"No, the 'sticky plates' are part of an electrified fence that gives the sheep a nasty buzz when they wander too close to it. But occasionally one of the Goodfellows gets too close to a 'sticky plate' and gets sucked right onto it. Then they have to stop the game while someone reverses the field to release him and allow him to shake himself back together."

Roscoe laughed at her description of three cursing Goodfellows tripping over sheep as they struggled to free their comrade from a Detainer. Having finished her report and slipped Roscoe the videotape of Fremont's conversation with Punchinello, Rose visibly relaxed. They enjoyed a comfortable moment of silence as they sipped their drinks. She looked even more beautiful in her white cutaway. Her hair had been clipped and swept behind her ears in a masculine, duck-butt style. She gazed at him shyly, as though asking whether he approved of the way she looked. He felt a passion and tenderness he had never felt for Barbara or any other woman. He slipped his arm around her waist and drew her closer to his side.

"I think we should look like lovers," he whispered in her ear. "What do you think?"

"Are you proposing this as strategy to deceive Stuckey's spies?" she asked coyly.

"Yes...and no."

"No?"

Roscoe took a deep breath. "I'm attracted to you, Rose. Strongly attracted...I...." He struggled with embarrassment.

She turned her head away. After a moment she faced him again, on the verge of tears.

"I'm attracted to you, too, Roscoe. With my whole heart. You're sweet and decent and caring--everything I've always wanted, but it's hopeless. I'm dead. You're alive. It could never work."

"We could make it work. I'll just keep coming back in my astral form and staying as long as I can. Then, before you know it, I'll be dead and we can be together always." His heart told him he meant that. He didn't care what his head wanted to tell him.

She looked doubtful but seemed unwilling to disappoint him.

"For now, let's enjoy it while we can. Come back to my place." She took his arm. They left the club, drawing envious looks from a dozen disappointed patrons.

Rose's place was not what he had imagined. She did not live in an ordinary apartment. She lived in a bower in a shady, fragrant grove. They had floated through a lush valley and passed into the cool dappled light of a forest with immense, primeval trees. A huge root arched out of the ground to form the doorway to the bower. It was a spacious, one-room dwelling, its walls made of rushes that bent to form a vaulted ceiling. A thick layer of newly picked ferns covered the ground. Windows in either wall and one in the ceiling admitted soft light and framed the passing of brightly colored birds. A rustic couch and fan-back chair, both made of woven branches, bracketed a mossy stone table against one wall.

She turned a dial on the wall, filling the room with soft music by an oaten reed ensemble.

They sat on the couch.

"I've always liked the Golden Age. The poetry and music of lovesick shepherds are so romantic," she said. "When I feel lonely, this bower helps me imagine I am being wooed from afar by the lyre of a handsome young shepherd on a hill top."

"Why imagine it? Couldn't you create a virtual reality in which this happens?"

She grew sad. "It would be too painful to do that. I can no longer bear to get too close to my fantasy. You see, in life, I was so completely driven by it I went to Albania as a young woman, looking for a shepherd who would fulfill my romantic dream...I found one, but he wasn't as young and handsome as I had hoped. He was middle age and balding. He had a large Arabic nose with a black wart on it. And he had a wife and three children in the village. Despite all this, I fell madly in love with him. I lived with him in his stone hut on a rock-strewn hillside. I helped him with the sheep. I taught him how to play the lyre."

She smiled wanly. Her handkerchief, which she clasped to her breast, released a strong scent of lilies.

"For a while it was wonderful. He learned to play 'Three Blind Mice.' Sex was rough, passionate, profoundly orgasmic. I would scream and pull out his hair and rake his hairy shoulders with my fingernails. He would bite my neck and my breasts and curse me in Albanian. But it didn't last. He drank, you see. He beat me when he got drunk. Then one night, in a towering drunken rage, my beloved Albanian shepherd cut my throat. I bled to death."

She was trembling. He put his arm around her so that her head rested on his shoulder. Roscoe could not detect where the fragrances came from, but he was now smelling--besides the lilies--an admixture of parsley, sage, rosemary and thyme.

He began to tell her his story of unhappy love. It was not so much his failed marriage with Barbara. That was an impulsive union between two people with no common interests or dreams, and even from the beginning, theirs was a lukewarm relationship.

The love that changed his life was his high school sweetheart, Bootsy Knockle. Her beauty had the robust freshness that came from being a dairy farmer's daughter. In later years, when he got lonely, he would remember how beautiful she looked in strapped overalls and mucking boots, her thick blond braid swinging like a horse's tail as she pitched hay or shoveled cow shit.

69

Sometimes he would picture the two of them stalking woodchucks, one of their favorite activities. Bootsy was a crack shot with a .22 rifle.

They did most of their necking in his father's faded black Dodge.

"We were virgins, but our hormones finally got the better of us. We went to the hayloft in her barn. I remember I could hardly breathe as we removed our clothes and began fondling each other. Almost immediately I couldn't wait another second. I climbed on top and entered her. Just at that moment the barn door flew open with a bang and her father stood in the doorway, with a shotgun, looking up at us. 'What the hell you doing up there with my daughter, you son of a bitch!' he roared. 'I'll fix your sorry ass!' He fired the shotgun and I saw the hay lift with the impact of the pellets. I am sure he was deliberately firing wide, but at that moment I thought he meant to kill me. I was terrified. I grabbed my pants and shoes and jumped through a side window to the ground. He came around the side of the barn and fired another shot in my direction, but I was off and running. Any other time, the stones and branches that punished my bare feet would have caused excruciating pain, but that night I didn't feel a thing."

Rose gently stroked his face.

"Right after this happened she dropped out of high school and enlisted in the Army. She was killed in Vietnam."

"She was a nurse?"

"No, a sniper."

Rose drew his face close to hers. They kissed.

She took his hand and placed it on her breast. He lifted her from the couch and lay down beside her on the cool ferns. They entwined, caressing each other hungrily. Between gasps of her mounting arousal, Rose explained that virtual sex was a commingling of their memories of great sex during their lifetimes. Roscoe scarcely had time to absorb this before their mutual need became irresistible and they coupled, there in the bower, amid liquid birdsong and the dulcet music of oaten reeds, she screaming Albanian curses at him as

70

she neared orgasm, he thrusting with wild abandon, but with his head turned away, looking over his shoulder. Ever since the episode in the barn, it was the only way he could have sex.

Afterward, Roscoe held her in his arms as they lay spent on the slightly crushed ferns. They marveled at what had just happened. She had experienced once again the tumultuous sex with her Albanian shepherd. He had finally consummated his interrupted coitus with Bootsy. Yet each of them, and not the ghosts of the past, had been the lover who made this historic recreation possible. It was an incredible, miraculous, soul-shaking kind of love between the living and the dead.

At length, Duffy rose and reluctantly began to put on his dowager clothes. Rose helped him squeeze into the dress and set the bustle straight.

"No more of this disguise for me," he said. "I can't breath in it, and I feel like a fool."

"If you come here, you won't need a disguise. It's so out of the way, almost no one passes by. You just need to make sure you're not followed."

Roscoe nodded. She made sure he knew the site number.

He drew her close. "Finding you has changed my life. We will always be together...we'll find a way.... " She sealed his lips with her finger.

" No talk of the future. We will enjoy the present for as long it lasts." Trying to lighten the gravity of her words, she grimaccd with mock pain for using this lover's cliche from war movies. Roscoe smiled at her light-hearted theatrics, but deep down they made him uneasy.

Chapter Five

"**A** catapult! Oh no...no, no, no!" protested Lance Petard. "That would *never* do. It is *way* out of keeping with the oceanic theme. Where *did* you get this crazy idea?"

Fremont Taylor slouched in his chair and settled his right foot on top of Petard's desk.

It's Colonel Stuckey's wish that a catapult be part of the grand finale," Taylor said.

"You tell Colonel Stuckey it is out of the question. No, no, no. Absolutely not! I have already acceded to his wishes by agreeing to put the mermen in wet suits with masks and tanks. That is *dreadful* enough, though of course I pretend it is a marvelous touch. But this catapult business...*impossible!* This is *not* the siege of Troy."

At the mention of Troy, Taylor snorted with laughter. This surprised Petard. He hadn't expected this cretin to know anything about Troy. Besides that, he didn't see what there was to laugh about.

"You really believe Stuckey will take 'no' for an answer?"

Petard nervously rubbed his forehead. "For God's sake, he's going too far. Tell him the catapult would ruin the Masque. Is that what he wants?"

"Certainly not."

"Why does he have this sudden interest in adding touches to the Masque, anyway?"

"He never told me. Maybe he has developed artistic

ambitions."

Petard got up from his desk and began pacing. "I never should have agreed to follow his 'little' suggestions in the first place."

"You forget, you had no choice. We know you stole a baby Basilisk from the Pagan Zoo by bribing a keeper. That's a serious offense. Stuckey looks the other way in return for your cooperation and your silence. But if you are no longer willing...."

"To be blackmailed, you mean...."

Taylor merely smiled. "And then, of course, there would be no more rabbits. But that would be the least of your problems, Petard. How is that thing, by the way. Has it grown much?"

Petard ignored the question. They had him by the balls, but he could take some small pleasure in not satisfying this bastard's curiosity. He sagged into his desk chair. He closed his eyes.

"All right. You win. Tell Stuckey he can have his catapult. But I'm too damned busy to build it. If he wants it, he has to make it!"

Taylor nodded. "You've made the right decision, my friend."

Petard glowered at Taylor, who responded with an insolent wink.

After Taylor left, Petard struggled to regain his composure. Amid the fear and anger roiling in him was a growing sense that Stuckey's blackmailing him must be more than an egomaniac's crude attempt to seize the Masque's directorial reins. There was something bad afoot in all of this, but he could not imagine what that could be. What the hell was going on?

In a remote corner of Heaven, next to the outermost wall that bordered Chaos, lay *Theatris,* the domain of dramatic works. Here were all the plays of the Greeks and Romans, all the plays of the French, German, Italian, Russian and English masters, as well as all worthy drama from lesser known playwrights around the world. In recent centuries it had become the least visited domain in Heaven. The older residents of Heaven who persuaded the Almighty to give characters and their plays life in Heaven had tired of seeing the masterpieces. Contemporary plays, of which only a few were deemed worthy of Heaven, didn't much interest them either. Nor did younger audiences care much for traditional theater. Their artistic palate hungered for sitcoms, explosions, car chases, and World Federation Wrestling. Among the younger souls, the most popular porthole in Heaven's floor was the one looking down on NASCAR races, described by one disgruntled character living in a Chekhov play as "a bunch of assholes chasing each other in a circle." Undaunted, however, the characters in the older masterpieces continued to play their parts, hoping an audience of one or two wide-wandering souls might chance into their theater.

The characters in *Hamlet* were upbeat this day because they did indeed have an audience, albeit a small one. It consisted of a newly arrived Jewish couple from Miami, a New York interior decorator and his boyfriend on holiday from their accustomed domain, and a former Harvard intellectual.

The play began well. On a platform before the castle at Elsinore, Bernardo relieved Francisco as he was supposed to.

"Have you had quiet guard?" Bernardo asked.

"Not a mouse stirring," Francisco replied.

"Well good night. If you do meet Horatio and Marcellus, the rivals of my watch, bid them make haste."

"I think I hear them," Francisco said. " Stand, ho! Who is there?"

From the darkness below came a whisper: *"Farsididdyfasgatagee"*

The two sentinels looked at each other, dumbfounded.

Bernardo cleared his throat and shouted boldly, as though he might be dealing with a drunken fellow actor who had forgotten his lines. "Do you not mean to say, 'Friends to this ground'?"

"And 'liegemen to the Dane'?" Francisco added.

"Farsididdyfasgatagee," the voice repeated.

Horatio and Marcellus had entered during this exchange. They hung back, not knowing how to handle this radical change in the drama. Bernardo, by now sweating and filling the awkward silence with indecipherable dramatic twitches, broke the unbearable tension of not knowing what to say by tossing the problem to Horatio.

"Look, it beckons to Horatio," he lied. "Thou art a scholar; speak to it, Horatio."

Horatio silently vowed to break Bernardo's neck when the play was done. He hesitated.

Bernardo had found salvation and would not relent.

"It would be spoke to," he said to Horatio.

Marcellus saw a rescue, too, and chimed in: "Speak to it, Horatio."

Horatio, livid, could think of nothing to say but the lines he was supposed to speak, even though the darkness below made it impossible to tell whether the speaker looked anything like Hamlet's dead father: "What art thou that usurp'st this time of night together with that fair and warlike form in which the majesty of buried Denmark did sometimes march? By heaven I charge thee speak!"

"Farsididdyfasgatagee."

"It is offended," Marcellus said tentatively.

The cobblestones below gave off the sound of horse's hoofs and the grating of wooden wagon wheels in motion. The voice in the darkness muttered something that sounded like "bullshit!"

"See, it stalks away!" Bernardo said with great relief.

The sound of the wagon faded in the distance.

"I don't remember it this way," Pearl said to her husband, Hymen.

Hymen raised his hands in resigned surrender. He didn't either, but then he reflected his memory wasn't what it used to be.

The Harvard intellectual was irritated. "Why can't they play

75

the damn thing straight!"

"Now, now. We must encourage creativity, mustn't we," countered the interior decorator.

"How now, Horatio? You tremble and look pale. Is not this something more than fantasy? What think you on't?" Bernardo asked.

Horatio was thinking about exacting bloody revenge upon his fellow characters for handing him the hot potato. Beyond that, he was angrily pondering how this embarrassing alteration in their familiar routine had come about.

Some miles away, the figure driving the cart was thinking along similar lines. He was cursing whatever dumbass was guilty of this royal fuckup. Colonel Stuckey wouldn't like this!

Roscoe, Bruno and the Professor finished looking at Rose's tape of the exchange between Sally Punch and Fremont Taylor.

"Why don't we just go there, threaten Punchinello with exposure if he doesn't cooperate, and take the sheep?" Bruno asked.

"It's too risky. If we go as ourselves, Stuckey will probably figure out how we discovered where the sheep are. He'd have to suspect Rose. I don't like to think what he might do to her."

"We could cut through thuh fence at night and make off with them," the Professor said.

Roscoe shook his head. "Not good either. We'd be trying to deactivate those Detainers in the dark, which would be dangerous. And even if we succeeded, Stuckey will figure we did it and still work back to Rose."

"So what do we do?" Bruno asked.

Roscoe suddenly realized he was making tough decisions, planning strategy. It was exhilarating. This was the Roscoe Duffy he had wanted to be during his days on the force.

"We have to make a deal with Sally Punch," he said.

"What! How you going to make a deal with that idiot!"

"When in Rome, do as the Romans do," Roscoe said.

"Whut's thet supposed tuh mean?" the Professor asked.

"Trust me." Roscoe said.

"Why the Hell haven't you caught this Duffy guy and the Professor! They can't be that hard to find, Mooch, or is this job beyond your limited ability!"

Sergeant Mooch had learned to control his temper when Stuckey insulted him. He liked his job too much to risk losing it. But each insult strengthened his resolve to somehow, someday, make his superior pay for the insults.

"Well, sir, our man followed them to Conklin's station house."

"And? You could have gone in and collared them. Only that angel, Bruno, has the power to protect them. Couldn't you have grabbed them when he left them alone for a short time?"

"My plan exactly, Colonel, but...uh...I never made into the station house. You see it was haggis night, and I can't stand the smell of the stuff. It makes me sick. In fact, I ran to the curb and vomited."

"Oh MY GOD!" Stuckey fumed, stamping his foot. It was bad enough that Mooch was a nincompoop. What enraged him more was that he had been foiled by haggis. He had never before heard of a commander being stymied by haggis, or any other dish for that matter.

Mooch decided he might as well give his boss all the bad news and get it over with.

"Ah....we also had a little trouble with that shipment of chemicals we need. Nothing that can't be fixed. It will just mean a little delay..."

"Don't tell me! Don't TELL me..." Stuckey shouted, meaning tell me you asshole because I am about to explode in your face.

Mooch edged toward the door. "The smuggler from Hell was supposed to get past the guardian angels at Heaven's wall by joining the siege of Harfleur in *Henry the Fifth*. He was to give the password to Ancient Pistol who would hold him ready until Henry cried 'Once more unto the breach, dear friends, once more; or close the wall up with our English dead!' Then Pistol was to lead him into the ranks charging the wall and the smuggler and his cart would rumble through in the melee and wind up on one of Heaven's main roads...."

Mooch had reached the open doorway.

"Go on! Go on!" Stuckey demanded.

"Well, this smuggler doesn't know much about drama. He misheard *Henry the Fifth* as *Hamlet the Fifth* and so he made his way to *Hamlet*."

"It didn't bother him that *Hamlet* has no 'Fifth' in its title?"

"That did puzzle him at first, but he reasoned that 'Fifth' meant the fifth *revival* of *Hamlet,* and that signs directing him to plain *Hamlet* must be leading him to the original play, which he figured would be just the same as the fifth revival."

With that, Mooch ducked out the door, leaving Stuckey to spend his wrath on the air.

The sound of the front door bumping against the wall as it opened drew Sally Punch's attention. He looked up from his antipasto to see three strangers enter the Goodfellows club in high Mafia style.

First through the door was a short man in a dark pinstripe suit, the jacket of which reached almost to his knees. He wore a dove gray fedora that pressed down the tops of his ears, forcing them to splay out slightly. He positioned himself a few feet inside the room, hands clasped behind him, and surveyed the scene. Then he nodded an "okay" over his shoulder and a tall, beefy man walked through the door.

This one wore a black turtleneck sweater under a black windbreaker. His brown leather cap was pulled down so low he had to raise his head slightly to see ahead of him. He stepped into the room to the right of the short man and looked around. Satisfied, he nodded over his shoulder to the third man.

Don Finnochio entered with deliberate steps, assessing everything around him. His camel hair coat was draped negligently over the shoulders of his dark, double-breasted suit. The elegant effect of his expensive clothes was compromised by his being tie-less with a white shirt buttoned at the collar. Sunday dress-up at a cheap boarding house. The don sported a bushy black mustache. He advanced into the room and took a commanding stance with feet wide apart. "Where's this Sally Punch?" he demanded.

The wannabe mafioso got up and walked toward Finnochio, not sure how he should react to this imposing figure.

"It's me," Sally said in a neutral tone. "Who are you?"

"Don Finnochio. You don't know me yet, but you will. Come, let's sit down. We have business to take care of." Finnochio led Punchinello to the banquette he had just left. Finnochio's men stood by either side of the table.

"You don't know me because I have just arrived. You heard of the Polenta family?"

"No, I ain't. I been up here so long I'm out of touch wit' what's what on earth."

"We are the biggest crime family going, and I'm the boss!"

"You mean 'were' the boss. You're dead."

" Hey, I'm *still* the boss! Just 'cause I had a fuckin' heart attack don't mean I can't still run the organization. Look how Gotti ran his family from jail. And The Chin, Gigante. Listen, believe me, I still fuckin' run it. There are *ways!*

Sally Punch was impressed. This guy was the real article.

"You wanna drink?"

79

"Yeah, Amaretto," the don said.

"Yuh kin make thet two," the short guy said.

Sally Punch looked at the short man.

"What kind of Italian is that?"

"He ain't Italian. He's a Scot. The only one in the Mafia. I brought him in myself. He can shoot the eyes outa a pigeon."

"Wit' that cauliflower schnozzola, it's a wonder he can see around it to aim!" Sally quipped.

The short man gave Punch a steely glance, then looked away.

"So what business you got wit' me?" Sally asked.

"I'm takin' over up here," Finocchio said. "All the other families are with me."

"Hey! You ain't takin' over my family, pal."

Finocchio leaned forward, his eyes hard and unblinking.

"I'm gonna lay my cards on the table, Sally. I can do anything I want to you because you ain't shit. You never were a mafioso...."

"How'd you know that! You been talkin' to that fuckin' Fremont?"

"Doesn't matter how I know. I don't want to do this the hard way, Sally. I'm really a nice guy. So I'm offerin' you a deal. You come with me, you get to stay head of your family *and* I open the book and make you a made man. Then you're legit. Stuckey won't have nothin' he can hold over you. Nobody can question your menace."

Sally's facial expression relaxed and brightened.

"I can live wit' that," he said. "I'd love to tell Stuckey to shove it up his ass."

"Good! Then we've got a deal. And if you want to get back at Stuckey, here's a way to begin. Those sheep you're keeping for him. Give them to us."

Sally Punch frowned. "Believe me, I'd love to get rid of those fuckers, but when Stuckey finds out they're gone he'll find some way to kick my ass. What's so important about those sheep anyway? Why do you want them?"

"You don't need to know. But I will tell you they'll help me put a leash on Stuckey so he won't ever bother us again."

"Yeah, but in the meantime... ."

"In the meantime, he'll never know they're gone." Finocchio nodded to his Scots button man, who walked to the door, disappeared for a moment, and reentered accompanied by three sheep.

"Give us yours, and replace them with these. Stuckey's people will never know the difference." Finocchio said. He leaned closer, smiling.

"Best of all, Sally, these sheep eat grass!"

"Hey, you're somethin,' you know that! You know the whole picture and you got all the angles covered! It'll be a pleasure workin' wit you."

The exchange was made in minutes. Finoccio and his men led the rescued sheep out the front door and into the back of a small truck. The Scots button man climbed in with the sheep. Finocchio slid behind the wheel and started the engine while the other man closed the rear door, then joined the don in the front seat. Within minutes they were out of Brooklyn and driving across the grassy plains of the adjacent domain. The turtleneck mafioso leaned forward in his seat.

"You're a genius, Duffy! It went down just as you said it would," Bruno said.

Roscoe laughed. He had never felt better in his entire life. He had conceived and executed a bold plan that had rescued his best friend. He unbuttoned the collar of his shirt and took a deep breath. He wished the detectives in his old precinct could see him now!

"How're they doing?" he said.

Bruno turned to look through the cab window into the back of the truck. "Looks like the professor is injecting one of them now.

You want to stop and watch the transformation?"

"I better keep driving. We're going through *Land of the Pioneers*. Nothing but horses and wagons here. I don't want get cited for trespassing in a truck. But damn it, these ruts and potholes are slowing us down!"

Just as Roscoe finished saying this, the truck bucked violently out of a pothole, lifting him and Bruno out of their seats.

"Shit!" Roscoe said.

Bruno looked back through the cab window.

"That knocked them all on their asses, but they seem okay. Looks like your friend Benny is back to being his old self."

Roscoe pounded exultantly on the back window. *Welcome back Benny.*

Meanwhile, at *Eccentrics' Corner,* Michael the Archangel was meeting with a delegation of eccentrics about the disappearance of a colleague, William "The Great" McGonagle, Britain's worst poet.

Michael hated dealing with missing person cases. They were boring and a waste of effort. The subjects always turned up somewhere, unless they had fallen over the wall into Chaos. But, short of God, Michael was the supreme authority for the well being of Heaven's residents. He had to deal with such cases when they were brought to him.

What made this case especially trying was that the delegation complained that Colonel Stuckey, to whom they quite properly reported the problem first, had done little or nothing to find McGonagle. He had, in effect, blown them off. The Archangel sympathized with Stuckey, although it irritated him that the Colonel's brusqueness had forced the case to become Michael's problem. He would have to appear concerned and somehow mollify these oddballs. Given their natures, that would not be easy.

82

They were in a shady corner of a small park. Michael and the group sat on metal chairs in a circle before the low stage that served as the platform for crackpot declamations and dramatic performances.

Seated to his right was "Liver-Eating" Johnston, who had killed 300 Crow Indians and eaten their livers. He later made peace with them and became a preacher.

Next to Johnston was Chauncey Dalton, the "Holy Shouter." Shouting praise of the Lord at the top of one's voice got Heaven's attention, he had told his followers. He was famous for getting hundreds of them shouting at once, and in their fervor, being seized with severe jerks. "I have seen more than five hundred persons jerking at one time in my large congregations," he proudly told a reporter.

The tall white haired gentleman to the Shouter's right was Lyman Foster Digby. He had formulated the theory of Left-Right-and-Roundabout, the principle governing all movement in the cosmos. Digby propounded that any formation moves in multiple directions according to the movements of many increasingly greater formations, each depending upon the great formation for direction, and upon varying changes caused by counteracting influences of Suction and Pressure of different proportions. More simply put, Suction and Pressure govern all that happens in the universe. The eye sucks up light. "The lungs suck in air, and so forth," he explained. Excretion is a prime example of the action of pressure. The earth itself is nothing more than a great sucking machine that draws in nutrients from the sun, sea and air through a "mouth" at the North Pole, distributes these through "arteries" inside the earth, and then expels the wastes, with pressure, though the earth's "anus" at the South Pole. Additional excretion is accomplished through volcanoes.

In the next chair sat a bearded figure in a Union Army uniform bearing a general's fringed gold epaulettes and a row of medals. He wore a stove pipe hat surmounted by a droopy plume of indeterminate origin. He rested his hand on the hilt of a sword buckled to his waist. This was Joshua Norton, self-proclaimed Norton I, Emperor of the United States and Protector of Mexico.

Beside Norton was the hermit, Titus Spivey, the "pumpkin scratcher." In life, he had avoided almost all contact with people and lived in a cave that flooded each spring with the rising of a nearby stream. Apart from his infrequent visits to town for a few necessities, he was seldom seen, but evidence of his approximate whereabouts was to be read in the arcane signs and numbers he carved into pumpkins in farmers' fields.

Completing the circle, on Michael's left, was Montrose Pangborn, an execrable Shakespearean actor of the Victorian era. His signature role was Romeo, a part he augmented during each performance with his own pathetic doggerel. He was famous for the death scene, wherein he laid himself atop Juliet and expired, only to rise again, bow to the derisive laughter and booing of the audience, and die a second time in extended and even more pitiful agony.

None of the eccentrics liked McGonagle.

Pangborn said: "He bored one to tears with his strutting and posturing and his wretched poetry. He was compelled to write about whatever prosaic thing crossed his field of vision and to assault our senses by reciting every composition. Utterly without poetic talent. Master of the boring."

"Look who's talking," Titus Spivey said. Pangborn ignored the pumpkin scratcher.

"Allow me to recite a typical McGonagle poem," Pangborn said.

There was collective groan as Pangborn stepped onto the low stage and struck a histrionic pose, hands on hips, head thrust upwards to the heavens.

"This is about a newly opened railroad bridge in Dundee," he said.

Beautiful new railway bridge of the silvery Tay,
With your strong brick piers and buttresses in so
grand array,

And your thirteen central girders, which seem to my eye
Strong enough all windy storms to defy,
And as I gaze upon thee my heart feels gay
Because thou art the greatest railway bridge
of present day,
And can be seen for miles away,
From north, south, east or west of the Tay

"That man is better off lost!" intoned Left-Right-and-Roundabout Digby.

"Pray, sir, to whom do you refer?" challenged Pangborn.

Norton I intervened with majestic benevolence: "Come now, Pangborn, he meant McGonagle. I am sure we all are grateful McGonagle is gone, but like him or not, he is one of us and we are obligated to find him if we can."

"NO EXTRAORDINARY MEASURES NEED BE TAKEN TO FIND THE AUTHOR OF BAD POETRY," said the Shouter. "LOOK FOR HIM, MICHAEL, BUT DON'T LOOK TOO HARD!"

"Damn it all, preacher, you don't need to shout anymore. You've made it to Heaven," groused Liver-Eating Johnston. "You give me such a headache I get a craving for liver."

"Ah shit, don't start that again," Digby said.

Michael raised his hand to quell further arguments. He asked the routine questions about McGonagle's disappearance, but they yielded no useful information. No one had seen him for a week, and no one had an idea where he might have gone. "He can't have relocated in another domain. No other domain will tolerate him," Pangborn explained. "That's how he wound up here. When he could find no place to go, the Administration said we *had* to take him in."

At length, Michael promised to renew the search for McGonagle, but in his heart he knew it would be perfunctory. Britain's worst poet would show up in time or he would not. For the

85

time being, at least, no one would have to suffer McGonagle's inept I-am-the-camera-of-the-commonplace poetry.

Roscoe tried to lift Benny off the ground in a great bear hug as Benny tried to hug back and pummel his old partner with back slaps, but the violence of their attempts merely forced their etheric bodies to commingle wispily. They separated, laughed, and called each other a schmuck. Bruno joined the celebration with vigorous congratulatory blows through their arms.

"Hey, Bruno, you big asshole. Good to see you again," Benny said.

The professor did not join in the celebration. He stood in front of the truck looking unhappy, with two sheep at his side. Roscoe and the others paused, realizing something was wrong.

"There's no antidote   left tuh transform these two," the Professor said. "Thet header we took back there smashed thuh bottle holdin' thuh rest of thuh liquid. Ah kin make moor, but ah have tuh do it in my laboratory."

Benny frowned. "You trust this guy, Duff? He's the one made me a sheep! How do you know he ain't just gonna disappear with these sheep and do whatever with them--something bad maybe. I know he undid me from sheepdom, but I figured you had him by the short and curlies and he had to do it."

Roscoe reassured Benny the Professor was okay, promising to fill him in later.

"I'll have tuh sneak in at night and work by flashlight, but I kin do it," the Professor said.

"I'll go with you," Bruno said. "Protect you along the way and keep a lookout for any guard Stuckey may have posted at the lab. Besides, someone will have to hold the sheep while you're inside."

"Be careful, Professor. Bruno can protect you from a guard, but that would alert Stuckey you've been making something,"

Roscoe said. "Since you fled to avoid turning people into sheep, he'd have to figure you're making the antidote, and he'd have to wonder why. Wouldn't be to hard to suspect you plan to use it on the sheep you somehow tracked down. He'd probably check at the Goodfellows, see if all was okay. It wouldn't take much to get Punchinello to spill the beans."

The Professor nodded.

"We'll take the truck, keep you and sheep out of sight inside," Bruno said. "You and Benny will be on your own but you'll have the Detainer. That'll be some protection unless you're outnumbered."

"We'll hide out at Rose's. We'll wait for you there," Roscoe said. He gave Bruno the site number of the bower.

As the truck drove out of sight, Bruno turned to Benny. "And now, you little schmuck, we're going to ground for a while and you're going to tell me how the hell you got us into this godawful mess."

"Hey, Duf, what's to tell? I screwed up!"

"I know that, you moron. I want the details that lead to that bottom line."

They made it to the bower without incident. Benny unzipped his blue nylon warm up jacket and lifted his Yankee cap to rub his bald head. He surveyed the bower.

"Man, what a weird place. This Rose must be a real cuckoo bird. She an informant or something?' Benny said. "They're usually a little off."

Roscoe hesitated. Should he confess his love for Rose now? He decided to wait.

"Yeah, she's an informant, but she's not a cuckoo bird. She's special, but we'll get to that later," he said. "What *happened* to you?"

"Hey Duff, don't say it that way, like it was *my* fault. Dealing with these people up here is all new to me. I was an innocent victim." Benny explained how Lance Petard had fallen in love with

Benny's idea of making *Paradise Lost* into a musical, and how he promised to let Benny watch the final rehearsals of the Masque.

"When I left him I was flyin' high. After he promised to put on my *Paradise Lost,* I couldn't wait to see how they do productions up here. So when I hear this Taylor guy say that site 321 is 'just about ready for show time,' I decide I just got to see how much their show biz is like ours. I take off on my own because I don't want to be chaperoned. I want to be free to move around and see what I want to see. It was an impulsive move, Duf, but I couldn't help it. It was the artist in me."

"So what happened?"

"It was a strange place. First I was on a wooded hillside looking down into a small valley. I couldn't see anything in the valley except what looked like tree tops. Where is the production site? So I moved down the hill and I began to hear sounds. When I get closer I see I had not been looking down on tree tops but on a huge camouflage net. And under it there are lots of people in black scuba suits with tanks on their backs coming out of this big lake. They look to be rehearsing a routine. They come out of the water in two files that separate and run onto the land. Each has two tanks and two air hoses--one hose in the mouth, the other in the hand. The one in the hand they keep waving about as they run. Maybe it was part of a dance routine. Weird dance routine, if you ask me, but maybe they choreograph differently up here."

Benny paused and spread his hands, palms up, they way he typically did when reporting something amazing.

"Then there were these people in those old-time Greek or Roman costumes who were building this humungus ball. It was like one of those gezundheidt spheres at world-of-the-future fairs ...

"You mean a geodesic dome."

"That's it. The frame was all wooden triangles and they were applying the outer shingles, or whatever those plates were. But where they hadn't covered it yet I could see the inside, and braced in the center was a kind of big egg cup structure. Looked like a holder of some sort."

"But the egg cup was empty?"

"Yeah."

"What else did you see?"

"There was this big wooden contraption on wheels. It had a long wooden arm. Sorta like a folded down cherry-picker. And that's all I had time to see. Next thing I know...these two guys are shouting and running at me with these huge tennis racquets. Before I can run, one of them whacks me with a racquet, and wow...was THAT an experience! Suddenly I feel all prinkly and, whoosh, I'm sticking to the racquet, only it's not my body sticking to it, its me in tiny pieces like sand. I try to move but I can't. I have no body parts to move!"

"They caught you with a Detainer, a 'sticky plate.' "

"A what?"

"Later. Then what happened?"

"I don't know how long I was stuck to that thing. Could have been a few minutes or days. I was like one of those suspended animation things, you know? No sense of time at all. Then all of a sudden I feel this prinkly feeling again, and *kazam,* I'm back to my normal self. But these two guys are standing right beside me, ready to swat me again if I move...And there's the professor in front of me. I tell him I ain't done nothing wrong, and if this is some kind of game they play up here, I don't like it. It's a hell of a way to treat visitors...He just gives me this sad look and sprays me with something. Next thing, poof, I'm a sheep. How can you trust a guy like that? And what's going on here? It's crazy."

"You're right. It is crazy, and I don't understand it either." Then Roscoe explained about the Detainer and the Professor. He told Benny everything that happened during their search for him, including the part Rose played in finding him. He didn't spell out his relationship with her.

When Roscoe finished, Benny smacked his hands together. "Okay! We got a lot of questions here, Duf. Just like the old days. Feels good, don't it?"

Roscoe smiled. "You bet."

"This astral thing is even better than I thought it would be," Benny said. "I'm gonna get *Paradise Lost* produced, and you and me are gonna solve a real good mystery. Maybe the most important one of our career."

Roscoe gazed fondly at his former partner. Benny was his old self. Excited. The eternal optimist. Always expecting to break a big case, even though he never got the chance to work on a big case. Back in the Precinct, he had been tagged as a screwup. There was some truth in that. But maybe, up here, the dice will roll in his favor at last.

"You'll have to wear a disguise," Roscoe said.

"That figures. How about I wear a mustache?"

"You'll need more than that. Got to get rid of those plaid pants."

"But hey, these are me!"

"A guy wears pants that loud, people wonder if maybe he shot a couch. They remember him."

"Okay, smart ass, what do you suggest?"

"We'll see what Bruno can come up with."

They sat down on the couch and began considering how they should proceed. At length, Benny got drowsy and lay on the ferns. He was soon snoring. Roscoe decided to wait up for Rose. An hour later he too was sound asleep.

Roscoe awoke to the sound of birds chirping. The sun was just rising. He knew Heaven had night and day, a concession to the circadian rhythms of humans, but this was the first time he had slept at night, and in fact the first night he remembered being up here. How long had he been in the etheric state? Had everything he'd experienced occurred in a single day? A single hour? Time seemed normal up here, but it clearly wasn't. Day turned into night and night into day, making it seem time was passing. But if you were dead, or in the etheric state, you didn't change. The passage of time had no meaning. It's day-to-night movement was simply a comforting illusion. Yet contradicting this was the fact that events moved forward, unfolded. Actions were followed by consequences. Situations played out sequentially, through time. So there was time and there was not time. How strange! But that's Heaven for you, Roscoe thought. The ultimate weirdness. There's no point in trying to figure it our because you can't.

Benny grunted in his sleep and turned on his side.

Roscoe sat up, fully awake now.

Rose was not there. The coppery taste of panic rose in his throat. Had Stuckey picked her up? Or was he confused about her working hours? Maybe this time/no time thing had got him all screwed up. Where was she?

He shook Benny. "Get up. Get up. We've got a problem," he said.

"Whuuh...." Benny mumbled, raising himself on an elbow.

There was the soft sound of approaching footsteps and Rose appeared at the entrance to the bower, her head down, lost in thought.

" God, Rose, are you all right?"

She looked up, startled. "Of course I am. Of course. Don't I look okay?"

"Yes, but...I was worried...you didn't come home last night...and I was afraid maybe something happened to you. Where were you?"

Rose gave him a strange look, as though she resented his demanding tone, or perhaps wasn't sure how to answer the question. She hesitated a moment.

"I spent the night with a friend. I didn't know you were here."

The way she said it made him uneasy. Too tentative? Evasive? He couldn't say what exactly. He wanted to ask who the friend was, but his instinct warned him to back off.

Benny studied them both for a moment, sensing something was going on. Then he stood up and shook her hand. "So this is Rose," he said. "I ain't heard much about you, except Duff says you helped him big time when he was looking for me. I owe you one for that. You can't imagine what it's like being a sheep."

"At least you had company," she said, smiling.

"Yeah, but all we could say to each other was 'baaahhh.' Worse part was that one of others wouldn't shut up and he kept going 'bah, bah, bah...baahhh...bah, bah, bah...baahhh' or sometimes 'baahh...bah bah...baahhh...bah, bah, like it was morse code, but I couldn't make nothing of it. Me and the other sheep stayed as far away from him as we could get."

The professor and Bruno appeared in the doorway.

"Maybe they'll tell us who the talkative sheep is," Roscoe said.

The professor shook hands with Benny. "I'm glad tuh see yer all right, laddie. I'm sorry I had tuh turn yuh intuh uh sheep, but I no had uh choice, as I hope Roscoe has told yuh."

"No hard feelings, Professor. But I sure don't want to go through that again! I love veal piccata, but it doesn't taste the same on a sheep's tongue."

The little Scot gave Benny a sympathetic smile. Then he turned to Roscoe.

"Everythin' went well. Willem's fine and I'm gretly relieved aboot thet. He's off tuh hide out wi' friends fer thuh time bein'."

"Who was the other sheep?" Rose asked.

"A strange one, believe me," Bruno said. "Name is McGonagle."

"He was still dazed, just as he was when I turned him intuh uh sheep," the Professor said.

"Dressed funny in one of those purple velvet smoking jackets with a black satin collar," Bruno said. " Wore a red tassled fez. Says he is the true Poet Laureate of England. Couldn't get anything more out of him. He kept spouting doggerel I couldn't understand."

"I can't figure out whut he was sayin' either, but I wrote it down anyway," the Professor said. He pulled a paper from his lab coat and handed it to Roscoe, who read it aloud:

Row on row the barrels stand
Girded round with iron band
Staves of each count twenty-five
And rounded are they to my eye.
Oh barrels brown that look so grand
What stuff within thee draws my hand?
I faint, I swoon with eyes wide open

Roscoe shook his head. "I can't make sense of it either. But if 'barrels' are barrels and not some figure of speech, he saw some barrels at the site and apparently opened one out of curiosity. But what he found is anybody's guess."

"It was something overwhelming, something stunning," Rose said.

"I didn't see any barrels," Benny said

"You couldn't get anything else from McGonagle but this?" Roscoe asked Bruno.

"The Professor made him repeat the poetry so he could write it down. After he repeated it, he did this little twirl and stepped forward on one leg like a tap dancer finishing a routine. 'And there, gentlemen,' he said, 'you've had the honor of being the first to hear the latest divine creation of the true Poet Laureate of Victorian England. And with that I twitch my mantel blue, tomorrow to fresh woods and pastures new.' Then he turned and sort of staggered away. Didn't seem at all concerned about being picked up again. Definitely a bit looney tunes."

"Nobody's gonna believe I ate with a sheep that was a poet," Benny said.

"We've got to find him. He's got to tell us more about what's in those barrels," Roscoe said.

"I'll have Conklin organize a search and alert all the other police stations," Bruno said.

93

Roscoe rubbed his forehead, considering the idea. "But that will alert Stuckey that McGonagle's been freed and he'll quickly discover the fast one we pulled at the Goodfellows Club."

Rose said: "Not if McGonagle is reported simply as a missing person. Stuckey would have to expect that after all the time McGonagle has been a sheep, *someone* would report him missing."

Roscoe agreed that was the way to go. Bruno said he would take care of the details. "Trouble with this bird," Bruno said, "is that he's dotty enough to be someplace we would never expect him to be. We'll need a bit of luck."

"Maybe we should consult the Oracle at Delphi in the *Ancient Greek Domain,*" Rose said.

"Nah, that's all a crock of bull. Some ancient god supposedly answers your question in winds or rustling leaves or entrails that a so-called priest has to interpret. You might as well consult a carnival fortune-teller," Bruno said.

Rose laughed with the others at Bruno's dismissal of the oracle, but privately she was not convinced it was all nonsense. It might be worth a try.

Chapter Six

Rose Trautman's bower lay in *Arcadia,* the virtual domain of the Golden Age. It was a pastoral world of shady grottoes with sparkling fountains and grassy hillsides topped by ancient copper beach trees. A river wound serenely through a valley of gently swaying flowers. From a distance came the melancholy strains of an oaten reed played by a lovesick shepherd to his indifferent mistress. Upon a nearby hillside, a flock of sheep sat contentedly on the grass, mesmerized by the sweet sounds of their shepherd's lyre.

Colonel Stuckey sat in the cool shade of a hilltop tree. What a bunch of crap, he thought. This was a panseyland, all tootely-toot pennywhistle instruments and fattening milk and honey. None of these curly-haired, soft-bodied shepherds had the makings of a soldier. They looked like girls in their flowing cotton gowns, although as he scanned the hills with binoculars, he spotted one that was darker and leaner than the rest. Probably not a real shepherd, he thought, but a wannabe shepherd who in life had been a sun-burned camel jockey in the Sahara.

He looked at his watch. Just as the second hand reached the appointed hour, a large snake dropped from the tree and landed in front of him with a heavy plop. Its lettuce-green scales glistened even in the shade. It raised its head, fixing one of its glassy red eyes on Stuckey.

"Oof," it said. "Dropping like that always knocks the wind out of me. I hate this disguise!"

"You're not the only one, Satan. I wouldn't want to be seen talking to a snake."

"Not to worry, Stuckey. The simple shepherds and shepherdesses out here wouldn't think it odd. They talk to animals and plants themselves."

"That doesn't surprise me."

"So...how are things going on your end?"

"Your men have got the real finale down pat. They bitch about going to Petard's rehearsals and pretending to learn his choreography. But that's to be expected. If the troops don't grumble, you've got a real morale problem."

"And the chemicals I sent?"

"There was a brief mix-up, but we finally got them."

"And our 'special' machinery?"

"Both pieces will be finished on schedule."

"So everything is going as planned."

Stuckey hesitated before answering. "Well, there is a small glitch. The Professor is still missing and we haven't been able yet to catch that nosey detective, Duffy." What Stuckey could not know was that the pair he was after were less than a mile away.

"Hmmmm. That is worrisome, Stuckey. Most worrisome. You assured me you would take care of these matters."

"Believe me, I will. In the meantime these two have not caused us the slightest problem."

"I see. Yes. But it is still worrisome, and not just for the threat they pose. My staff has always had doubts about your ultimate loyalty, I am sorry to say. I have been able to quell their doubts up to this point, but I fear your failure to catch these two may seem to their suspicious minds...well, possibly collusive...."

"What! They think I might be a traitor! That is outrageous! Preposterous!"

"Of course, my friend, of course. *I* know you are loyal, but they are the ones with doubts. And we cannot have them bothered by the slightest doubts about their confederates, can we."

Stuckey's face clenched with anger. "And?..."

"And I think you need to offer some proof of your loyalty."

"Such as?"

"A sacrifice would be appropriate."

The Colonel's head snapped back as though hit by a punch.

"Oh, it needn't be anything personal, like an arm or a leg," Satan said. "It should be a person. Someone you depend on. A trusted aide, let us say. I don't especially care which one you choose."

Inwardly, Stuckey felt enormously relieved, but outwardly he played the outraged victim, at first fuming, then bitterly frustrated, and finally bending his neck to the sword. This wasn't bad at all. Here was a chance to get rid of that dummy Mooch. That was something he had been seriously considering of late.

The Colonel looked at the ground and turned his head away from the snake as though he did not want to hear the answer to the question he was about to ask.

"How is this sacrifice to be carried out?" he said.

The snake hissed, pleased with this response.

"Quite simply. I will tell you when and where to bring him to the outer wall. Two of my men will be there to toss him into Chaos. And of course there will be cameras there to record the event for my staff."

"And that will do it?" Stuckey said.

"I should think so. Naturally, it would help if you also caught those two."

"That will be done, I promise you."

The snake lowered its head and began to slither away. Then it paused and looked back at Stuckey.

"Oh, one more thing," it said. "From now on, call me Bob."

At the mouth of the Congo River in the *African Domain,* two paddlewheel steamers boarded an excited crowd of tourists for a trip to the interior. The tourists were a mixed lot spanning the human time line--pagan celebrities, Neanderthals, puritans in white collars and black waistcoats, Victorian ladies, World War I doughboys in campaign hats, and backpack-laden moderns in birkenstocks who carried water bottles.

At a nearby dock the coal-fired steamer, *Conrad,* heaved up dense black smoke as it prepared to head upriver. In front of the dockside warehouses, a handful of friends and relatives waved goodbye to those already on board. Deeply tanned Company officials in pith helmets directed a final trickle of passengers up the *Conrad's* gangplank. Last to board were a half-dozen black soldiers employed by the Company. They wore white tunics and red fezzes. Each had a Martini rifle slung over his shoulder.

Roscoe and Benny stood at the rail, their khaki bush shirts dark with artificial sweat. They waved goodbye to Rose, Bruno and the Professor.

"Good hunting," Bruno shouted to them.

"Try tuh stay cool en keep yer helmets on in the sun," the Professor yelled, then laughed at his poor attempt at humor. The sun couldn't affect their etheric bodies. The helmets were simply *de rigeur* costuming for travel in this domain.

Rose simply blew them a kiss which Roscoe chose to believe was really meant only for him.

The *Conrad's* whistle shrieked and the boat pulled slowly toward mid-river. It soon rounded a bend, putting the station out of sight.

Benny slipped his arm through the strap of his pith helmet so it hung on his shoulder like some giant beetle. He looked down ruefully at his pudgy white legs exposed by his shorts. Some disguise. He longed for the concealment his plaid pants would have provided.

"I'm not crazy about this idea, Duf. We should have waited longer to see if the police were able to find McGonagle."

"They didn't come up with any leads at all. And if they couldn't come up with them on the first go around, I doubt they'll have better luck as they continue the search. As Bruno said, this guy is probably in some unlikely place, and the heart of the Congo is certainly an unlikely place."

"Yeah, but we're going to this unlikely place for a crazy reason. Back at the Precinct, they'd laugh at us if we said we're following a lead from a voice that came out of a cave. A voice that stirred up leaves interpreted by some hokus-pocus guy who told Rose that McGonagle is in the Congo...This is misuggah...."

Benny paused. He looked Roscoe straight in the eye. "You're hooked on this Rose, ain't you. That's why we're going on this wild duck chase. This is all to please her!"

Roscoe tipped his head back, smiling, his eyes almost closed. *Touche!*

"Nothing gets by you, Benny. I am hooked on her. I can't help it."

"This is no good, no good. How the hell can it work? I heard of long-range love affairs. I heard of sicknicks doing things to dead bodies. But I never heard of a live person carrying on a real love affair with a dead person. How you going to do it? By séance?"

"I don't know how we can work it out. But we will. She is the first woman I have ever truly loved."

Benny fell silent. He rubbed his hand back and forth over his bald crown. He looked away from Duffy when he spoke.

"I'm gonna tell you something else. You ain't gonna like it, but I gotta tell you." He paused, then said: "Back there, when she walked into the bower? I knew there was something going on between you two. It was obvious you were stuck on her...but the way she reacted to you...my gut tells me there's something wrong here...Trust me, she's gonna break your heart, Duf."

Benny's words caused Duffy's stomach to churn. Benny almost always had good instincts. Worse yet, Benny's gut feeling magnified Duffy's own sense that Rose had somehow changed, drawn back.

He took a deep breath, trying to shake off these painful forebodings.

"Hey, this isn't like you. You're the guy I depend on to be upbeat. Get with it, man."

Benny frowned and studied the distant shoreline. He shook his head.

"I hope I'm wrong and everything works out. But I'm sorry, Duf. Dead women are nothing but trouble."

The *Conrad* moved slowly toward the interior. The river began to narrow. The forest on either side grew denser and taller, leaning out over the water as if to embrace them. At length the boat arrived at the Central Station. Roscoe and Benny remained on board as tall blacks in loin cloths unloaded supplies for the station. On shore, three white men sat on the steps of their combined office and living quarters, a large screened-in platform raised on stilts. A wooden sign hanging from the rusty tin roof bore the word "Depot" in sun-faded letters, and in smaller print below, "Sorry, No Public Restrooms." As the natives carried boxes and burlapped goods from the boat into the quarters, the white men looked on languidly, occasionally shouting directions for the placement of certain goods. To the right of the screened platform a large open-sided hut covered piles of ivory tusks. Workers moved slowly in the heat, sorting the tusks by size and grouping them in jumbled piles.

"All very realistic," Benny said. "But I don't know why anyone would choose this virtual reality. Go figure! This is what *they* want, okay, but why do *we* have to go through this steamboat charade! Why don't we just teleport ourselves to the Inner station?"

"You should know the rules by now, Benny. When in a Domain you're supposed to abide by the conventions of its virtual reality. This is Africa of the 1800s, and here we travel the Congo in a steamboat."

"Okay, but what's with these soldiers?"

"They will protect us when we are attacked."

"Attacked ?"

"It's all part of the scenario. The natives will shoot arrows and hurl spears at us from the shore. The soldiers will drive them off with gunfire. Everybody has a good time and nobody gets hurt."

"How do you know this?"

"In the ticket office, this guy named Marlow told me. Seems he had something to do with the conception of this domain. Strange, sad-looking man."

Benny sighed. "Hell of a way to have fun, if you ask me."

"Oh, there's more to it than that," Roscoe said, "There's the lottery."

"I'm not even going to ask what that is."

"When you boarded. They write your name on your ticket. Everybody's ticket goes in a hat and the Captain pulls one out when we reach the steamy part of the river."

"I don't remember anyone writing my name on a ticket. But what's special about the steamy part of the river?"

"Full of mosquitoes and crocodiles."

"God, I hate crocodiles."

"The person with the lucky ticket gets thrown to the crocodiles. Virtual crocs, of course. But they say it's great fun to watch."

Benny's eyes widened. He looked hard at Roscoe.

"You're kidding me, aren't you. Come on, tell me you are." Roscoe couldn't restrain himself. He laughed. "Gotcha," he said.

"You are a mean son of a bitch, Duffy."

Both river banks were closer now. The sun began to dip below the horizon of tree tops, muting the glare from the river's surface. It was now possible to see the true mocha color of the Congo's muddy water. The shoreline vegetation began to take on three-dimensional form, revealing small openings in the forest and offering glimpses of the terrain behind the first line of trees.

Benny saw it first. A flash of color behind the shoreline's screening leaves. "What's that?" he cried.

Roscoe scanned the tree line. He could make out shadowy forms partially hidden by the foliage. They followed the boat as it moved up river.

"I think we're in for some fun," Roscoe said.

A moment later the air was pierced by the chilling war cries

101

and ululations of attacking savages. They were running onto both river banks, firing volleys of arrows that hissed by with astonishing speed. With an authentic *tunk* and a quivering *twang,* they drove themselves deep into the wooden superstructure of the *Conrad*. The soldiers fired at the attackers, forcing some of them to retreat. Benny ducked and dodged about, desperately seeking shelter. He was so busy scrambling, he didn't see the spear that suddenly drove through his chest and embedded itself in the wall of the pilot house. He stood there, shocked, unable to move.

"God! I'm hit, I'm hit!" he cried. "Help me, Roscoe!"

Roscoe, who had made no effort to avoid the arrows, moved to Benny's side. By now the *Conrad* had passed beyond the gantlet of savages and entered the safety of wide water.

"Just walk sideways or straight ahead. Remember, you're not flesh and blood. You're like air. It can't hold you," Roscoe said.

"No, it will hurt!"

Roscoe cocked his head impatiently. "Does it hurt now?"

Benny considered for a moment. "No," he said.

"Then it won't hurt when you walk away from it."

"You're sure?"

"Absolutely."

Benny tried a little twitch to see if it hurt. Then, gingerly, he walked sideways. The haft of the spear moved outward through the left half of his body like a wand passing through a column of dense smoke, then the separated parts reunited. Benny managed a sheepish grin.

"What the hell, it was so realistic I believed it. I even felt pain there for a moment, I really did."

"This is going to make a great story, Benny. Wait until Bruno hears this!"

Benny threw up his hands in exasperation and concentrated on the shoreline. Far behind them the yelling and gunfire resumed. The tourists were getting their money's worth.

The humid heat pressed heavily on them. A few of the soldiers unbuttoned their tunics and removed their fezzes. Most had propped their rifles against the rail, their job apparently done for the time being.

It was dark by the time they tied up at the Inner Station. Torches flickered from several dock pilings, creating an eerie corridor of light and shadow. As Roscoe and Benny disembarked, jungle drums began beating in the darkness.

"I'm glad this isn't real," Benny said.

They were met at the end of the dock by a party of natives. A half dozen with spears grouped themselves behind a tall, sleekly muscled black who appeared to be their chief. Bare-chested, he wore a woven skirt of some coarse material and armbands of small, multicolored feathers. Around his neck hung a string of what looked very much like teeth, though in the flickering light it was hard to see them clearly. A band of black pigment crossed his nose and cheeks. He and his retinue bowed to Roscoe and Benny.

"Welcome Mr. Duffy and Mr. Spielmacher," he said in surprisingly clear English. "We have been awaiting your arrival with great eagerness." Their astonishment drew a smile from the chief.

"Oh yes, we got word of your visit from the Outer Station some time ago. The jungle telegraph is ancient but very effective. Translating 'Spielmacher' into tomtom was quite a challenge, though."

"You also know why we have come?" Roscoe asked.

"You've come for that wretched poet, McGonagle. Yes, he's here, I'm sorry to say. I have tried to get rid of him, but he won't go. Perhaps you can persuade him to go back with you. Come, I'll take you to him."

With torch-bearers leading the way, the chief took them along a path crossed by vines and large fronds . Benny was short enough to pass under the fronds but Roscoe was repeatedly smacked in the face with them. These slaps passed through his face painlessly but the momentary gaps they created between sections of his head were annoying. The chief talked as he walked just ahead of Roscoe.

"The attraction of this domain for us is the culture of our

ancestors. We like its simplicity, its rituals, its traditional ways of doing things. We are keeping our heritage alive," he said. "The tourists are a boon, too, because they buy the artifacts we make, and that keeps us busy and feeling that we produce useful things...."

"Like those ebony statues of naked women with pointy boobs," Benny said. Roscoe grimaced with embarrassment.

The chief seemed to take the remark in stride. "Yes, along with colorful cloth, pottery, baskets and other items. But unfortunately, that nitwit McGonagle is undermining our culture, as you will see."

They walked on in silence. At length they heard drums mingled with the rhythmic chanting of voices. They soon reached the source of these sounds in a large clearing lit by a surrounding circle of torches.

Natives were performing a rap number. In their midst was McGonagle, an incongruous figure in a purple smoking jacket and tassled fez sitting on an elevated throne of ivory tusks and lion skins. In front of him a native wearing gold chains and a baseball cap turned sideways chanted rapper lingo. He strutted and crouched and sidestepped to the beat, slashing the air with extended forefingers to dramatize unintelligible words. Two sullen women pranced around him with pelvic thrusts and hip flips, their hands brushing suggestively over their breasts and thighs. Other natives shuffled among these performers, apparently understanding the rap artist's babble, and acting out key words with sexually suggestive posturing. McGonagle was caught up in the rhythmic recitation, tapping his foot in time to the beat and chanting words Roscoe could not decipher. Britain's Worst Poet beamed with maniacal ecstasy.

The Chief scowled at the performing natives. "This is the consequence of bad poetry," he said. "At first our young people made fun of McGonagle's wretched verse by chanting unintelligible words. But gradually they came to like their mocking gibberish and regarded it as a new musical genre. Now look at them. Instead of wearing traditional skirts, the men scuff the ground in dungarees two sizes too long and spin on their ass. They've shed their bandannas in favor of gimme caps. And the women, instead of being innocently nude above the waist, wear provocative tops with low backs and cutouts around the nipples. They shimmy and shake in the most indecent ways."

" 'Shimmy and shake'?" Benny said.

"You know what I mean!" the Chief snapped back. "Look at them. Hump, hump and waggle your ass."

"Benny, shut up." Roscoe said.

The rapper finished his recitation and the drums stopped. Members of the ensemble cheered, their arms raised and swaying in the air like bending saplings. Roscoe and Benny approached McGonagle. His eyes were wide with excitement.

"Did you hear that? Did you hear that? I finally got it!" he said.

Benny raised his eyebrows at Roscoe. *What's he talking about?*

Roscoe didn't know either, but he nodded to McGonagle as if he understood. *Go along, get along.*

The poet favored them with look of mad triumph. "I've journeyed to the very origins of poetry...to the emerging language of Cro-Magnon man. Here's how I use it to invigorate modern verse:

> *Boomalay, boomalay, boomalay BOOM!*
> *Wimaway, whamaway, shamaway TOON!*
>
> *Motherfucker BOOM, motherfucker BOOM*
> *Boomalay, boomalay, motherfucker BOOM*

The horror, the horror, thought the Chief.

"See how that catches the very essence of our ancient forebears! I have revolutionized modern poetry!"

Roscoe responded to McGonagle with an ambiguous smile like that of a man experiencing gas pains. "Yes, I can see that," he said.

McGonagle beamed.

"And now you must go down river with us, back to the domain you left," Roscoe said. "You must not deprive its poetry lovers of your new art."

"Yes, yes, please go," the Chief said.

McGonagle thought about this for a few moments. Then he nodded: "Yes, it is time for me to return. I will henceforth call myself England's only Cro-Magnon Poet."

The Chief looked greatly relieved. He smiled his thanks to Roscoe. After waving a regal farewell to the rappers, McGonagle joined Roscoe and the others as they filed back onto the trail that had brought them to the clearing. Once again Roscoe endured the annoying slap of fronds. McGonagle was frond-slapped as well but seemed oblivious to the repeated partitioning of his head. Benny, walking behind the poet, again passed beneath the fronds, unaware his taller companions were being struck by them, although he was puzzled by the way McGonagle's head kept pulling apart and then closing back together. He though the man must have a tic of some kind.

The *Conrad* was fired up, awaiting their return. The Chief thanked Roscoe profusely for taking McGonagle with him. The poet took this as an insult, turned his back on the Chief, and proceeded with stiff dignity up the gangplank.

"I wish there were some way I could repay this great service you have rendered us," the Chief said.

"Absolutely not," Benny said. "But maybe you can tell me if there's someplace around here I can buy a shrunken head. I always wanted one of those."

"Ah, I am sorry, but we don't do those anymore. I mean how could we? Up here with only etheric bodies to work with? Not to mention the political incorrectness of decapitating people to make souvenirs. But you can buy fabricated ones at the Outer Station. Big sellers. But made by the Chinese, I'm afraid. They make them better, faster and cheaper than we can. Business is business, even up here."

Roscoe and Benny said goodbye and boarded the *Conrad*.

Traveling down river in the dark they passed slowly beneath

106

a spellbinding canopy of glittering stars. How very human to include stars in a created domain, Roscoe thought. Even in Heaven we want our glorious stars.

The *Conrad's* searchlights illuminated the river ahead, sweeping over the scuted backs and glowing eyes of crocodiles and startling four-footed creatures at the water's edge. McGonagle leaned against the rail, smoking, his face silhouetted against the brightness of the night sky. He was calmer now. He had unbuttoned his smoking jacket. He began talking before Roscoe had a chance to ask questions. He had an audience once more and telling his story was as much a compulsive performance as reciting his poetry.

"It began with those *strange* barrels," he said with theatrical gravity. "I was simply curious to see what was in them, and as the top of one was open, I looked in. It was white powder. I thought it might be *sugar,* and almost without thinking I took a pinch of it, sniffed it, and tasted it. Great Jehosaphat! I immediately had the *weirdest* sensation of being suspended in time and space. I could see and hear and talk but I wasn't *there,* if you know what I mean.

"Then I saw these men running toward me, yelling, and waving these big fly-swatter things. I didn't care. With complete indifference, I just watched them rushing at me."

"Then one of them hit you with a racquet and you went all prinkly," Benny said. "Next thing, you were standing in front of the Professor and he jabbed you with a needle that turned you into a sheep."

"I'm not entirely clear on that, but I have dim memories of something like that happening, yes."

Roscoe said: "Do you remember being turned back into yourself."

"I remember that prinkly feeling and then standing in front of this short Scot and a burly angel, not really knowing where I was or what I had been doing. I reacted automatically, doing what was most familiar. Reciting my latest poetic composition. Then I wandered off, still in a daze."

Roscoe asked whether he wandered into the Congo

accidentally.

"My thinking was distorted. I got this notion I wanted to bring poetry to the natives...a beacon in their darkness, so to speak. Besides, I had never been in the *African Domain* and was not a *persona non grata* there, as I am in so many of the cretin domains up here! You know the rest. It was serendipity of the most exalted kind. It has changed me *utterly!*"

McGonagle sighed and fell silent. Roscoe began to speak, but the Cro-Magnon Poet silenced him with a raised hand and a look that said, *Can't you see I wish to be alone!*

The two detectives moved to the other side of the deck.

"I don't believe it. A mind-altering drug in Heaven?" Benny said. "Who needs to get high on drugs up here?"

"I don't think it's for getting high. McGonagle didn't say anything about it making him feel good. What surprises me is that it had an effect. How can a drug affect someone who no longer has a physical body?"

"You can ask the same thing about turning people up here into sheep," Benny said.

"Good question with no answer for the moment," Roscoe said. "But let's put together what we *do* know. Stuckey's behind it. He took you and McGonagle down because he though you might have learned something you shouldn't about what he's up to. And those guys in wet suits and tanks are part of it...."

"So are the geodesic ball and the folded-down cherry-picker thing."

"Something bad is about to go down," Roscoe said.

"Yeah, but how can anything bad happen up here? The Almighty's in charge and He knows everything that's going on."

"That's supposed to be the case. But what if it isn't."

"C'mon, Duf. You gonna tell me God don't always know what's happening everywhere? That don't make sense."

"Look at it this way. Would Stuckey be doing this in secret if it were something innocent? No. And if he knew God would surely find out he's up to no good, would he even consider doing something evil? No. So he's got to know that God doesn't always know everything."

Benny slowly rubbed his chin. "If you're right, you know what this means?"

"What?"

"When I get back I'm going to live my life differently. Especially with women. What a time I'll have!"

"You're forgetting the Eye In The Sky Bureau I told you about."

"Damn!" Benny said.

Lester Mooch flunked out of ninth grade in a backwater Mississippi town. Disgusted with his stupidity and convinced he'd never amount to anything big like a snake-kissing preacher, his parents, who were first cousins, abandoned him and moved to Appalachia. Mooch earned enough to feed himself by working on local farms. At eighteen he joined the Army. He was surprised to discover it harbored a lot of rednecks like him, and that his assignments did not require much education or intelligence. Being slow-witted and willing made him attractive to superiors like Stuckey, who exploited aides ready to do what they were told, no questions asked. But if Mooch was slow-witted, he was not stupid. He had street sense and the intuition of a survivor. Right now, his instincts were telling him something was wrong.

Stuckey was being suspiciously nice instead of railing at him. He actually spoke in a paternal tone when he said: "Lester, you have a lot on your plate and you need some relief. I'm taking you off the search for the Professor and that detective. I've got something else in mind for you, never mind what just now."

He won't even look me in the eye. This sonofabitch is going to screw me somehow.

"We'll get to that tomorrow. Right now I want you to carry out an important mission." He opened his desk drawer and withdrew a letter-size envelope with the flap tucked in. "At 1400 hours today I want you to be at our secret breach in the Heavenly wall--you know, the one where the wagon finally came through."

Mooch nodded.

"Dress in civies. Two of our Friend's men will be there. Give them this envelope with our 'special' powder in it. Our Friend wants to test it to make sure it works. Got it?"

"Right, Colonel," Mooch said, struggling to hide his anger.

The sergeant dressed in blue jeans and a loose Hawaiian shirt. He left early for the rendezvous. He wanted to observe Satan's men before they saw him. He didn't trust anyone from Hell, especially when there was something fishy about this mission. The Devil must already know the powder works. Hadn't McGonagle had proved that? He was being sent on a needless errand! Why?

The breach in wall of Heaven lay in a remote part of *Theatris* not far from the theater staging of *Henry the Fifth*. It was hidden behind a dense patch of tall bushes. The guardian angel who patrolled this section of the wall had been last in his class at the Angel Academy. He was miffed at being passed over for promotion several times, and bored with this job in the sticks. From a distance, the 10-foot-high wall looked okay to him. It disappeared behind the bushes on one side and reappeared on the other. He was not disposed to make the extra effort it would take to check behind the bushes.

Mooch hid in a nearby copse of trees. After the guardian angel passed on, he worked his way closer to the bushes in front of the breach, careful to screen himself behind the foliage of the copse. No one was about. He quickly crossed the open ground to the wall and crouched in the shadows to the right of bushes. He could see into the opening, which partially concealed its width by being cut at a 45 degree angle. Fifteen minutes passed. Then with a *kwack* sound the two from Hell hurtled into the breach, each compressed pupa-like inside a large, transparent capsule. The capsule, contrived by an anti-Christ alchemist who had been burned at the stake, emitted a continuous electronic burble that repelled the furies in Chaos. But once at the base of the wall, Satan's legionnaires still had to scale it without being intercepted by guardian angels with flaming swords. The concealed breach had thus far eliminated that problem.

Mooch watched the legionnaires flip open the capsule cover and emerge like newly hatched butterflies, unfolding arms and legs and wings until they had attained their full stature. Tall and muscular, they were dressed like the English soldiers besieging Harfleur in *Henry the Fifth.* Anyone spotting them would take them for actors in the play taking a break near the Heavenly wall. One with blond hair reached back into the capsule and withdrew a Detainer. Mooch's heart froze. But then, why shouldn't they carry one for self- protection? As the two advanced into the opening the one with the Detainer concealed it beneath his blouse. Maybe that was okay, Mooch thought, but maybe not. He stood up and moved to the mouth of the breach. The two legionnaires saw him and waved. They approached at an unhurried pace. When they were within 30 feet, they suddenly began rushing toward him, the blond one swinging the Detainer in his hand. Mooch jumped to one side barely avoiding the swipe. The miss threw the assailant off balance just long enough for Mooch to recover and throw the "special" powder in his face. The blond instantly froze and dropped the sticky plate. This startled the second legionnaire into pausing for a heartbeat to fend off a similar attack. In that split second, Mooch scooped up the Detainer and swatted him squarely in the face. His entire body atomized with a sizzle as it stuck to the plate. The "powdered" blond did not move or show emotion as his comrade disappeared. He looked on indifferently as Mooch approached him. His expression changed to a look of mild curiosity as Mooch slowly drew the Detainer back, then swung it hard into his chest. The fight had taken less than thirty seconds. With the two assailants reduced to atoms clinging to the plate, Mooch extended the device over the wall and pressed the countercharge button on the handle. The atoms of legionnaires dropped from the plate with a crackle and began to reassemble themselves, but it was too late. They were falling into Chaos unprotected. He saw flailing arms disappear into the mist and shuddered at the terrified screams of the "unpowdered" legionnaire as he plummeted downward. His comrade made no sound at all. Seconds later, Mooch heard the horrible roaring of furies devouring

111

their prey.

He slumped against the wall. Only now did his fear rush through him at full flood. Stuckey had tried to off him! His anger burned like hot bile. *It's payback time, you sonofabitch. Now it's my turn to fry your ass.*

The journey back to the Outer Station was uneventful. McGonagle kept to himself. He paced the deck with hands behind his back, deep in thought.

"I wonder what he's thinking about," Benny said.

"No idea. Don't care either. He gets on my nerves," Roscoe said.

Benny studied his friend. "What's bothering you?" he asked.

Roscoe looked up at the stars. "I'm thinking about what we've got ourselves into. We're way over our heads, Benny. We're meddling in stuff the living aren't meant to mess with."

"Yeah, but that's why it's so exciting. No living person has ever done what we're doing."

"And what good is it? Tell me! I fall in love with a dead woman... and you're drooling to stage *Paradise Lost* for dead people. That's a big whoop! Dumbest of all, we're trying to figure out what kind of a bad-ass plot some dead Colonel is cooking up against *whoever* for *whatever* reason. What difference does it make whether he succeeds or fails? It won't affect us either way. It's none of our business."

"Maybe so, but maybe not, Duf. And you're forgetting we're detectives. This is the biggest case any detective has ever worked. We can't just walk away from it because it's none of our business...and maybe we can make a difference... maybe even save God!"

"Save *God*? Us save *God*? That's ridiculous, Benny."

"Think a minute, Duf. You're right that Stuckey must know the Almighty does not always know everything that's going on. But carry that further. Say his plot succeeds. Whatever he does won't stand up once the Almighty finds out about it. So it figures...he's got to get rid of God."

"But that's impossible!"

"It doesn't figure any other way."

"It's unthinkable. I can't buy it."

"Suit yourself. You can go back to the boring life you were leading. Not me. I'm going to see this through. How many people get the chance to save *God!* I don't know how you can walk away from that."

Roscoe fell silent.

"By the way, producing my musical *is* a big whoop for me. I don't care if the audience is dead."

"Save God! Save *God?*" Roscoe said, shaking his head.

"Damn right. Walk away from this, you'll always regret it."

Roscoe snorted dismissively but Benny could tell he was weakening.

He said, "You've just slipped back into your old ways, Roscoe. You get down on yourself and go into a black funk. You think everything's negative...But hey, up here, *anything* can happen. You know that. Forget what I said about you and Rose. It could work out, who knows?"

"You're always the optimist, Benny. That's part of the reason we flopped as detectives. You were overly optimistic when you should have been skeptical, and I was too pessimistic when I should have seen possibilities. I never had the guts to go out on a limb while you were always way out on a limb. What a pair we are."

"There you go again. We weren't as bad as all that. Even if that's true--and I ain't agreeing it is--here's our chance to change things. Look, we're experienced detectives. Those are in short supply up here. We've got something to offer."

"And save God?"

"Absolutely!"

Roscoe sighed and shook his head. He felt himself in the grip of the old self-doubt that had kept him from making decisions. Benny might be all wet about saving God, but suppose he wasn't.

113

Then the responsibility for saving the Almighty rested on the shoulders of two screwups. Why us? Why me? Why am I dogged by such bad luck? Why can't somebody else save God, or not save god! *Somewhere it must be raining.*

Lance Petard almost cried with despair and anger. The dress rehearsal was one gigantic jumblefuck. With the Masque scheduled to be staged tomorrow, it was too late to straighten everything out. They would have to go with the mishmash this had turned into. The Masque ought to be called *Seafood Salad* instead of *Poseidon Triumphant.* He struggled to console himself with the thought that it wasn't his fault! He had been forced to delegate too much responsibility to others, Fremont Taylor chief among them, and had lost control of the production. Too many bad ideas foisted upon him by Stuckey. Too many odd people he did not remember casting were largely ignoring his directions. Absolutely unheard of!

But right now he had to put the best face on things for Rollo Glotz, the most feared reporter from the supermarket tabloid, *Saucy Tidbits.* Glotz had been tipped that things were not going well and he was sniffing around for titillating morsels.

Glotz stood on the beach, watching the dress rehearsal. He was a small, balding man with the pointy rodent face. His thick glasses in oversized black rims made his eyes look large and fishy.

"I don't get it," he said in his thin, whiny voice. "If this is *Poseidon Triumphant* what is Polyphemus doing out there?" The giant with an empty eye socket in the middle of his forehead stood a hundred feet offshore, up to his waist in the sea. Even with his lower half in water 30 feet deep, his upper body towered over the neriads and mermen swarming in front of him.

Damn Glotz for asking that question! Damn Fremont Taylor for insisting the giant be part of the Masque as a "favor" to some of Stuckey's pagan friends!

"What's his role? He's just standing here with his hands on his hips," Glotz said.

114

What indeed was this giant's role? That challenge had driven Petard to distraction. This oaf had no conceivable role in the story line of the Masque. Besides that, he was absolutely useless. How could you direct a giant who couldn't see? Worse, he was cranky and unpredictable, unleashing tremendous roars for no reason; rock-cracking roars that scared the daylights out of the cast, reminding them that this monstrosity had devoured four men before Ulysses had driven a stake into his eye. No matter that they were no longer vulnerable flesh and blood; no one in the Masque wanted to experience even the virtual sensation of being eaten. But desperation had forced Petard's imagination to come up with a minor role for the giant, preposterous and dangerous though it was.

"He is going to do mock battle with Poseidon. It will be an exciting cliffhanger, but of course Poseidon will finally win," Petard said. "We are not running through the fight in this rehearsal. Poseiden and Polyphemus have their parts down pat. We need to concentrate on other aspects of the Masque that need to be smoothed out."

He was lying. He had no idea whether Polyphemus even understood the directions he had given him. And if the giant did understand them, would he cooperate, or would he have a quirky moment and go on a rampage? Nor did Petard know whether the new Poseidon would in fact go through with the mock battle.

The Poseidon originally cast had, at the last minute, flatly refused to "fight" the unpredictable monster. In desperation, Petard replaced him with a lotus-eater. This smiling idiot was so strung out he wouldn't care if his hair were on fire.

"That's cool, man," he said when Petard asked him to take the part.

Petard could not think of any excuse to avoid the interview. He forced himself to smile at Glotz and summoned Flower Power, the name he gave the lotus-eater in his own mind. Flower Power's real name was Ganymeade of Gophlopsy. He was a soft but shapely youth with the smooth white skin of someone who has not known hard labor under a hot sun. Tangled strands of wavy blond hair reached his shoulders, a few of them falling over his eyes as though

115

he had just emerged from the shower or a wind tunnel. He wore a red and blue body suit festooned with sequins and cockle shells and a conch helmet that looked vaguely Napoleanic.

Glotz and Ganymeade settled down in a rowboat beached at the edge of the water. Petard stood beside them, nervously rubbing his hands together.

Ganymeade, reclining on one elbow, spelled his name for Glotz and then half-closed his eyes as though ready for a nap.

"So what do you do in Lotus-land?" Glotz asked.

Ganymeade opened his eyes a little wider and smiled languidly.

"Mostly muse and brood in sweet melancholy. Sometimes I write poetry."

"What kind?"

"I sing of ocean ripples and zephyrs. Not waves, not surf. Only ripples. And not gusts or winds. Only zephyrs."

"One doesn't see ocean ripples or zephyrs everyday," Glotz said

"Exactly. You have to wait and wait and wait. That's when I eat lots of lotus and immerse myself in sweet melancholy."

"So you are stoned all the time. What does that do for you?"

"Do? Makes me mellow, dude. I don't worry about anything. I don't fear anything. Just kinda flow along dreamy and pleasantly sad."

"Can you remember things'"'

"Man, who needs to remember things? Everything is now. Who needs to remember what happened yesterday?"

"I mean stuff like directions. Like what you're supposed to do with Polyphemus."

"Polyphemus?"

"Yes, that giant out there. The one you are going to fight in mock combat."

"Oh? Oh, sure!"

"So how will you fight him?"

Ganymeade couldn't remember anything about fighting the

giant. He had agreed to be Poseidon because he liked the spangly costume he would wear. Sashaying around in it would be a big kick. Maybe Petard had said something about the giant, he couldn't remember. It didn't make any difference. It was all funzies, and he loved fun. If he was supposed to fight a giant, then he would fight a giant. But he couldn't remember how he was supposed to do it, so he decided to wing it. Keep this Glotz guy happy. And Petard, who was glaring at him.

"No need to keep it a secret from him, Ganymeade," Petard said through clenched teeth.

"Well, okay then. But I'll do better than tell you. I'll show you !"

"No!..." Petard began. But it was too late. Ganymeade hopped from the boat, picked up his triton, and pushed the rowboat into the water so quickly that Glotz toppled out onto the sand.

With a sinking feeling Petard watched Ganymeade row toward Polyphemus. He smiled bravely at Glotz and added a faint *wait-till-you-see-this* nod.

Polyphemus could not see Ganymead approaching but he could smell him, just as he could smell the other players swimming by him. But this one had a funny sweet smell about him and it pricked the giant's lumpish brain in a spot where his curiosity had lain dormant for ages. His great hands began sweeping the water around him for this strange being.

Petard watched the groping with alarm. One pass of the giant's hand headed straight for Ganymeade but the lotus-eater pulled hard at the last moment and escaped. He turned toward Petard and Glotz and waved his triton triumphantly. Petard's heart gave a violent thump. What an idiot! There's no telling what Polyphemus will do if this fool provokes him!

Ganymeade managed to keep the rowboat a couple of feet away from the giant's midsection as he surveyed him, considering how to proceed. Should he stick him with the triton? Swat him with the oar? This was terribly confusing. Damn! He should have paid attention to the directions for this combat. A sudden wave lifted the boat and carried it closer to Polyphemus' middle, so close that the tip of one oar momentarily penetrated his abdomen, leaving a wispy hole that immediately began to fill in. The giant roared and reached blindly for the source of this annoyance. His hand snared the boat and immediately lifted it to his cavernous mouth. He swallowed the boat and Ganymeade in one gulp.

Petard stood speechless.

Glotz stared wide-eyed for a moment. "Wow," he said. "That is a cliffhanger! What happens next?"

Next? Petard had no idea. The script called for Poseidon to circle the giant, stabbing and running until Polyphemus tired of vainly trying to catch his tormentor and slouched off, angry but defeated. Swallowing Poseidon was not in the plan. That stupid giant! That stupid lotus-eater! He was trapped. How could he possibly explain this unwelcome development to Glotz!

"Wait and see," he said, buying time. Surely something more would happen. Something had better happen!

And it did.

A deep rumble shook the water around the giant. This was followed by an upwelling behind him that released the vile gas of a tremendous fart. Petard gagged and tried to hold his breath, and it was not until later that he was able to regard this as The Fortunate Fart. In the midst of the upwelling the rowboat popped to the surface followed by the flailing, gasping Ganymeade.

"Oh, excellent!" Glotz said, applauding with delicate hand claps.

"But why is he swimming back toward us? Isn't he going to finish off the giant?"

Petard's heart was still racing madly but he rose to the challenge.

"Ah, that's a surprise we will save for the actual performance. A little tease never hurt attendance, did it Mr. Glotz?"

Ganymeade by now had staggered out of the water and joined the reporter and Petard.

"Man," he said with a foolish grin. "*That* was a trip!"

The *Conrad* docked at the Outer Station at mid-morning. The Professor and Bruno stood onshore, waving to Roscoe and Benny. From the rail of the *Conrad*, Roscoe could see that Rose was nowhere in sight.

"Welcome back, you three," Bruno said as he greeted them. The Professor mumbled something similar and flashed a brief smile.

Bruno extended his hand to McGonagle who, in the manner of royalty, accepted it without much return effort.

"I was most happy to hear they found you," Bruno said to him. "I trust you have provided detectives Duffy and Spielmacher with helpful information."

McGonagle straightened slightly like an actor whose moment to speak has come. "I do not know whether the information was helpful or not. I simply told them what happened," he said, his tone implying that no one could possibly expect more of him than that.

"He was most helpful," Roscoe said.

"Good. Very good. It may please you to know, Mr. McGonagle, that your friends at *Eccentrics' Corner* were worried about you and petitioned Michael to search for you. Nice to know how much you are missed, eh?"

McGonagle was not moved. "They are idiots. I never should have been forced to share their domain. I will never return to the company of those crack-brained pettifoggers!"

"Ah, just what I was coming to," Bruno said, relieved they had come so easily to what he was coming to, which was informing McGonagle he was being assigned to a new domain. It was never pleasant to tell people where they must go.

"You won't have to go back to *Eccentrics' Corner*. Michael wants you to move to a new domain that was just created. It's called *PSHAW*. That stands for *The Permanent Shelter for Hapless and Abandoned Words*. He feels you could be of great service there, since you are such a lover of words."

McGonagle was wary. "What are these...hapless and. what?... that I am to help?"

"*Hapless* and *abandoned*. Hapless words whose misfortune has been to fall out of use. Words like "slumgullion," "trimotor," "hickey," and "dun." There are also abused words, like split infinitives, wrong tenses, malapropisms and words wrongly forced to take on the meaning of close cousins, like "imply" and "infer" and "pour" and "pore." It is heartbreaking to see them all languishing at the Shelter, their hopes of being restored to their proper selves and returned to current usage fading day by day. You could offer them counseling and encouragement. You might even find a place for some of them in your poetry."

McGonagle's face brightened at the quaint prospect of words clamoring to become part of his poetry. What greater endorsement could a poet get!

"I am persuaded to try it. No promises, mind you. But we will see if it suits us."

Bruno congratulated him on his decision, which in fact was no decision at all. As an outcast in so many domains, McGonagle became a ward of the Heavenly Administration and *had* to go where it sent him. The poet knew this as well as anyone. Allowing him to pretend it was his choice was a face-saving kindness on the part of Bruno.

The angel gave McGonagle *PSHAW's* site number and wished him luck. Britain's worst poet, now also the Cro-Magnon Poet, nodded farewell to everyone and strode off.

"Ah, there's one problem solved," Bruno sighed.

"And perhaps another one averted," Roscoe said, thinking of McGonagle's notions of reinvigorating modern poetry.

Roscoe recounted what McGonagle told them.

"So it's obviously some kind of anesthetic or powerful tranquilizer that leaves you conscious but pretty much immobilized and somewhat disoriented," Bruno said.

120

"Must be something like the stuff used during a colonoscopy," the Professor said. "Yer not aware they're pushin' this cable up yer colon and yuh have no notion of time passin', but yuh can obey commands like "roll tuh the right" or "raise yer hips."

Roscoe posed the question that had been bothering him all along.

"I don't understand how drugs can affect anybody up here. They are all etheric beings. They don't have flesh or blood for drugs to work in."

The Professor nodded. "An excellent point. What yuh have tuh understan' is thet everythin', including etheric bodies, is made uf atoms. Thet's why the detainer works. It sucks in thuh electrical components uf a victim's atoms. My sheep-makin' serum also affects thuh atoms, though ah di no know quite how it does thet. The drug McGonagle discovered must somehow affect thuh atoms, too. So yes, it's quite possible fer drugs tuh affect bodiless persons."

"But not necessarily *all* bodiless persons," Roscoe said. "Look at the Detainer. It doesn't work on everybody up here. Higher ups like Stuckey are immune to it unless it is used against them by a superior. Why wouldn't higher ups be immune to drugs as well?"

"Immunity to the Detainer is provided by a chip that Stuckey and the other brass carry on them," Bruno explained. "A superior wishing to catch Stuckey with a Detainer would simply program it with a code that will override the chip--a code that only the superior knows."

"Detainer immunity, in uh word, is mechanical and therefore alterable," the Professor said. "Drugs are uh different story. If their atomic structure is compatible with etheric atoms, no one is immune tuh them. Theoretically, anyhow. In fact it remains tuh be seen how far up thuh heirarchy drugs and my sheep serum are effective. They may cease tuh work at some higher level, or they may not."

Benny flashed a knowing smile at Roscoe. "Then it's possible even God isn't immune to drugs," he said.

"Possible, yes." The Professor said.

They all contemplated the implications of this revelation.

121

Roscoe could read the dark expressions on the faces of Bruno and the Professor, could see them rising to an alarming conclusion.

"No one would dare..." Bruno began.

"Aye, Stuckey couldn't pull off somethin' like that," the Professor said.

"Right. Stuckey couldn't. He's only one of the plotters. Someone much more powerful is behind this," Roscoe said.

The others looked at him, the unspoken "who?" in their expressions.

"Think a moment, gentlemen. There is only one candidate," he said.

They saw his point immediately. They responded almost with one voice: "Satan."

That was the first step. Then they sat down and fitted together the pieces of information they had until everything fell into place. Satan, Stuckey, and others would attempt a coup against the Almighty tomorrow during the Masque. It was an incredible and terrifying prospect, but they knew it was real. The Second War in Heaven was about to begin and the odds were stacked against the Almighty.

The four quickly agreed on a course of action. They would have to persuade Michael the Archangel that the plot was real. He could forewarn the Almighty, who would act in time to stop the rebels before they started. Even if Michael were too skeptical to take the matter to God, he at least might take the precaution of having his legions at the ready--just in case. They would also pressure Petard to cancel the Masque.

"Let me approach Michael," Bruno said. "I might carry more weight with him than any of you. The Professor can come with me to explain the scientific side."

"Fine. Benny and I will deal with Petard," Roscoe said. "By the way, anybody seen Rose lately?" Bruno and the Professor shook their heads.

They did not seem concerned by her absence, but Roscoe felt his stomach tighten. He had expected her to be here when he returned. She never *said* she would be, but he assumed it was an unspoken agreement between them.

Bruno and the Professor departed after agreeing to meet the two detectives at Petard's after they spoke to Michael. Then Roscoe turned to Benny: "Let's make a quick check on Rose before we see Petard. I'll go to her bower. You check *EITSB*."

"What are you worrying about, Duf? She's probably been busy at work."

Roscoe wanted to believe that, but the anxiety in his heart would not go away.

The Department of Heavenly Security lay at the end of a marbled corridor in the Heavenly Administration Building. Bruno and the Professor passed through a pair of twenty-foot mahogany doors adorned with intricate carvings of battle scenes, and an ornate golden handle in the shape of a sword hilt. The handle was strictly decorative. Callers simply ignored it and passed through the closed doors.

The lobby they entered was more like a hall for Roman senators than a waiting room. It held a half-dozen red velvet couches and black granite end tables positioned at the bases of marble columns. The gilded molding of the coffered ceiling gleamed under indirect lighting. Heraldic shields hung on the walls. This majestic setting conveyed an unmistakable sense that only matters of the highest consequence ought to be brought here. The Professor sat on one of the velvet couches while Bruno walked ahead to a dais upon which a stern-faced archangel sat behind a white Louis XVI table. There was nothing on the table except a white telephone.

Bruno looked up at the archangel and said he needed to speak to Michael. The archangel looked at him with disdain for a few seconds. Then he arched an eyebrow and said: "And who are you?"

"I'm Chester Conklin's deputy. Name's Bruno."

"Do you have an appointment, Chester Conklin's deputy?"

"No I don't, but it is urgent, incredibly urgent."

"Oh *incredibly* urgent, is it? Well then, let me get right to the point, Deputy Bruno. You may *not* see Michael without an appointment. We simply do not operate that way. Good heavens, if everyone who comes here with an *incredibly* urgent matter were allowed to see Michael, he would never be able to leave his desk."

Bruno strained to suppress his anger. He was tempted to simply walk through the large golden door behind this ass. That would put him among the hundred offices of the Department's hierarchy, but without a guide, he and the Professor would never find Michael's office, or get past the guards sure to be standing outside it. He had no choice but to deal with this arrogant oaf. "Perhaps if I tell you the terrible thing about to happen, you'll let me see him."

The archangel closed his eyes and raised his hand as if to ward off something that would be insufferably offensive.

"No, no, *no*! I am not here to listen to everyone's sob stories."

"All right, you nitwit. I want to speak to your boss."

The archangel, head back and sneering, shoved the white telephone toward Bruno. "Dial 9," he said.

Bruno did so.

"Please listen carefully to your options, as our menu has changed," said a voice with a heavy Indian accent. "If you know the extension of your party, you may dial it now. For job applications, press one. For our most recent catalog of angelic apparel, press two. For tour prices, press three. To order a CD of the Music of the Spheres, press four. For the Hosanna schedule, press five. To speak to a representative of this Agency, press six. To repeat this menu..."

Bruno pressed six.

A minute passed. Then a voice said: "How may I help you?"

"I want to speak to whoever is the superior of the archangel on the lobby desk."

There was a pause, during which Bruno heard a muted conference in the background.

The voice returned. "What's his name?"

Bruno looked across the desk. "What is your name?"

The archangel closed his eyes, crossed his arms and looked

away.

"He won't tell me."

The voice sighed. "I can't connect you with the superior of an unnamed archangel."

"Look, just connect me with *someone* who can authorize me to see Michael!"

"That would have to be his Deputy, Israfel. I'll connect you."

There was a long silence followed by electronic clicks and buzzes. Eventually Israfel's phone rang. And rang. And rang. At length Israfel's voice said: "Your call is important to me. I'm sorry I'm not at my desk right now to take it, but if you'll leave your name and number after the beep, I'll get back to you as soon as I can."

Bruno slammed the handset into the cradle.

"Satisfied?" the archangel said with a smirk.

Bruno was at a dead end. What now? He couldn't go directly to the Almighty. No one could unless through the intervention of Michael.

The Professor had walked up to the dais halfway through Bruno's encounter with the archangel. Bruno turned to speak to him, but before he could say anything, the Professor silenced him with narrowed eyes which said *keep quiet.*

"Very impressive, I must say," the professor said, smiling at the archangel. "Yuh handled this one precisely as he deserves. We can't have everybody and his brother takin' up Michael's valuable time, kin we?"

The archangel was taken aback but smiled graciously at this odd little man who complimented him.

"And you are?" he said.

"Ah yes, my apologies fer not introducin' myself. I thought yuh might recognize mey. Name is Ross Mcgregor. I'm senior reporter fer *Heaven's Nightly News.* I'm usually on yer TV screen at least once durin' our daily broadcast. Yeh must not watch thuh news if yeh haven't seen mey."

"Oh, I watch the news all right, believe me. Part of my job, you know. And now that I think about it, yes, I have seen you many times. Yes indeed."

Bruno stood dumbfounded.

"I'm doin' a story on Heavenly security and thuh people responsible fer it. We're going tuh cover it from bottom tuh top and you'll be thuh one we will start with. Thuh first level of contact with the public, yeh might say."

"You don't say. . . .Me, on television? Me?"

Bruno could not believe what was taking place.

"Absolutely. My cameraman should be here shortly. Of course, I'll also need tuh interview Michael. Thuh piece won't fly unless I talk tuh him. It'll only take 10 minutes or so. Kin yuh slip mey in, duh yuh think?"

The archangel looked crestfallen. Then he flushed and seemed torn by indecision. At last he said:

"Believe me, I would get you in if I could, but Michael's not here just now."

"Where is he?" the Professor said.

Once again the archangel seemed to wrestle with his conscience.

"He's out conducting field exercises with his legions. Readiness is all, eh!"

"And where are these exercises being held?"

"I really don't know. They're usually in several places, and those could be anywhere. Locations are classified for obvious reasons."

"When will he be back."

"Have no idea. Could be days, a week."

"Ah, too bad. Then we'll have tuh wait."

The archangel's face sagged with disappointment. "Perhaps you could interview me when your cameraman arrives...get that part of the story done, eh?"

"Afraid not. Loss of continuity thet way."

"Ah yes, of course."

"So then, we'll just have tuh come back another day...."

"I'm here on Monday, Wednesday and Friday," the archangel said with servile petition in his tone.

How the mighty are fallen, Bruno thought. But that reflection passed quickly as he was seized by the chilling realization that without Michael and his forces at hand, and no way to warn the Almighty, Heaven had no defense against Satan and his legions.

Roscoe paced back and forth outside the tall iron gate of *Showtime in Heaven* lot, waiting for Benny. The foreboding that had been gnawing at him now gripped his heart in a vice. He had teleported himself to Rose's bower only to find it empty. Where was she? Had Stuckey taken her? Was she a prisoner on a Detainer stored in a secret place? Once again he cursed himself for getting into this whole business of saving God. What hope did a mere mortal have of saving the Almighty? It was preposterous. It was the Vanity of vanities. If he had steered clear of this affair, Rose would be with him right now. They would be working out a way to remain together. Or was that hopeless, too? He felt as though a great stone were pressing on his heart.

He saw Benny walking toward him. A fragile hope rose in him that his partner had good news.

"Man, you look terrible," Benny said. "You look like you lost a winning lottery ticket."

" Did you find Rose?"

"She wasn't at work. Darlene hadn't seen her. The Permitted Absence book, though, shows Rose signed out for vacation time yesterday and today."

That eased some of Roscoe's anxiety, but not all of it. What was going on? She had never mentioned any vacation plans. Something unexpected must have come up. There probably was a simple explanation for her sudden absence. Still . . . to leave at *this* time?

Several feet away a thin man in a pinstripe suit was studying them with interest. One arm pressed a clip board against his chest.

"Ah, gentlemen," he said as he came up to them, "would you be interested in signing my petition to keep Elvis in supermarkets?"

The two detectives were too startled to speak for a few

moments. Benny finally said: "You mean Elvis really is alive and hiding out in supermarkets?"

The man frowned at Benny as though he were impossibly out of touch with what goes on.

"Of course not. He's dead as a doornail, but the outfit I work for, the *Keep 'Em Laughing* division of *Showtime in Heaven,* sends his etheric self back to supermarkets now and then. Folks up here get a kick out watching the reactions it gets from shoppers and the media. That's our job. Keep folks up here laughing. Being in Heaven can get to be boring after a while."

"Why the petition?"

"Oh, Elvis is tired of these performances. Doesn't want to do them anymore. But if my colleagues and I can get enough signatures to keep him doing them, he'll have to do them. That's a rule up here."

Roscoe turned to Benny. "I don't like the idea of Elvis being forced to do this."

"Me neither. In fact, I was against him doing it in the first place, voluntarily or not. Dressed in one of his costumes--like the white one with all the rhinestones and spangles on it--he looks silly sitting on a pile of rutabagas, or slouching among the pancakes. It's even worse when he shows up among rolls of toilet paper."

"Right then," Roscoe said. "So we'll do our bit to keep Elvis out of supermarkets. No sir, we won't sign your petition."

The petition man shot them a look of disgust. "If we can't force Elvis to do this, some undesirable will steal his place. Like some dead rapper. You'll *so* not love it when that type is spotted in hat stores and jewelers' showcases." Then he turned and walked away.

"Man has a point," Benny said.

"Forget it. We've already wasted too much time."

As Roscoe and Benny were about to pass through the iron gate, the Professor materialized with a small "whoosh." He carried a Detainer and the insecticide sprayer containing the sheep-making elixir. He looked grave.

"Forget aboot Michael," he said. "He's away in thuh field

somewhere on maneuvers with his legions. Bruno's gone tuh search fer him, but he'll have tuh be very lucky tuh find him in time. We'll have tuh count Michael out, I'm afraid."

Roscoe cursed and looked glumly into the distance. Benny slapped his hands together like a man whose horse has just run out of the money. The three eyed each other, waiting for someone to break the silence. Benny suddenly brightened and snapped his fingers. "Hey, you Christians have been overlooking the obvious solution. And I, a Jew, have to point it out to you? How ironic!"

"Skip the gloating, Benny. What's your point?"

"You forgot Jesus! If He really is the son of God, He can certainly knock Satan and all his legions on their asses with a wave of his hand, right? How could you two not have thought of that? We simply need to tell Jesus what's up."

Roscoe and the professor looked at each other.

"Good thought, but too late, Benny," Roscoe said. "Before we rescued you, Bruno mentioned we could not expect any help from Jesus. I forgot to tell you that. Jesus has been resorbed by the Almighty. The Son of God is reposing in the bosom of his father enjoying a well earned break from his duties."

"And thuh Holy Ghost went with him," the Professor added, "which means thet if Satan wins, he neutralizes not just thuh Almighty but thuh entire Holy Trinity. Thet would be an unspeakable catastrophe."

No one spoke again until Roscoe took a deep breath and turned to the gate. "Our only hope is Petard. He's got to stop the Masque."

Chapter Seven

Lester Mooch made his way to the Pearly Gates by a route that meandered along the outskirts of the Golden City. The shorter way, directly through the city, would have increased the chances of being spotted by Stuckey's men.

He had been at the Pearly Gates only once, when he arrived for judgment, and he had no desire to revisit them. The sea of trembling applicants, wailing and moaning as they awaited their fate, brought back unpleasant memories of his own anguished wait to be judged. He did not wish to relive that tribulation, even though he had been incredibly lucky. The screams of those condemned to Hell had haunted him for months.

Lester was headed for the Gates only because he had learned that Jeremiah was there monitoring the admission procedures for the Heavenly Administration. Jeremiah's efforts to warn Michael of a gathering plot had worried Stuckey, although that worry was mitigated by the knowledge that Michael scoffed at the old man's prophecies.

But Jeremiah still had influence in high places, and armed with what Lester would reveal to him about the coming coup, Jeremiah might be able to warn the Almighty in time to crush it. *And how will you like that, Stuckey, you bastard!* He imagined the Colonel's rage when he realized that know-nothing Lester Mooch was the architect of his destruction. Although he savored the sweetness of his anticipated revenge, Lester's motive was not solely the desire to get back at Stuckey. He was also trying to save his own skin. If the plot succeeded, Stuckey would eventually find him and toss him into Chaos. But if he, Lester, were the key to foiling the coup, he would be forgiven his part in the plot and perhaps even be regarded as hero, which would be very nice, indeed.

Mooch heard the Pearly Gates before he saw them. They came to him first as a high, indistinct sound in the distance. As he drew closer, the sound grew louder and he could hear the jangling voices of souls weeping and crying out in terror. At last he crested a hill immediately behind the Gates and looked down on the sea of the newly deceased. Thousands of naked men, women and children crowded together, shuffling slowly forward to cordoned lines that led to processing stations. The seething mass was like a giant amoeba that kept changing its outline and pushing slender pseudopods into narrow spaces ahead of it.

Lester walked toward an elevated reviewing stand overlooking the processing stations. As he mounted the steps he noted the crowd of souls awaiting judgment was larger than he remembered it. So much for efficiency! The administration had tried to speed up the judgment process by issuing an electronic ticket to each soul. Inserted in a machine, the ticket automatically called up the *EITSB* watcher's report and calculated good deeds against bad ones. Trouble was that every soul who flunked the calculation wanted his videotape reviewed. This slowed matters up considerably because protesting souls had to wait for judges dressed as football referees to review the tapes and signal touchdown--a pass to Heaven--or false start, which meant a trip to Hell. Some of the white-robed administrators loudly insisted this procedure be discontinued in the interest of eliminating the bottleneck, but they were being harangued by lawyers protesting the injustice of doing so.

The tall, gaunt figure of Jeremiah stood apart from the administrators and the lawyers, apparently indifferent to their debate. Mooch walked up behind the prophet and tapped him on the shoulder. When Jeremiah turned to face him, Lester was startled for

131

a moment, thinking perhaps this was not Jeremiah. Mooch had never seen the old man when he wasn't scowling. This Jeremiah was smiling a serene smile. He looked at Mooch as though he couldn't quite get him in focus.

"Oh, yes," he said slowly, "you are one of Colonel Stuckey's assistants." Then he giggled.

Mooch found this unsettling but forged ahead anyway.

"I have some profoundly alarming information, sir. And I believe you are the only one with authority who will believe it," he said.

Still smiling, Jeremiah closed his eyes and nodded. He did not seem in the least bothered by the prospect of dire news.

"You were right about a plot against the Almighty," Mooch continued. "It will be launched tomorrow at the Masque. Satan is behind it and Colonel Stuckey is one of the key conspirators!"

Jeremiah's eyes opened half-way as though he were having trouble coming fully awake. He sighed and smiled again at Mooch.

"Ah, no, my dear young man. You cannot possibly be right. God would discover a plot as soon as it was conceived and punish the plotters. And Colonel Stuckey a conspirator? Preposterous. He is one of the finest and most loyal members of the Administration. I had the most pleasant time with him at lunch yesterday. Fine fellow. Nothing to worry about, dear boy! No plotsy wotsy afoot, trust me."

Plotsy wotsy? At the mention of lunch with Stuckey, it suddenly dawned on Mooch why Jeremiah was so utterly changed. The Colonel had somehow slipped the prophet a dose of the "special" powder. Mooch had to admire Stuckey's cleverness. With one stroke he had made *absolutely* sure Jeremiah would not be a threat *and* proved that the powder worked on the hierarchy. If it worked this far up chain of command, the likelihood of its working on the Almighty was high enough to persuade Satan and his cohorts to proceed with the coup.

Mooch was crushed. Where to turn now? Michael would never believe him--and anyhow, a low-ranking person like himself had little chance of speaking to the archangel without going through a lengthy petition process.

He turned away and headed for the platform steps. As he did so, he passed an official with the bullhorn, who was addressing the throng. It was another attempt by the administration to speed things up. "Every hundreth sinner gets amnesty," the official announced. Mooch had been a hundreth sinner. He had been lucky then, but now it appeared his luck had run out. He scarcely heard the mighty sound of rejoicing that rose to the vault of heaven.

Satan's legionnaires were a mixed lot. The fallen angels who had sided with Lucifer during the First War in Heaven stood out as the tallest and handsomest ones. The shorter, hairy legionnaires with paunches had been angels as well. But they had disobeyed Divine law by copulating with mortal women and producing athletic phenoms revered almost as deities by millions of sports fans. The Almighty, who did not want mortals to worship any god but him, hurled these angels headlong into the flaming pits of Hell.

The rest of the legionnaires were thin, fat, short, tall and average mortals, all of them depraved, who had come from the countless ranks of men condemned to Hell from after Adam's fall to the present day. Superior air-conditioning units in the barracks, or the power of legionnaire uniforms to excite lust in women, had induced many of them to enlist. A few had been drawn into service by a love of marching in parades, while others, the slow-witted five percent, who were still innocents in this kingdom of duplicity, had been duped by the obviously false promise of travel to exotic places.

In the barracks housing the Fifteenth Phalanx, a.k.a. the *The Devil Dogs,* Satan's troopers filled the time before D-hour in soldierly fashion. A crowd of men in one corner tried their luck in a crap game. A rather skinny legionnaire named Baggio was hot, making his point again and again with loaded dice, provoking cheers and shouts of dismay from the other players.

Other men reclined on the chain-mail mattresses of their bunks, hands behind their heads, reliving the pleasure of incest or rape, murder, pedophilia, marketing, advertising, corporate malfeasance or other sins that brought them here. A few wrote scatalogical letters to the Heavenly Administration. Others leaned on an elbow in their bunks studying dirty French postcards from the 19th Century. From the shower room came the sounds of sodomites enjoying what could be their last go, should fortune turn against them on Heaven's battlefield.

Camaraderie was in the air. Men hunkered down in small groups, exchanging details of their lives as they bonded ever more closely with their depraved comrades. Their voices carried over the medley of disparate sounds in the barracks:

"Hey, Brooklyn. Where you from?"
"Brooklyn."

"Me? Speared through the heart at Thermopylae. You?"
"Drowned in a malmsey butt in the Tower of London."
"A what?"
"It's a big wine cask."
"No shit! How'd you squeeze through the bung hole?"

"Listen. My girlfriend is a knockout. What tits! What an ass! And she can suck a golf ball through a garden hose, believe me! She was runner-up in last year's *Whore of Babylon* contest.

"Why don't you write her a last letter and give it to me. If you buy the farm tomorrow, I'll deliver it personally."

"Really? That's asking too much of you, ain't it?
"Nah!"

"Listen, you jerk, I was an electrician. You gotta have a lotta smarts to be an electrician."

"Bullshit! Any moron can become an electrician. I was a plumber, and let me tell you, you gotta know a lot to be a plumber."

"Get outta here. A plumber only needs to know three things. Cold is right. Hot is left. And shit goes down!"

134

"What's wrong with Joe? I never seen him so down in the dumps."

"He just got a Dear John letter from his girlfriend."

"Yeah? What's her name again?"

"Semolina. She's the Goddess of Macaroni. Says she's waited for him 500 years and she ain't gonna wait no more."

"Yeah? Well he's lucky she sent him a Dear John letter. Goddesses are bad news. Piss 'em off and they turn you into a frog or something else."

"Amen, brother. You got that right."

"I knew a guy was going with this Goddess of Disinfectant. Named Methiolate or something like that. She caught him screwing around with other women and turned him into one of those cakes they put in the bottom of urinals."

"No kidding!"

"When she finally restored him, his hair had turned blond."

"No shit!"

The barracks' door slammed open. The First Sergeant strode in and assumed his command-giving stance, legs apart, hands on his hips.

"All right, listen up. Put on your wet suits and tanks and form up. We're moving to the jumping off position, like we did in training. But this time when we're ordered into the vacuum tunnel to Heaven, it's the real thing!" He turned and started to leave. Then he spun and faced them again. "And remember, we're going to be packed shoulder to shoulder in that Z32T- H47 Series E Large-Transport Tunnel Capsule. Get all your farting done before you climb in!"

The crap game stopped. A hush fell. Seconds later the *Devil Dogs* broke into song. They sang "Home on the Range" in four-part harmony.

Lester Mooch walked through the outside wall on the south

side of the *Showtime* lot. This put him among buildings storing fabricated bedrooms, store fronts, living rooms and a variety of other large props--an area not busy with a lot of actors and production people.

Keeping his distance from the few people he passed, he made his way across the lot to Lance Petard's street. He walked on the side opposite Petard's building, his head down, deep in thought. Passersby hardly noticed him.

His plan to reveal the coup to Petard, he realized, was risky. Maybe Petard had been pressured into joining the plotters, and would immediately call Stuckey's men. And if he hadn't joined them, would he believe there *was* a plot? Would he have the guts to stop the Masque?

Unsettling though these questions were, he knew he could not turn back. There was no one else who could help. Yet in truth it was more than desperation pushing him on. There was something else, deep inside, that drew him to Petard. He had been smitten by the head of *Showtime in Heaven* the first time he laid eyes on him. Revealing the plot to Petard--an innocent Petard, he fervently hoped--might not only foil the coup; it would also be their first intimacy, their first dizzying step in a waltz of love. Why not? A lowly sergeant and a gorgeous show biz executive could find happiness in this mad, mad Heavenly world! He was sure of it.

Mooch was so absorbed in these thoughts he almost crossed the street to Petard's building without noticing two of Stuckey's security men stationed on either side of the front entrance. He continued straight ahead as he watched the sentries out of the corner of his eye. One of them glanced at him, then looked away, uninterested.

He walked to the corner, crossed the street, and made his way past several buildings. At the next intersection he turned left and kept going until he reached an alley that ran back to Petard's street. It also ran along the side of Petard's building. Mooch approached cautiously. There was no security man at the back of the building. He caught a glimpse of someone moving past a partially open window in what he figured was Petard's office. Checking once more to make sure he was alone, he quickly moved beneath the window and then levitated until he could just see into the room.

What he saw startled him. He was looking at the back of Stuckey's head. The Colonel was leaning back in the leather chair of Petard's desk, his bald spot almost touching the glass. Across the desk, Roscoe, Benny and the Professor faced Stuckey with angry looks. One of the Colonel's enforcers stood behind them with a Detainer in his hand. He had a squat weight lifter's body and a large head with buck teeth. Petard sat pale-faced in a chair to one side of the desk.

"Your deductions are quite right, Mr. Duffy," Stuckey said. "You lack one or two details, but you know our essential plan....By the way, that sheep switch you pulled on Punchinello was brilliant. I rather enjoyed pitting myself against a man of your high intelligence. It's a pity our cat and mouse game ends with this chance encounter. I would have preferred a hunter's satisfaction of running a wily prey to ground at last," Stuckey said. He laughed. "But I won't reject winning by dumb luck." He and his accomplice had spotted Duffy and the others entering the building and jumped them before they could defend themselves with the Detainer or the insecticide gun.

"You sound like the villain in a bad melodrama," Benny sneered.

"Really! Here you and Mr. Duffy have been playing the pious heroes, telling me that *I* can't defeat God. And you accuse me of melodramatic cliches!"

Benny's face flushed as he strained at the edge of self-control. He glanced at the Detainer and the insecticide gun they had been forced to relinquish, both of which lay on the desk. He looked at Roscoe, nodding toward the weapons without trying to conceal his unspoken appeal. *Let's make a grab for these and take our chances.* Roscoe put a restraining hand on Benny's arm. "Negative, Benny. Let it go."

"Very prudent, Mr. Duffy. I doubt you could get to those

weapons before Oswald caught both of you with the Detainer. Even supposing you did hit me with the sticky plate, it wouldn't work on me, as I assume you know. But there is a much better reason why it would be foolish to attack me...I have Rose."

Stuckey paused, reading the shock and anger this brought to Roscoe's face.

"She is on a Detainer safely tucked away in a place known only to me," he continued. "So you see, even if you sprayed me with the Professor's elixir, you would lose Rose. I mean, if I were a witless sheep, how could I have any idea where I am holding her?"

"He don't have Rose, Duf, he's bluffing!" Benny said. "Darlene said Rose signed out for vacation days."

Stuckey sighed. "She did sign out—with Oswald's Detainer at her back." He unbuttoned the flap on his shirt pocket and pulled out a photograph. It showed Rose wide-eyed with fear. Behind her Oswald held a Detainer, ready to strike.

"She can't do anything to stop you," Roscoe said.

"Perhaps. Perhaps not," the Colonel said. He closed his eyes in thought for a moment. Then he looked at Roscoe.

"You're a practical man, Mr. Duffy. I am sure you can guess the simplest way for me to ensure that none of you threaten the success of our plan."

Roscoe glared at him but said nothing.

"It would be to slap all of you with a Detainer and dump you into Chaos. End of threat...That is the fate I had planned for you." He glanced at Petard. "You were to end the same way just before the Masque began, you whiny little pervert." Petard's lower lip trembled. He was sweating.

Stuckey inclined his head and spread his hands in mock apology. Then he said: "But there may be a more pleasant solution for all of us." He turned to the Professor. "I need quantities of your serum and the antidote you used to restore Spielmacher and the other two. Will you make them for me?"

The little Scot did not hesitate: "Ach, no!"

"That is what I thought. So I will put the fate of your friends

138

in your hands. If you refuse to produce more serum and antidote, these two, Rose, and Petard, will be hurled into Chaos. If you comply with my request, I will release them once the coup is successful."

"You expect us to believe you'd keep your word!" Roscoe said.

"Put yourself in my position, Mr. Duffy. If the Professor does what I ask, why would I *not* let you go once we are in power. At that point you will no longer pose a threat. The coup will be a *fait accompli.* I would have no reason to concern myself with any of you, or your beloved Rose...it would be wanton of me to dispose of you all when I had no reason to do so. I am a practical man, not a beast."

Stuckey looked at his watch. "I must go. I leave you in the care of Oswald while you consider my proposition. When I return in two hours I will expect your decision, Professor."

The Colonel rose, nodded to Oswald, and walked out through the closed office door.

"Sit in a semi-circle in front of the desk like sensible people," Oswald commanded. "No, don't put your backs against the desk. Move away a couple of feet and face the desk."

As Roscoe and the others repositioned themselves, Oswald warily picked up the Detainer and insecticide sprayer that had tempted Benny. He leaned them against the wall behind the desk. Holding his Detainer in one hand, he rolled the leather chair from behind the desk and set it in front of the seated captives.

"Don't mind me. Go right ahead and talk as though I'm not here," he said with an arrogant grin as he eased himself into the chair. "If any one makes a move to stand up, I'll swat you before you raise a knee."

Except for Petard, who looked away and hugged his knees abjectly, the others stared back at their guard, their eyes blazing with anger and frustration.

The Professor spoke first. "Yuh know whut it'll mean if I cooperate with Stuckey," he said to Roscoe and the others. "It'll give him thuh power tuh be an absolute tyrant!"

"Wait a minute!" Petard cried. "You're thinking of *not* cooperating with him? For God's sake, Professor, you can't do that to us!"

The thought of Chaos sent chills rippling through Roscoe as well. Yet, to his surprise, he also felt the surge of something else, something that had grown as he faced the dangers of this world: a kernal of optimism and the courage to make a decision he knew to be right.

"You can't give him that power, Professor," he said. "What do you think, Benny?"

Benny winced. He wagged his head one way and then the other as he struggled to decide. At last he sighed and turned to Roscoe. "I'm sorry, Duf. I'm scared shitless of Chaos. I say we let the Professor give Stuckey what he wants and then go back where we belong."

Oswald smirked and shook his head. *You are such pitiful assholes.*

"Yes, yes! That is the only sensible...." Petard began.

He suddenly stopped. He jerked backward with a gasp as though struck by a heart attack. Oswald sprang up with the Detainer, unsure what to expect.

Petard was not having a heart attack. He had been startled by what he saw over Oswald's shoulder: Lester Mooch coming through the wall, grabbing the Detainer behind the desk, and lunging toward the guard's back. The sergeant needed only four or five steps to close with his former colleague. With a great shout he drew back the Detainer as he rushed forward. Oswald snapped around instinctively, throwing up an arm to ward off the blow he barely had time to see coming. It was too late. The racquet hit his elbow and instantly caused the rest of his body to disappear with a small "plink." His Detainer rattled on the floor as it settled down.

Roscoe and the others sat frozen with astonishment.

Mooch sucked in large draughts of air, trying to catch his breath. He lowered himself into the chair Oswald had occupied. He would answer the questions already forming on their lips. But first he settled his gaze on Petard, whose eyes were fixed on him, moist with adoration. *How sweet it is to be loved by the one you love!*

Bruno did not find Michael and his legions in any of the half-dozen likely places he visited. He asked locals in numerous domains whether columns of archangels had passed their way. No one had seen any. He was beginning to think it was a waste of time to question locals out here in the boondocks. Many were so quirky they wouldn't have noticed an earthquake. The last one he interviewed was an oddball artist who was completing the fifty-seventh portrait of his own handlebar mustache in color-infused Vaseline on masonite. He seemed completely unaware that overflowing water from a nearby creek had risen over his ankles and was moving up his legs.

At the moment, Bruno was surveying yet another valley hemmed by low hills that would make an ideal place for field maneuvers. He looked down on the valley floor and scanned the tree line on each side but found no sign of Heaven's legions. *Where the hell is Michael?*

As Roscoe and the others recovered from the shock of their startling rescue, Mooch explained how he came to be there and why he wanted to join them. His past association with Stuckey made them a little wary at first, but there was no denying he had rescued them at considerable risk to himself.

"I think he has redeemed himself," the Professor said.
Roscoe and Benny nodded in agreement.

Petard was overjoyed. He moved quickly to Mooch and rewarded him with a passionate kiss on the mouth and an embrace. Mooch put his arm around the director and stared soulfully into his eyes.

"Do you know where Stuckey has Rose?" Roscoe asked.
"Sorry, no. I wasn't in on that," Mooch said.
Benny said, "Never mind that now. First we have to get out

of here and find some place where Stuckey wouldn't think of looking for us. Any ideas?"

"Stuckey will have informants in just about every domain," Petard said. "I can't think of anywhere that would be safe..." He paused. He frowned and looked away, wrestling with a thought that had suddenly occurred to him. "Well..." he began, then stopped and shook his head. "Nothing," he said.

"Damn it," Roscoe said, "You obviously have an idea. Let's hear it."

Petard hunched his shoulders forward, drawing inward with reluctance to speak.

Mooch looked at him tenderly with silent prompting. Petard grasped the sergeant's hand for support.

"We could go to my place," he said.

"But that's one place Stuckey will be sure to check," Benny said.

"Maybe not," Roscoe said. "It's so obvious a place not to go, he might skip it in his rush to search as widely as possible."

"I dinna think so. He's uh meticulous man. He wud send at least one ur two men tuh check it," the Professor said.

Petard dismissed this thought with a wave of his hand. "It doesn't matter if they check my house. Doesn't matter if they see us. They won't be able to get us. We'll be protected...."

The others stood silent a moment. "And who will protect us?" Benny asked at last.

"I...it's illegal, you see...I shouldn't be telling you about it."

Mooch put a comforting arm around Petard's shoulder. "Illegal is the least of our worries now, Lance. Tell us who at your house will protect us."

Petard rolled his eyes. *Utterly impossible.* "You wouldn't believe me if I told you. You have to see it."

Roscoe and Benny exchanged glances. *It?*

Petard seemed to revive a little, a man of the theater once more. "You'll just have to trust me," he said, managing to make his words sound like both a plea and an ultimatum.

142

Mooch smiled his approval at Petard. He nodded vigorously to the others. "Trust him," he said.

They did. They had no choice.

Chapter Eight

Roscoe and the others stood in Lance Petard's kitchen, horrified by his explanation of what was going to protect them. Is he mad?

"You're not going to get me down there with that basilisk thing," Benny said, backing away from Petard. "I'll take my chances up here!"

"You'll be perfectly all right if you do exactly as I say."

"I'm not sure about this either, Lance," Mooch said. His feelings for Petard were one thing. Being eyed to death or incinerated by his basilisk was quite another.

The professor, however, was all for trusting Petard's assurances. Ever the curious scientist, he was thrilled by the chance to see this legendary beast.

"He has managed this serpent wuth no problems so far. If he says we kin get tuh thuh safe room by goin' down thuh aisle, I'm ready tuh believe him," he said

The "safe" room, where Petard sometimes spent hours observing his pet, was a small fireproof enclosure just beyond the rear edge of the pit. Its two-way window was mirrored on the outside to reflect the basilisk's gaze back at the beast itself. The problem was getting to it. Entering it by passing through the room's back wall, or down through the ceiling above it, required absolute mastery of body movement. Veering only slightly off course when descending through the ceiling would drop the traveler short of the room and into the pit.

144

The traveler passing through the rear wall had to make an immediate stop once in the room, or he would go too far, hurtling through the mirror into the serpent's den. Petard was highly skilled in aerobatic movement; his entrances, usually through the ceiling, were by now virtually risk free for him. Mooch and the Professor, however, were not accustomed to making precise passages through walls and ceilings. They needed a generous margin for error. Roscoe and Benny had no experience at all in close maneuvering. Entry through the ceiling or back wall was quickly ruled out.

The only other way to enter the safe room was by the aisle the Professor mentioned. It ran beside the low cement wall on one side of the pit. Petard again reassured them they could safely negotiate it.

"If you're crouched down with your back to the beast its gaze can't hurt you," Petard said. "It's lethal only when you look at its eyes."

"What happens if you meet its gaze?" Roscoe asked, dreading what the answer would be.

"Yuh instantly turn tuh stone," the Professor said.

"Oh, really? I thought it simply killed you," Petard said. "That's what I was told. I'll be darned!"

Petard's easy acceptance of being misinformed upset Benny. "Hey, you didn't know that? You're asking us to take our chances with a beast you don't know all that well?" he said.

"Uh small detail," the professor said calmly. "Bein' turned tuh stone is just as bad as bein' kilt."

Roscoe was more worried about incineration. The waist-high wall along the side of the pit offered some protection, provided they duck-walked down the aisle; but if the serpent rose to its full height, towering over the wall, it would be able to incinerate them with a downward blast of fire. "We could all be grilled in a second," he said.

"I thought fire couldn't hurt us," Mooch said.

"Normal fire can no hurt us, but this beast's flames are much hotter than normal fire. It's thuh same superheated fire carried on thuh swords of Michael's archangels in battle. Which is tuh say, hot enough tuh melt our atoms and send their electrons zoomin' off ever which way," the Professor said. "Something like an explodin' firecracker. Complete dissolution."

"But that won't happen," Petard said. "I'll toss it a dead rabbit when we go in. That'll keep it occupied for the few seconds we need to reach the room. We only have to take this way once. We can leave the safe room through its back wall."

The Professor was ready to go but the others were still doubtful. While they discussed it, Petard disappeared behind the door to his rabbit room and reemerged holding a brown rabbit gently in his arms. Its eyes gaped wide with alarm and its nose twitched querulously. He lightly stroked it.

Petard tilted his head coyly and appealed to Mooch.

"Would you help me, dear boy? Hold Fluffy and cover her eyes while I do this rabbit." As Petard moved to the sink, Mooch picked up the dog, covered its eyes with one hand, then turned his head away and closed his eyes. The others watched with morbid fascination as Petard wrung the rabbit's neck. Benny flinched at the snapping sound.

"We're all set. Let's go," Petard said. He held the limp rabbit by its ears.

"Nah, not me. I'll stay up here," Benny said.

"They catch you, you won't like what they'll do to you," Roscoe said.

"I've got the Detainer. And I have the advantage of surprise," Benny said without much conviction. He turned to the Professor, raising the Detainer holding Oswald. "This can hold several bodies at the same time, can't it?"

The Professor nodded. It could.

Roscoe said: "You might surprise one of them, but if there are two or three, you're in trouble. Look, at least come down to the cellar with us and size things up before you decide to stay here," Roscoe said.

"I don't like this. How come they let beasts like this into

Heaven, anyway? It's not right," Benny said.

"It's because the Pagan gods demanded to have their mythical beasts," Mooch said. "They're like children who need their teddy bears."

The Professor explained why the Almighty allowed the pagan gods to keep basilisks and other mythical monsters. As when He granted them the right to keep oracles, enchantresses, and vestal virgins, and allowed them to engage in thunderbolt-throwing, adultery, incest and eating their own children, this was another attempt to silence their bitter complaining that He was trying to turn them into monotheists.

Petard added: "Basilisks, however, are not allowed anywhere but in the zoo in *Pasture of the Pagan Gods and Heroes.* The one downstairs is illegal. I bribed someone to steal it for me. That's what Stuckey was holding over...."

Petard stopped abruptly with a sharp intake of breath. His attention fixed on a blinking light above a cabinet. It was an alarm he had rigged to detect intruders.

"They're here already...passing through the front gate. Hurry!"

Petard rushed them down the stairs to the cellar, cautioning in a tense whisper to keep their backs turned to the pit. A familiar sound of nasal breathing right behind Roscoe told him Benny had abandoned his plan to stand and fight.

With their backs to the front wall of the pit, they shuffled backward several feet from the bottom of the stairs and waited for Petard's commands. He stood with his back to them, looking at the reflection of the pit in the mirror he held at shoulder height. They heard a hissing behind them that began to grow louder at an alarming rate.

"When I toss it this rabbit, wait for me to say 'go.' Then back into the wall, crouch down beside it, and move along the side aisle as fast as you can. Got it?"

They murmured their assent.

Petard hefted the rabbit twice, gauging its weight and how

far he had to throw it. Then he pitched it high over their heads and into the pit. The basilisk reacted immediately. With a tremendous roar it lifted its green crested head above the wall and followed the trajectory of the falling rabbit. When a short blast of fire from its nostrils turned the falling animal into a smoking black morsel, Petard shouted "Go."

They scrambled into the aisle, with Roscoe in the lead and Benny behind him. Roscoe found it easier to crawl on his hands and knees than duck-walk. He moved as fast as he could, but not as fast as his frightened partner, whose head ran into and momentarily merged with Roscoe's buttocks and gastrointestinal tract. This intrusion startled Roscoe into a small burst of speed that pulled him away from the hapless Benny. It took less than fifteen seconds for all of them to gain the safety of the fireproof room.

Petard strode boldly to the viewing window with the Professor right beside him. The other three hung back for a few moments, then inched cautiously toward the window like tourists approaching the edge of the Grand Canyon for their first look down.

The basilisk had finished the rabbit and wanted another. It was now fully erect. Its crested serpent's head moved sinuously from side to side, its tongue flicking out to detect telltale signs of nearby prey.

"Whut uh beauty," the Professor said.

Beauty?

Roscoe saw nothing beautiful about it. It was damn scary. It had the neck of a dinosaur, and the wings and wide body of a dragon. Its heavily muscled forelegs gave its body an upward tilt while the stubby hind legs balanced a reptilian tail that tapered to a point. The red eyes in the green crested head were the most chilling. An eerie flickering light within them caused Roscoe's heart to freeze, and yet he could not look away from them. *Thank God the glass is mirrored on the outside.*

The basilisk had grown annoyed and seemed to sense the presence of people in the room. It suddenly reared back and loosed a huge blast of fire at the mirrored window, causing Roscoe and the

148

others to jump back instinctively. The flame did not melt the glass but some of the blistering heat passed through.

Roscoe was so awed by this incredible beast he momentarily forgot why they were hiding in this room. But the fear that had driven them here flooded back moments later when two men in combat fatigues appeared on the other side of the pit, each with a Detainer. Still at a short distance from the edge of the pit, they could not yet see the basilisk, which had returned to a crouching position below their line of sight. They had heard the noise as they descended the stairs but didn't know what had caused it. The two approached cautiously, their Detainers raised. Roscoe didn't want to see this. Despite his fear of what Stuckey's men could do to him, he still felt the pull of sympathy for fellow creatures about to be destroyed.

It was over almost before Roscoe could comprehend what he witnessed. The sudden, nightmarish rise of the crested head. The serpent mouth opening with a shattering roar. The twin flames jetting from the beast's nostrils, enveloping the two bodies. For a few seconds the dark figures in the flames jerked in an uncontrollable dance of dissolution, their bodies bursting apart with great popping sounds. Within seconds all that remained of them were two small black piles. As the flames subsided, the residue of Stuckey's men spiraled upward like paper ash rising in the heat of embers.

Sickened and speechless, Roscoe and the others took several seconds to recover. At last Roscoe said: "Jesus, Petard, how did you manage to handle that thing when you brought it here?" Roscoe asked.

"It was just a toddler then, with no more fire than a cigarette lighter and a gaze that could be painful but not fatal. I didn't handle it, in any case. That was done by the Blue-faced Hag of Glamis, an enchantress I bribed to steal it. She bottle-fed it at the Pagan Zoo after its mother was killed and it bonded with her."

"Man, if we could harness that firepower, we could take on all of Satan's men," Benny said.

The Professor's eyes narrowed as he considered what Benny

said. He turned to Petard. " The Hag of Glamis. Wud it still remember her, duh yuh think?"

"Hard to say. It might, but who knows?"

"Do you know where she is?" Roscoe asked.

"Last I knew she was bartending at the *Suds and Salty Tears.* I sponsored her for that job so she could go on a work-release program from *Pasture of the Pagan Gods and Heroes.* That was how I paid her for snatching the basilisk."

"Work-release?" Benny said.

"Right. If she takes her punishment without doing any mischief, she gets to stay here permanently."

"Punishment for stealing the basilisk?" Roscoe asked.

"Nah, they never caught her for that. Those puritanical zealots who control the Parole Board wouldn't let her in here without suffering for the witchcraft she practiced when she was an active enchantress," Petard said. "Her punishment is to listen to the hard-luck stories of every one of her customers. She probably hates it, but if she endures this until those tight asses decide she has been punished enough, she can stay here and choose work that is more congenial."

"It's a long shot, but maybe she can still control the basilisk," Roscoe said.

Petard raised his shoulders in a shrug. *Why not?*

"Follow me," he said.

They left the safe room through the back wall and teleported at the fastest possible speed to an inner-city slum Petard identified as *The Wretched Refuse of Your Teeming Shore.* It had been created by souls who had been down and out so much of their lives they were not comfortable anywhere but in the trashy kind of neighborhood they had inhabited. They slept on folded cardboard in garbage-strewn alleys and begged food money from the handful of social workers and lost tourists who passed through this domain. Roscoe saw one figure wearing three coats who held a sign reading "No More War."

In fact, as everywhere else in Heaven, no one in this domain needed money or food, and there was no war to protest. "These people simply want to be among the friends they knew and continue doing what they did most of their lives. Change is too frightening," Petard explained.

"This is bizarre," Roscoe said.

"Many souls up here choose bizarre lifestyles,' Petard said. "Take the ancient Egyptians. A few of them prefer to be sideways people, like the figures in their art. Makes it hard for them to get about because they can't walk toward you. They can only walk right or left, which means they have to keep turning corners until they get themselves headed in the direction they want."

"And they like it that way?" Benny said.

"Absolutely, even though all their corner-turning keeps them bumping into each other," Petard said.

The *Suds and Salty Tears* was not much wider than a railroad coach, with a long bar along the right wall and red naugahyde booths back to back along the other. The padded bar stools were faithful imitations of their real counterparts; they appeared to have lost their plumpness to years of use and showed glimpses of stuffing through tears in their red coverings.

The booths were empty. Three patrons at the near end of bar sat several stools apart from each other. Two of them stared blankly at an episode of Lassie on the television set. The third glowered at his reflection in the bar mirror and muttered to himself. At the far end, a derelict with long white hair harangued an old woman in black behind the bar. He said: "That wasn't right, was it. Was it?" He fixed her with a glare as though she were somehow part of the conspiracy against him, and put the questions to her again in a louder voice.

Roscoe studied the Blue-faced Hag of Glamis as she responded with indifferent nods to the derelict's effort to enlist her sympathy. Of average height, she had the withered, stoop-shouldered body of a crone. Only her wrinkled face was blue, a pale blue that contrasted eerily with the whiteness of her hands and arms.

Roscoe found it uncomfortable to look at that face. Its blueness reminded him of the cyanotic pallor of some dead men he had seen. The eyes were also disconcerting; a heavy upper lid on the left one covered all but a sliver of white eyeball. The other eye bulged almost out of its socket as though swollen from the effort of doing all the seeing. Her blue scalp shone through thinning black hair that hung down in thready tangles. Roscoe felt sorry for her. With her frightening blue face and ungainly features she could not have appealed to any man, even in her youth. She must have lived a life of great loneliness.

Petard caught her attention and beckoned to her. She left the derelict, brusquely shaking off the restraining hand he placed on her arm. "Circette, Circette, I'm not finished!" he cried. She frowned with annoyance at this but said nothing in return as she walked toward Petard.

She smiled but offered no word of greeting to Petard. Ignoring the others, she studied his face for a long moment, then grabbed his right hand, turned it palm up, and began tracing its lines with the fingertips of her free hand.

She looked up and peered at him with her good eye.

"Ah yes, I have not lost my powers entirely. It is in your face and your hand, Petard. You are being drawn to some critical event, something dangerous, and you have come to me for help."

She turned to Roscoe and his companions. "I'm not supposed to practice any of my arts," she whispered with a naughty smile, "but sometimes I can't resist doing a little, just to keep the rust off. The magic of an enchantress wanes with age, you know." She looked at Petard, tipping her head to the side for a moment, waiting for him to offer a flattering protest that such a sad thing could not happen to her. He responded with a theatrical *It can't be so* look and a dismissive wave of his hand. She seemed pleased.

Petard came right to the point. "We desperately need your help, Circette. You're absolutely right about a dangerous event looming ahead. It will have unspeakable consequences if it happens. You may be the only one who can save everyone in

Heaven," he said.

Circette drew back in surprise. "Save everyone in Heaven? Me? An old enchantress here on work-release and forbidden to use any of my old powers. What could I possibly do? And what is this dangerous thing that threatens us all? Tell me."

"Time is short. Come with us and I will explain along the way."

"But I can't leave without official permission...."

"I'll take responsibility for that. Come!"

She went with them.

Satan stood before a three-sided mirror in the large room containing his vast wardrobe and countless disguises.

"What do you think? Does it make my ass look fat," Satan asked Fremont Taylor and Max Shapiro. He wore the Poseidon costume Taylor had just delivered. The red and blue body suit sparkled with sequins. A black mask covered his face from the nose up. The mask joined a headpiece piled with shells, starfish and sea horses. He looked like a comic book superhero dressed for a Fruit of the Loom commercial.

Taylor and Max Shapiro studied the fit.

"It needs a tuck here and there in the seat," Shapiro said.

"Yeah. That lotus-eater, Gophlopsy, has a big ass," Taylor said, remembering that the young man also has a big drug habit. He was quite happy to surrender his costume and his role for the generous amount of lotus Taylor had given him.

Satan studied himself in a mirror. He didn't like the extra material in the seat. It made his buns look droopy. "You're right. Got to be fixed," he said to Shapiro.

"Absolutely, Bob," the PR man answered.

"Everything ready?" Satan asked.

"Everything ready, Bob. We launch in two hours," Shapiro said.

"Did you check Polyphemus?"

153

"Done. The pagan gods will see that he does what he's supposed to," Taylor said.

"He's not absolutely necessary," the Devil said, "but I thought he would add a nice theatrical touch. And maybe scare the shit out of the crowd, make them a little more unwilling to oppose me," the Devil said.

"You haven't lost your devious touch, Bob. You always have a nasty kicker behind whatever you do," Shapiro said.

The Devil winked at him. You can count on that my good man. Then he turned to Taylor, frowning,

"By the way, Colonel Stuckey was supposed to send me one of his men. I haven't seen that man or the two legionnaires I sent to escort him. What happened?"

"Don't know. You'll have to ask Stuckey."

"Believe me, I will when this is over. He is proving unreliable and I will not tolerate that."

"Easy, Bob. Don't get riled up now. You must look calm and magisterial when you step from the chariot," Shapiro said. "Right now, first things first." He turned to Taylor. "Where can we find a seamstress to fix the seat of his pants? We can't have the new Almighty show up in baggy pants."

Taylor shrugged. He had no idea where to find a seamstress. Inwardly, he guessed there might be one in the Pasture of the Pagan Gods and Heroes, like that what's-her-name...Ariadne. You could maybe get some thread there, but could she sew? He doubted it. A long shot would be the Fatal Sisters, the ones that spun, measured, and cut the thread of a person's life. Could any one of them sew? Not likely. Using them was too dangerous, anyway. They were known to be capricious. Satan could end up cocooned in thread or bare ass where the seat of his pants had been cut out. Taylor wanted no part in that! Let Shapiro find a seamstress! If he couldn't...well, the new Almighty would just have to make his debut with baggy buns!

"Oh, my. He's certainly grown," the Hag said. She gazed down on the basilisk from the safe room.

"You should have seen him after his mother was killed. Mewing pitifully like a motherless kitten."

"How was his mother killed?" Roscoe asked.

"Some errant knight from the Fairy Queen wandered into our domain and thought the mother was another of those dragons he had been slaying. Caught her by surprise as she lay there nursing this one."

"Can you still control this beast, Circette?" Petard asked.

She pursed her lips and considered this.

"There's only one way to find out," she said. Before Petard could stop her she darted out the door of the safe room and around its corner to the rear edge of the pit. The basilisk had its back to her.

"Hamish! It's me, Auntie Circette! Auntie Circette!" she cried. The beast rose and swung its huge neck toward her as she turned her back on it. It snorted as though suppressing an urge to blast her with flame. This momentary hesitation passed and it loosed a jet of flame at her, but one that fell short of the pit wall.

"Hamish! You naughty boy! Stop that or I will be mad at you." But Hamish was no longer a helpless infant subject to the discipline of its nanny. It reared back and shot a defiant blast of fire against the two-way window. A basilisk with an attitude. Being captive so long had probably made it nastier and more vengeful than it normally was, Roscoe thought.

"He remembers me, but I think he's angry with me. I could tell he didn't want me to leave him when I brought him here. And he didn't want to be left in this pit...can't blame the poor thing," the Hag said.

"Can you control him?" Petard asked.

"I would need a couple of days to win back his affection...if that is possible. Then maybe I could control him."

"A couple of days!" Roscoe said.

"At least. He'll have to let me sit behind his head so I can stroke him between his eyes...he loved that as a baby...then I'll have to get him to accept a bridle so I can control the movement of his head...and then the toughest part..."

"Which is?" Roscoe said.

"Tying a codpiece over his genitals..." she said.

"What's a codpiece?" Mooch asked.

"It's uh pouch thet Elizabethan gentlemen sometimes cupped over their genitals on thuh outside of their pants. Something like uh jockstrap worn externally," the Professor explained. "It was regarded as decorative, among other things."

"Why does the basilisk need the codpiece?" Rosco asked.

"It's like a safety on a gun" the Hag said. "When it's on, he can't breath fire. Pull it off and he's ready to blast away."

"What about his gaze? How can you control that?"

"Sunglasses."

Petard shook his head wearily. "It would be worth a try if we had two days to do all this. But we don't. The Masque begins in less than two hours."

This news left them all deflated and silent. Then Benny snapped his fingers. He had an idea. "What if we turn him into a sheep with the Professor's serum, lead him to the Masque, then turn him back to a basilisk with the antidote."

They all looked at the Professor. He shook his head.

"Ah doubt it 'ud work on uh basilisk. In any case, I don't have any more serum or antidote. I'd have to make more and I couldn't do thet in thuh time we have left."

That seemed to be the final blow. But Benny's idea had inspired Roscoe to think of another possible solution, bizarre though it was. He turned to the Hag.

"You're an enchantress. Can you turn him into something else...and then break the spell and restore him to being a basilisk?" he said.

She protested: she was old and her powers were not as strong as they once were. Moreover, if the authorities discovered she had used those powers, she would be forced back to the *Pasture of the Pagan Gods and Heroes.*

156

"But surely, anything you could do to foil the plot would win you great honor and a place of your choosing," Roscoe said.

The Hag closed her good eye and thought for several seconds.

"Okay, maybe you're right about being rewarded. But it's not as simple as you think," she said at last. "I have never enchanted a gorgon, a griffin, a sphinx or any other creatures of their ilk, much less a basilisk. If I can transform him, I'm not sure how long the spell will last. We could be walking down the street with him in altered form, and poof, the enchantment wears off and there we are, holding the leash of one huge, pissed-off basilisk. On the other hand, the spell could last forever and I would not be able to revoke it."

Roscoe looked at the others. They were not happy, but they knew this was their only hope. Take the chance, or fail to prevent the unthinkable for the Almighty and themselves. And Rose...what would happen to her if they failed, Roscoe thought. The rush of events had kept him from searching for her but he was never without a pulsing fear that he might never see her again. They had to succeed!

"Give it your best!" he said to the Hag. The others nodded their agreement.

She hesitated at the door of the room for a moment, collecting her thoughts. Then she walked with determined strides to the back edge of the pit. She extended her arms toward the crouching basilisk as if embracing it with her powers, and uttered a long fluttering wail which seemed to calm the beast. She followed this with an incantation of words Roscoe could not make out. Then she shook violently as if in the grip of a powerful force rising from somewhere beneath her feet. Her good eye pulsated as she focused on the basilisk and pointed at it with both forefingers. "Now!" she cried.

It was as if an electric shock hit the basilisk. It jolted into a series of violent convulsions that made it smaller and smaller until it disappeared in a mist. Roscoe and the others stood transfixed as the mist cleared. The basilisk was now a large brown mastiff.

Its trim body stood waist-high on long legs. Its large head

was regal but it walked clumsily as though it were still a puppy that hadn't quite learned to control its leg movements. There was a gentle sadness in its look, but Roscoe could imagine that, if provoked, it could knock a man down and tear his flesh with its formidable teeth. Roscoe named it Big Galoot.

Getting the dog out of the pit was the next challenge. It was too large and heavy to be hoisted out by its front legs or pushed up from below by Benny and Mooch. Petard finally fetched a blanket which was fashioned into a sling that enabled them to hoist the animal up and over the pit wall. The hag carefully attached a leash Petard had brought and petted the dog on its head. It seemed to like her. When she gently scratched between its eyes, Big Galoot gave unmistakable signs of loving to be scratched in that spot. There was no doubt they had Hamish the basilisk inside the body of a dog.

The transformation had taken precious time. It took another ten minutes for Petard to find the makings of a bridle and a codpiece. By the time they emerged from his house, only forty-five minutes remained before the Masque was to begin. Petard had supplied everyone with sunglasses. Mooch carried the bridle and Petard the codpiece. The Professor had the Detainer with Oswald on it. Benny reluctantly held the mastiff's leash. They were ready to go.

"Teleportation should get us there just in time," Mooch said.

"Hold it!" the Hag cried. "We can't teleport the dog. It might compromise the spell. We'll have to walk him there."

When troubles come, they come not as spies but in battalions, Hamlet would have said. But Roscoe and the others responded much less eloquently with a ragged chorus of "shit!"

So they set out in a fast walk with Roscoe and the Hag in the lead, followed by the Professor, then Mooch and Petard, and Benny with Galoot at the end of the line.

They reached the corner of Petard's street when Benny shouted "Wait a minute." Roscoe looked back. Galoot was urinating on a fire hydrant. They waited impatiently for the dog to finish, then set off again. Halfway up the next street Benny called another time out. This time the dog was on somebody's lawn straining to defecate. Nothing came out. It inched forward, its rump still positioned for evacuation. Still nothing. Roscoe anxiously looked at his watch.

"No time for that," he shouted to Benny. " Pull him along."

"No, no!" the Nag cried. "It's too dangerous to force it to do anything it doesn't want to do. He's constipated. His schedule and the basilisk's apparently don't coincide."

So they waited. At last the mastiff gave up trying to void itself and resumed walking. But not for long. Around the next corner the dog found another fire hydrant that it had to mark with its urine. The minutes ticked away. The basilisk in dog's clothing proved to have an inexhaustible supply of urine and an irresistible urge to piss on two more fire hydrants it encountered. By the time it had christened the last one, time had run out. The Masque had already begun. A dog's bladder had sealed the fate of the Almighty.

The crowd assembled for the Masque stood a half-mile deep around the foot of the golden stairs that ascended to the throne of the Almighty. At the distant top of the stairs, His presence manifested itself as a rainbow spanning billowing clouds. A cadre of Michael's archangels in dress-parade wings and bearing shields of hammered gold formed a ceremonial cordon along both sides of the first dozen stairs. Thousands more of the audience crowded the hillsides of site three-twenty-one, which by an act of legerdemain possible only in Heaven, had been moved with its lake to the foot of the golden stairs.

Stands reserved for dignitaries stood next to each other along each side of the stairs. It was the custom to add a new group of dignitaries to existing ones each year. The coveted designation this year had been conferred upon illustrious baseball players. They stood in a colorful array of uniforms, the older ones with the short-brimmed beany caps and socks worn to knee height, the younger ones with crowned caps and pants that reached their ankles. All the greats were there. Walter Johnson, Smokey Joe Wood, Wee Willie Keeler, Honus Wagner, Mel Ott, Lou Gerhig. Babe Ruth leaned on a bat with one hand and ate a hot dog with the other. Ty Cobb stared at his colleagues with a belligerent sneer. DiMaggio and Williams stood shoulder to shoulder in their familiar pose for newspaper photos. The many names in this group were displayed on a wide banner attached to the front of their stand. Where a player chose to stand within this group was up to him, provided he abided by the Masque committee's insistence that, for everyone's comfort, compulsive spitters stand in the front rank and crotch-grabbers stand anywhere from the second row back, so their ball-hoisting would be shielded by someone in front of them.

Not everyone was happy with the custom of adding a new dignitary stand each year. Critics argued the growing number of stands obstructed the view of the multitudes behind them. They wanted to suspend the practice altogether, or at least limit new dignitaries to smaller groups like the great chefs of fast-food chains or sincere movie stars. There was some merit to this argument. The stands were now so numerous they climbed side-by-side twenty or thirty steps up the golden stairway, partially blocking the view of people behind them. Among the stands were those for the saints and martyrs, for the champion televangelist fund-raisers, for the prophets, the meek, the peacemakers, the Samaritans, the great philosophers minus Nietzsche, and NASCAR fatalities. For a growing number of citizens, however, this practice had gone too far. They complained Heaven already had too many dignitaries, and too many of them were merely arriviste celebrities.

Nevertheless, some stands were popular with the host of tabloid readers fascinated with celebrities and scandal. The perennial favorite in this category was the one reserved for the pagan gods and heroes.

It was the only time of year when pagan luminaries appeared together, their old animosities barely in check. Grudges were a way of life among the gods and heroes. Who had not injured

160

kith or kin by committing parricide, fratricide, infanticide, rape, adultery; or by changing into bulls, swans, cuckoo birds, and other creatures, to seduce objects of their lust? For the eager onlookers, there was always the delicious possibility that a jealous husband or a betrayed wife would exact gory revenge on the seducer who had caused them heartache; or that murdered sons, fathers, wives or daughters, would chop their treacherous kin into bloody gobbets. Even if mayhem did not occur it was fascinating to watch how grudges and griefs dictated the social dynamic of the group.

Smoke-smudged Vulcan, his brawny arms exposed in his sleeveless leather jerkin, stood apart from the others, a *persona non grata*. The god of fire and metalworking had forged the thunderbolts that helped Zeus defeat the Titans. This earned him the everlasting enmity of those giants, some of whom were present. Among the beautiful people, Vulcan was tolerated because he supplied them with thunderbolts for their tournaments and war games, but they did not consider him their equal. They regarded him as an uncouth lout. His true love was not blacksmithing but herpetology, and he had been irresistibly drawn into marriage with the hideous, snake-haired Medusa, thereby violating the custom that gods and goddesses should marry only beautiful people. The unpleasant consequences of this offensive marriage surprised no one. The union produced two disgusting children, Caca, the goddess of latrines, and Cacus, a fire-breathing giant. Poor Vulcan could do nothing to win esteem. Even his annual festival repelled his fellow deities because it called for small fish to be thrown into a fire to assuage him. This literally produced such a stink he had been forced to hold his festival outside the city.

One minor deity drawing attention was Priapus, the god of fertility. Short, hairy and rather ugly, he titillated the crowd by walking around with a huge red penis that was perpetually erect. He loved to sneak up behind goddesses and poke them with his member, which always earned him a slap or a rebuke and lusty huzzahs from the crowd.

The supreme god of the pagan gods, Zeus (a.k.a. Jupiter on

161

Mondays, Wednesdays and Fridays) was the riveting figure in the group. His awesome majesty compelled attention, but more from the crowd than from the other gods, few of whom shared his company. His sour personality and relentless holding of grudges caused most of them to fear his sudden and capricious wrath. Prometheus, everyone could plainly see, kept his distance from Zeus, who would not forgive him for stealing fire from his hearth and giving it to men. And everyone knew how angry Zeus continued to be that his ingenious punishment of Prometheus was cut short by Heracles. Chaining Prometheus to a rock on Mount Caucassus was a brilliant stoke, Zeus thought, and having an eagle stop by every day to peck away at his liver was the crowning touch. But then that meddler Heracles freed him just as the liver damage was causing a serious case of jaundice. Zeus was a very bad loser.

He had also been a very naughty womanizer, which thrilled the tabloid crowd. His lovers and mistresses were legion and his offspring beyond counting. He sired at least a third of the pagan deities and heroes, and did so with an abandon that knew no bounds. Some critics faulted him for committing incest with his sister and debasing himself by turning into a bull, a swan and a cuckoo bird to seduce women. *A cuckoo bird! Has he no sense of godly decorum?*

But these faults were generally considered the eccentric prerogatives of a mighty ruler. If he was a little bent, his defenders said, blame his horrific childhood. He was raised in a cave on Mount Ida, hiding from his father, Cronus, who wanted to swallow him as he had his other children. Later, with the help of the Cyclops and lightening and thunder he overthrew Cronus and the Titans, to found the Olympian dynasty. Was usurping his father an act of revenge, or ruthless ambition, or merely self-defense? Whatever the truth, his relationship with his cannibalistic father scarred him deeply. He was counseling to heal that damage but so far, no breakthroughs had occurred. He still could not bear to watch Cronus swallow even water. Nor could Cronus bear to look upon Zeus. The sight of him filled the old god with bitter regret. If only he been able to swallow his son he would still be the supreme god. And so father and son stood at opposite ends of the platform with their backs to each other.

Veteran observers such as Rollo Glotz noted a small change in this year's assemblage of gods and heroes. There were Titans in the group. Since Zeus released them from imprisonment in Tartarus, the Titans had largely scorned the other gods and seldom appeared with them at public occasions. But here they were. Ten or twelve of them. They stood close to Cronus and frequently whispered things in his ear that made him smile and nod approvingly. Was something up, Glotz wondered, or were these giants merely looking forward to the show? Upon reflection, he doubted the Masque was that interesting to them. Giants are churls with no interest in art. His reporter's instinct told him there just might be something developing here for *Saucy Tidbits.* He would keep an eye on them.

But right now, his attention was drawn to six of Gabriels's herald angels who stood on the lower steps signaling the beginning of the Masque with a fanfare on their long golden horns.

Amid the clouds at the top of the golden steps, the Almighty turned off His omniscience and leaned back comfortably on His throne. He relished the chance to be surprised by whatever unfolded in the Masque.

The crowd below and on the hills surrounding site three-twenty-one eagerly fixed their eyes on the water. The calm face of the lake suddenly erupted in an aquatic tapestry of small splashes, as hundreds of mermaids, neriads and other water sprites popped to the surface and began a coordinated water ballet they had learned from an old Esther Williams film. To dulcet strains of "La Mer" they formed moving circles and figure eights, lifting their legs and fish tails in unison. A brace of lovely mermaids joined hands in a line and flippered themselves into the air like leaping dolphins, turning a graceful somersault in unison before knifing back into the water with such pointed form they hardly created a splash. The crowd made a sudden *ploof* of delighted surprise and applauded.

As the ballet continued, the giant figure of Polyphemus emerged in the distance in water up to his waist. He moved ponderously toward the rear ranks of the swimmers, his hands raking the water as he advanced.

Glotz turned to the cub reported who accompanied him, a young female who had chosen the *nom de plume* Lois Lane.

"Wait until you see this!" he said.

The blind giant had now reached the rear phalanx of swimmers. He paused as though unsure what to do next. Then he snorted as it came to him. He groped the water until he scooped up two neriads whom he immediately popped into his mouth. The crowd gasped. It was only make-believe, but it was such a delightful frisson.

But Polyphemus did not stop. He scooped up more swimmers and swallowed them. The forward ranks of the water sprites suddenly became aware of what was happening behind them. They broke formation in a panic and swam desperately toward shore.

"This is disgusting," Lois Lane said.

"Pure theatrics, I assure you." Glotz said. "A rescue is at hand."

He pointed to Poseidon in his Fruit of the Loom costume with the baggy seat emerging from the depths in a golden chariot. Drawn by four large sea horses, the chariot pulled what looked like a large boat trailer with a geodesic dome secured to a backward tilting wooden frame.

"What's that thing?" she asked, pointing to the catapult bearing the dome.

"It flings the ball high in the air, where it bursts and releases a hundred white doves."

Polyphemus continued his slow advance through the swimmers, eating handfuls as he went. The front ranks of swimmers reached the beach and ran screaming into the crowd. Their fear alarmed the first rows of onlookers who fell back away from the advancing giant, no longer sure this was just playacting.

Poseidon did not approach Polyphemus but proceeded straight to shore. In the wake of his chariot a legion of "mermen" in black wet suits surfaced and followed him until they knelt on the beach in even ranks. Each wore two air tanks, one connected to a mouth piece, the other to a long tube that looked like part of an insect fogger.

Glotz was perplexed. "They must have changed the script...I don't remember being told about this," he said.

Polyphemus stepped onto the shore. The crowd shank back in fear. But he simply stood there, a menace eager for an order to proceed.

Poseidon stepped slowly from the chariot. He stood for a moment with legs spread and hands on hips, then raised his arms and spread them wide as if to signal he commanded all who beheld him. He turned to look at the catapult and gave a decisive nod with his head. A merman beside the catapult drew a sword and severed a thick rope that held its arm to its frame. The arm sprang upward with tremendous force, throwing the dome high into the air. It traveled over the golden stairway and disappeared into the clouds surrounding the Almighty. Seconds later, a mighty explosion rent the air, causing the startled crowd to flinch instinctively and cry out. No doves appeared. The rainbow in the clouds slowly dimmed. The Almighty had been anaesthetized.

Seeing this, Satan signaled his men to advance. They rushed up the stairs, a column on either side, dousing the crowds immediately before them with a cloudy mist from their tubes. Those wetted by the mist immediately ceased to be agitated and stood almost immobile with dreamy smiles on their faces. Michael's few legionnaires charged down the steps to battle the mermen, but they were quickly transformed into smiling zombies by blasts of the anesthetic.

The coup was over in seconds. As the stunned crowd began to realize something terrible had just happened, they erupted with a gathering roar of fear and dismay. Those at the rear of the throng tried to flee but were stopped by a line of mermen who threatened them with their tube sprayers. As word spread that they were all being held captive, their voices rose higher with hysteria.

In the midst of this din, Satan took off the Poseidon costume and tossed it aside disdainfully, silently cursing its baggy seat! Now he stood proudly in ceremonial dress that plainly identified who he really was: A collared red cape embroidered with a large black triton. A ruby red silk blouse split open to mid-chest revealed a golden pentangle on a neck chain. Seamless red satin briefs with a Ralph Lauren logo over black tights. Mid-calf silver boots with small wings on their heels.

He climbed the stairs with erect majesty until he reached a point slightly above the dignitary stands. He turned and beckoned to platforms on either side of him. Cronus and three of his titans along with Dionysus and Mars walked out to join him. From other platforms came more conspirators--the fundamentalist preacher; the representative of the concerned Elders; the PR man, Shapiro; Colonel Stuckey; Freemont Taylor; and several others. Satan shook hands with each of them as they gathered behind him.

The noise abated a few decibels as the crowd was given pause by the appearance of these others. Some co-conspirators, like Shapiro, were unfamiliar to the crowd, but others were well-known as honorable men. Why were these virtuous souls supporting the arch fiend? Was there something noble in all this that they, the onlookers, did not yet understand? A sudden eagerness to hear an explanation, a reassuring one they hoped, calmed them somewhat. Satan raised his hand for silence and the multitude immediately grew quiet and attentive.

"My friends, change is always a little frightening," Satan began, using a line Shapiro had picked up from a manual advising CEOs how to inform employees of a downsizing.

"First, let me assure you this transfer of power was absolutely necessary. You need not take my word for it, my friends, because these honorable men behind me, men you trust, they will tell you why it was necessary. You will come to understand it is necessary for the well-being of Heaven and earth."

He paused a beat. He leaned his head to one side, eyes reverently closed, and nodded slowly in a manner indicating he understood their pain.

"I know. I know you love the Almighty and fear for his well-being." He straightened and extended his arms compassionately.

"But be at rest. God is not dead. Nor is he in any pain or emotional discomfort. He is merely taking a well-deserved rest from his daily duties. And I promise you we will see that he continues to enjoy this serene peace." By which Satan meant the Almighty would be kept perpetually under the anesthetic.

"Now I know many of you have been taught to hate me. But you have been misled. I have been the victim of an unspeakable injustice. If you have read *The True History of Satan: The Never-Before-Told Story of His Innocence and Wrongful Damnation,* you already know the facts of the case.

"If you haven't read it, I want you to listen to Jimmy Cagney. He became a lawyer after he arrived here and will set the record straight for you."

He looked toward a stand on his right. James Cagney stepped briskly forward, smiling and offering a humble bow. As he approached Satan, he jauntily played to the crowd with a few stiff-legged steps from his tap routine in the film *Yankee Doodle Dandy.* Then he harkened back to his Cody Jarret bit from *White Heat*:

"Remember me on that burning oil-storage platform? he said to the crowd. "The flames leaping higher and higher. I lift my arms to Heaven like this and cry, 'Made it, Ma. Top o' the world!' Then BOOM, a huge fiery explosion obliterates me.

"Well here I am on top of the biggest world there is. And this time I'm not that tough-guy criminal you remember. I'm straight now, see. I'm a lawyer. And I'll give it to you straight why Satan got a bum rap."

He hitched up his pants using only the sides of his wrists--a signature Cagney tic. The pants weren't falling down, but show business is show business. He cockily assumed a belligerent stance with his feet set wide apart. The crowd murmured appreciatively. They were warming to him. He wouldn't steer them wrong.

"The Almighty made mistakes, see. His wrath was over the top lots of times. The Flood. Job. Abraham and Isaac, locust plagues, pestilence. And how badly did he treat Adam and Eve?' Cagney raised his eyebrows as if they all knew the answer to that question. Then he lowered them in a familiar frown.

"He treated them rotten. Here are two babes in the woods, never been here before, don't know anything about anything. What's this? What's that? How come you've got that thing and I've got these things? Even the strange looking creatures didn't have names. Ditto for the plants, see. The Almighty says don't eat fruit from the Tree of Knowledge. They have no idea what knowledge is. None whatsoever!" He crossed and uncrossed his extended arms in a nothing gesture.

"But here's this tree that looks like a million others around them, see. No sign on it saying 'Tree of Knowledge.' And even if there were a sign, they didn't know how to read. You don't let them have knowledge, how can you expect them to read! Anyway... here's this tree with tasty-looking things on it. They probably had already tried grapes and bananas and raspberries. Who knows, maybe they think they've found something at last that won't give them diarrhea! And then there's this talking snake egging them on. Yes, it's Satan. But did he want to egg them on? Absolutely not! The Almighty forced him to do it. If you don't do it, He said, you will remain a snake forever and I will tie a permanent knot in your tail. So what choice does Satan have? Who wants to live as a snake with a knot in its tail! So with tears in his eyes and a breaking heart he tells them, 'Go ahead. You'll be sorry, but go ahead.' They don't know what 'sorry' means, and they're hungry, so they go ahead. In perfectly innocent ignorance, they share an apple. WHAM! The Almighty gets steamed that the dummies he created did a dumb thing so he boots them out of Eden and condemns them to be mortal....

"Is that fair? Not in my book, brothers and sisters. And pretty soon the world becomes full of people and lots of things start to go wrong because He messed up. He put too much molten lava in the center of the earth so that it periodically erupts and wipes out villages. He mismatched the sea, the sky, the winds, and the climates so they clash and create floods, hurricanes and droughts. Ordinary

Joes get hit by lightening. And worse yet, He made men capable of bad things. Murder, genocide, rape, war, brutality and so forth....

"So what happens? Pretty soon people start to complain. God allows evil things to happen, they say. He is not the good guy we thought he was."

Cagney paused for effect. He did the pants tic, a sign he was about to roll big time.

"The Almighty doesn't like this. He wants to be loved. Don't we all want to be loved?" The crowd roared "yes."

"So he's gotta to find a patsy. You guessed it. He laid it on Lucifer, who was one of the brightest, most loyal mugs in Heaven. Why Lucifer? Jealousy. Angels jealous of his superior beauty and virtue framed him. These dirty rats persuaded the Almighty that Lucifer was plotting to take over his territory. One thing leads to another. Lucifer's friends stand by him and object to his treatment. God is fed more bad intelligence by Lucifer's enemies and moves to roust the angel and his cohorts. You know the rest of the story...but remember, Lucifer was only defending himself against a bum rap...and now at long last he is reclaiming his rightful place in Heaven. To me, that is only fair, and I am sure you will agree. Thank you. You have been a wonderful audience."

He received enthusiastic applause punctuated with whoops and whistles. It was hard to tell whether the crowd was responding to his performance or his defense of Satan.

The Preacher stepped forward next. His true reason for supporting Satan was simple: He wanted to influence Satan's policies--wanted to make sure those policies were more fundamentalist-oriented than the former Almighty's. But he dared not reveal this to the crowd--or to Satan.

So he looked sorrowfully at the crowd, his eyes brimming with tears. He praised the Almighty for his many wonderful works. He gave thanks for His love of mankind and His willingness to forgive sinners.

"But God has carried His burden a long, long time. He has grown old in his task," he said. "He has gotten weary and forgetful and inclined to take longer and longer vacations; so many that some who are weak in faith believe He has abandoned us. Such loss of faith cannot be allowed to continue. Now it is time for Heaven to be Born Again, with a vigorous new godhead, one as righteous as the God we knew long ago. The individual for the job stands before you! Satan, formerly Lucifer, the Almighty's favorite angel before he was falsely accused and condemned."

He walked a few feet to his right and turned to face the audience once again. He decided to save for his fellow clergy the God/Devil Yin-Yang concept he had explained to Satan. It was too sophisticated for the masses. He would offer something simpler.

"You say, ah yes, but if we accept Satan as our God how can we also denounce the Devil? My friends, we must separate the man from the office. The wrong person was condemned to be the Devil and forced, by the very nature of his office, and by threats from the Almighty, to act satanically. Now he has been restored to his rightful place. Some wretch in Hell, some truly evil sinner, will be chosen by his fellows to fill the office of Satan. We will revile him with complete justification. Brothers and sisters, fear not. We shall praise Lucifer and still condemn the evil ways of the new Satan."

The crowd murmured as the Preacher rejoined the group standing behind Lucifer. A few of the brighter souls perceived the sophistry of the Preacher's argument. Some others thought they could see logic in it, while still others, despite the simplicity of the argument, could not understand it but accepted it simply because the Preacher had made the case. He certainly knew more about it than they did.

Cronus spoke next. He also could not reveal his true motive for supporting Lucifer, which was to use him to regain power over the other pagan gods and then overthrow him. So he trembled as with great emotion and sought eye contact with the elderly in the crowd. And lied. He said the pagan gods supported Lucifer because he promised to grant them their due as the most senior citizens in Heaven. Their festivals would be put on the official Heavenly calendar of events. They would be allowed to open baths and fortune tellers' caves in any of Heaven's domains. They could send emissaries to U.S. southern states as farm animals or serpents to recruit devotees to offer sacrifices to them and read entrails. This is not much to ask, he said, and it is only fair. "Lucifer will be fair to us senior citizens and to all of you."

The fair-minded in the audience accepted this, but not all of the pagan gods and heroes clapped for Cronus. Many of them gasped incredulously or shot him angry glances.

The Elder who had enlisted Satan's aid shuffled forward to address the crowd. He wore the same coarse brown robe and multicolored headpiece he had worn during his conference with Satan, but the lower half of his face was now uncovered, revealing uneven black and white stubble and a newly missing upper front tooth.

As he spoke his tongue lapped against the gap in his teeth.

"The Elders fully thupport Luthifer. In time I will give you all of our rethuns for doing tho. But right now, I thimply want to assure you this change will be permanent only if you formally approve it. Yeth, there will be an open and free election! You will be able to vote for or against Luthifer's investiture as the Almighty, and for or against the rethtoration of the former Almighty. If you reject both options, you will be able to put forward other candidates for the job....A committee hath already been formed to dethide when and how the election will ake place!"

The crowd clapped and whistled their approval. This strong support for an election did not upset the Preacher. He smiled as if genuinely pleased with the idea, but his smile was a sly nod to other conspirators who knew an election would never happen. He and Cronus were on the election committee. They would ensure the matter would be tied up in committee long enough for Lucifer to establish a dictatorship.

Lucifer strode forward as the crowd began to quiet down. He smiled benevolently, nodding to indicate that what they had just heard was the absolute truth. He spread his hands.

"My friends, you must be wondering what to expect from

171

me. The short answer is a better Heaven." He had the crowd's full attention.

"Yes, you have had a good life up here. Let us thank the former Almighty for that!" This elicited waves of "amens" from the crowd.

"But the good life you've had can be even better. More is always better, and I will give you more. More pleasures. More freedom. More rights. More options. For example, maybe you're unhappy with the body you brought here and have been required to keep. You're too fat, or deformed, or you don't like your face. Friends, those days are over. In the new Heaven everyone will have the body and looks he wants without diets or plastic surgery!

"You're bored? Or maybe just starved for novelty? Then how does this sound! You'll be able to tour Hell and talk face-to-face with some of history's most notorious killers. Attila, Genghis Khan, Jack the Ripper, Stalin, Hitler--any villain you wish. You'll get to chat with Hollywood stars, kings and queens, temptresses and thousands of the beautiful and the damned. And that used car salesman who screwed you? You'll be able to pitchfork his ass good and proper!

"You say you crave earthly news coverage of gruesome murders and tragic accidents. You miss those interviews with grieving parents, with homeless victims of fire, flood and hurricane? We'll pipe that coverage up here. You won't miss one thrilling minute of human misery. And soaps! You'll get back all your favorite soaps. Hungry for news of movie stars and show biz celebrities? You got it!

"And there will be more. Lots more! I promise you. Just remember this. You've had a little of the good life under the old Almighty. And if a little is good, then more is better. Repeat that for me, will you. Say 'more is better,' 'more is better.'" The crowd began chanting the phrase. Satan urged them on until most of them joined in. *More is better. More is better*. Satan clapped and laughed and punched the air in a *that's the spirit gesture*. Then he raised his hand for quiet.

"And here's another promise. I will not be a remote God. My door will always be open to anyone who wants to see me. I want you to consider me a friend. And to demonstrate that I am just a regular guy, I no longer wish to be called Satan, or even Lucifer. Those are too high falutin for me. From now on just call me Bob! That's it, just Bob!" With that he removed his ceremonial garb and donned clothes held for him by Shapiro: black turtleneck sweater, charcoal slacks, black penny loafers without socks. He rolled up the sleeves of the sweater. A regular workaday guy by Ralph Lauren.

The crowd applauded and called out "Bob," " Bob," "Bob!" Bob was pleased.

More is better! More is better! Bob, Bob, Bob!

His co-conspirators gathered around and congratulated him on his speech. Max Shapiro clapped him on the back. "Hell of a good show, Bob. You've got them in the palm of your hand," he said. Bob thanked his comrades, then beckoned to his legionnaires to gather around him. He raised his fist in a victory salute and they all cheered.

"And now, you magnificent bastards, it's party time," he cried. "We'll kick back at the Central Administration building in the Golden City. Beer, chips and Slim Jims for all, plus a surprise. Show them Max!"

Shapiro signaled to a van that had been drawn up close to the stairs. Its doors opened and gorgeous women poured out, some of them bare breasted and wearing bikinis, others completely naked. "Here are your party girls, men. The Hookers from Hell," Shapiro cried. The legionnaires roared with delight. The Preacher pretended not to see the women.

As those around him began to disperse, Bob called Stuckey aside.

"Any news of Michael and his archangels?" he said.

"Nothing yet. But I've posted lookouts around the outskirts of the city. We should spot him in plenty of time for your men to take up defensive positions."

"Good. We may lose a few men to their fiery swords, but we'll overcome them with the anesthetic. They are not prepared for that!"

"Absolutely, Bob," Stuckey said. He straightened up and tendered a crisp salute. The slack latter days were over. This was the trig way to run things!

Lester Mooch had been sent ahead to the Masque when the others had returned to Petard's house with Galoot. Now he cautiously made his way back to the house, walking beside small groups returning from the Masque, hoping to appear inconspicuous.

"Isn't it wonderful!" a matronly woman remarked as he passed her. "All my life I've wanted to be thin. Wait 'til my ex-husband sees my new svelte self. I'll tell him 'Eat your heart out, you cheating bastard!' "

Farther on, a sallow man with wide, excited eyes caught Mooch's arm.

"Do you think Bob will make good on these tours of Hell? I can't wait to ask Hitler if he *shtupped* Leni Riefensthal."

Mooch was no saint, but these people depressed him. He smiled and nodded at the man, eager to avoid discussion.

He found Roscoe and the others in the cellar. Big Galoot had been returned to the pit.

"It's done. Satan has taken over." Mooch reported. The others remained silent, dismayed but not surprised.

"You won't believe how many people accepted him without hesitation." Mooch proceeded to give them a detailed report of the coup.

Roscoe closed his eyes and spoke quietly. "For a time there, I thought we were going to pull it off."

Benny shook his head wearily. "We were so close!"

Roscoe gazed blankly into the pit. He was seeing Rose's terrified face in the photo Stuckey showed him. Imagining what Stucky might do to her left him feeling hollow inside and weak in the legs. But at the moment Rose had to be all right. There was that at least. Stuckey wouldn't harm his bargaining chip for more serum

174

from the Professor. As he thought about this, he felt the vague stirrings of an idea forming in the back of his mind. He was beginning to see possibilities....

The heavy silence in the room was broken by the popping sound of someone coming through the wall. It was Bruno, entering head first, the dome of his policeman's hat appearing like the nose of a torpedo. He carried two Detainers.

"Ah, you are here. I was afraid Stuckey might have caught you."

"He did...for a time..." Petard began.

The Professor cut him short.

"Did yeh find Michael?"

"Yeah, finally. Took me so long because they weren't in any of the logical places. They'd finished maneuvers and were taking some R and R at Luciano's Lucky Horseshoe in the domain of *Fun and Games*. I just happened to spot them as I flew over it. Hard to believe, but these Simon Pures were playing poker, blackjack, roulette, slots. It must be stressful being so righteous all the time. I found Michael betting on the Centaur races. He was pissed at first that he and his men had been discovered *in peccadillo*, so to speak, but he got over it when I told him what was happening."

"Why didn't they rush here to beat back Satan's forces?" Roscoe asked.

"Too late. As I was briefing him, we got word the coup had succeeded."

"Still...it wasn't too late to attack..." Petard began.

Bruno shook his head.

"When I told him about the power of the anesthetic they're using, he realized he'd lose too many men if he attacked when they were armed and waiting for him...he needs to catch Satan's forces off guard. He and his men are on the outskirts of the city. They managed to surprise and eliminate three of Stuckey's lookouts without alerting the remaining guards....By the way, these two Detainers I brought are special ones. Michael changed their settings so they can be used against authorities like Stuckey. Would be just

the thing to have if you run across that bastard or Fremont Taylor."
He leaned the two against the pit wall.

"Michael can get them off guard now!" Mooch burst out.
"All but a handful of the legionnaires are celebrating with Satan and
his confederates in the Administration Building. I would imagine
they take their tanks off when they carouse...."

"But they wouldn't put them too far out of reach," Roscoe
said. "They know they're not out of the woods until they defeat
Michael in a battle that could come at any second."

Bruno said: "Say it took fifteen seconds to get their tanks
back on--and that's pretty damn fast. I doubt many could do it that
quickly. But say fifteen seconds. That's enough of an advantage.
Michael's forces could take out a lot of them before they armed
themselves."

"Michael wud gain even moor time if some distraction drew
thim farther away from thir tanks," the Professor added. With
eyebrows raised querulously, his gaze went from face to face. Any
ideas?

Roscoe was staring at the Detainers Bruno had brought. He
clapped his hands together. "I think I know how we can do just that!"
he said.

The plan he was about to propose was daring and based on
assumptions that could prove disastrously wrong. It would put two
of his friends at great risk. Were the chances of success worth that
risk? Doubts came crowding in as they always had when he was
forced to make a decision as a cop. But now he pushed them aside.
He had a solid feeling in his gut that they had a good chance of
pulling it off. With luck.

"Each of you will have to decide whether you are willing to
take the risks my plan entails. Especially you two," he said, turning
first to Benny and then to the Hag. Benny cocked his head to one
side, twisting his face into a sour expression that said *why me?* The
Hag frowned and said nothing.

Roscoe told them what he had in mind.

Three hours later the party in the second floor staff lounge of the Central Administration building was in full stride. Loud laughter and beery toasts of Satan's legionnaires poured through the open windows facing the main street below. While the Hookers from Hell were busy with their first customers in rooms elsewhere on the floor, those waiting their turn slumped in soft chairs, greedily gulping beer and exchanging comradely insults. Many of the sitters rested their sandaled feet atop the marble coffee tables as they drank. Although the beer was virtual in nature, if taken in quantity, its sheer volume deceived the drinker into feeling that he ought to feel drunk by now. That was a happy delusion now gripping most of the men. A line of burly legionnaires played leapfrog, frequently interrupting its progress to argue over whose turn it was to squat and whose to jump. By the open window a tall legionnaire with a bulbous nose led a cluster of boisterous comrades in a version of "Her Mother Never Told Her the Things a Young Girl Should Know." The noise level rose steadily as the drinking continued.

The anesthetic tanks lay haphazardly in corners and along the baseboards.

Satan and Stuckey sat on a red couch in a corner of the room. Rose Trautman stood at the Colonel's end of the couch. The Detainer in Stuckey's hand kept her from moving away. At the first sign of flight he would swat her with that terrible racquet.

"Why the girl ?"Satan asked.

"Unfinished business. She's going to get me something I've been after for a long time."

"That's what I like about you, Stuckey. You're the kind of devious bastard I want working with me," Satan said. He raised his glass. "Here's to good times ahead!"

One of the legionnaires standing by a window suddenly shouted "Get this!" and summoned Stuckey and Satan to his side. "Those the guys you been trying to catch?" Urging Rose ahead of him, Stuckey hurried to the window.

On the street below Roscoe stood looking up at them. Beside him were Benny and the Professor. Mooch and Petard stood

177

on either side of the Hag, who held Big Galoot's bridle and gently stroked his neck. Sunglasses were taped over his eyes. A string over his hindquarters held the codpiece in place.

Stuckey flashed an arrogant smile as he congratulated himself on correctly guessing that Duffy would show up here. That is why he had brought Rose with him.

"Ah, Duffy, good to see you again and my friend the Professor.

Satan laughed and pointed to Galoot and the Hag. "What is that...a blind dog led by a seeing eye person!" This got a big laugh from the legionnaires who by now were crowded at the windows of the lounge, eager for some entertainment.

Roscoe ignored the comment. "We've come here to bargain with you, Colonel."

"Bargain? It seems to me you are in no position to bargain! I could have you all scooped up in a minute. You don't have that angel to protect you now. And those Detainers I see won't work against us. You should know that."

"It would be foolish to try to seize us, Stuckey. Look at these." In each hand he held an uncapped jar filled with clear liquid. He raised his right hand. "This is the serum." He raised the other hand. "This is the antidote. These are all you need. Analyze them and duplicate them. No need to bother with the Professor and his determination not to work for you. But attack us, and I will spill both of these on the ground before you can reach us."

"Come now, Mr. Duffy, you insult my intelligence. You expect me to trade your woman for two jars of what may be plain water." He wagged his head like a school teacher catching a pupil in a foolish error.

"Of course not," Roscoe answered. "Watch carefully." He nodded to Benny, who winced and hesitantly turned sideways to the Professor. The little Scot withdrew a syringe from his lab coat pocket and filled it from the jar in Roscoe's right hand. Then he jabbed the needle into Benny's arm and pressed the plunger. Benny's face suddenly went pale. "Trust me, Benny. Trust me, buddy," Roscoe said in a loud voice. Stuckey and Satan watched Benny with such fixity they did not notice the Hag staring intently at Benny and muttering something as Roscoe loudly urged his partner to trust him.

Benny sank to his knees and then leaned forward on his arms. He shook his head as if trying to clear it. Then he suddenly blossomed into a sheep and began a pitiful bleating. The crowd at the windows cheered and whistled.

"Satisfied?" Roscoe said, trying to conceal the relief he felt that the Hag's enchantment had worked. But now an equally dangerous spell had to work. One that would restore Benny. Roscoe looked at the Hag. Her mouth was set in a firm line. She was ready.

"Very good, Duffy. Now prove the antidote works," Stuckey said.

The Professor withdrew a fresh syringe from his pocket and filled it from the jar in Roscoe's left hand. Roscoe and the others chanted "Come on, Benny. Come on, Benny," while the hag murmured words of her own and the Professor injected the sheep with the "antidote," which like the "serum," was merely water. Nothing happened for several seconds. A minute passed. With an almost imperceptible nod, Roscoe signaled the Hag to try again, then led the others in more loud chanting to cover her incantation.

This time the sheep quivered and yawned and twitched as though something were roiling in its gut, and then, with a small pop, it suddenly transformed itself into Benny. But there was something wrong. His eyes were wide with terror. He leaned close to Roscoe's ear and tried to whispered something. Roscoe's heart froze. Benny couldn't speak. He could only bleat.

Roscoe turned to the Hag and told her in a low voice what had happened. She closed her eyes and shook her head wearily. "I'll try to fix it later. I think I can do it."

Think you can do it! Roscoe's gut felt suddenly hollow but he forced a smile. He turned to Benny and gave him a wink and a thumbs up. You're going to be ok, pal. Hang in there. Benny looked doubtful, seeming to know that Roscoe pretended more confidence than he felt, but he straightened up and faced Stuckey with a smile as if everything were just fine. Roscoe felt a surge of affection for his partner. No matter what the circumstances, Benny never let you down.

"Bravo, Mr. Duffy. I am pleasantly surprised. Send the Professor up here with the jars and I will release Miss Trautman," the Colonel said.

Roscoe forced himself to laugh. "Oh   no, Stuckey. Now you're taking me for a fool. Send Taylor down here with Rose. I give him the antidote first. He   releases her. When she is safely in our hands, I give him the serum. But make a wrong move and I dump the serum on the ground."

The Colonel appeared to consider this proposal, but Roscoe knew it was an act. Stuckey would try to capture them all, once Taylor had the serum. He studied the Colonel's face trying to read his thoughts. If Roscoe's assumptions were correct, Stuckey would reason that if this were somehow a trick, capturing them would still give him the Professor and his friends to threaten, if the Scot did not do his bidding. And capturing them posed no problem. Bruno was not there protecting them now, which meant that for some reason the angel was not available to them. The Colonel would figure there was no way he could lose. Which was precisely what Roscoe wanted him to think.

"You are a clever man, Mr. Duffy. I have never underestimated you on that score. All right, it's a deal. I won't need her any more, and there's nothing you can do to stop us now. The coup is a success. Freemont will be right down with the girl"

While Roscoe waited for Freemont and Rose to appear, he scanned the parapet of the building. Bruno should be up on the roof somewhere, but there was no sign of him. Timing was everything. The plan depended on Michael's men infiltrating the city undetected and massing behind a large building a block away. At the right moment Bruno would signal them to attack. Why was there no sign of him? Had something gone wrong! But if Michael's forces had been detected there would have a general alarm, and there had not been one. Bruno, where the hell are you! If the archangels did not arrive at the right moment, the battle would be lost!

And if the Hag could not do her stuff, they would all be lost.

But the critical moment had arrived. Roscoe's heart hammered in his ears as Rose passed through the closed door of the main entrance. A second later, Freemont Taylor passed through right behind her with a Detainer. They walked slowly down the long flight of stairs at the entrance. Rose looked frightened. Taylor was smirking and turning the Detainer in his hand. The Devil Dogs crowding the windows looked on silently, waiting for something to happen. Stuckey looked down on the group, his eyes darting from person to person, alert to any suspicious movements. Satan stood beside him with arms crossed, smiling, finding this whole scene amusing.

Taylor and Rose stopped in front of Roscoe.

"Don't do anything foolish, Duffy. Just give me the jar and you get the girl," Taylor said.

Roscoe handed him the jar containing the "antidote". Rose ran to his side. Roscoe handed Taylor the second jar. Taylor turned and began to trot back to the building, but he slowed to a careful walk when the liquid in both jars threatened to splash over the rims.

"Oh, Roscoe...." Rose began.

"I know, I know...everything's okay now. But you've got to get out of here. I don't have time to explain. Go with Petard and the Professor. They'll see that you're safe. I'll be with you soon."

Rose hesitated, her eyes brimming with tears.

"Go! Go!" Roscoe cried.

She turned and hurried toward Petard and the professor. The three of them were about to teleport away when Stuckey shouted "Seize them all." Four of the Devil Dogs burst through the front door, almost colliding with Taylor. They were armed with anesthetic guns.

"Now!" Roscoe shouted to the Hag.

The old woman straddled Big Galoot. She grasped his bridle with one hand and reached behind her to untie the codpiece. "Innagadoom!" she shouted. "Innagadoom!"

Galoot responded with a deep bark and then began whining

as though in pain. His body began to swell, raising the Hag higher and higher off the ground. She stripped away the sunglasses. With a melancholy howl and a mighty shuddering the mastiff sprouted the long serpentine neck, and then the legs and huge winged back of Hamish, the basilisk. The Hag wrapped her legs tightly around his neck and pulled on the bridle to raise his head. She stroked his neck.

The incredible transformation from dog to basilisk drew a gasp of surprise from the legionnaires crowded at the windows. The onrushing Devil Dogs stopped, frozen with astonishment.

"Go on, go on. Get them!" Stuckey shouted to them. He was convinced Duffy would not have confronted him without some trick up his sleeve, and this must be it. A sleight-of-hand. Some flim-flam with virtual reality to scare them. He wasn't buying it!

The legionnaires exchanged frightened glances. They wanted no part of this weirdness.

"Damn you! Get after them or I'll have you shipped back to Hell immediately," the Colonel yelled.

Satan leaned slightly forward.

"Go ahead, men. Do as he says."

Cursing their fate, the Devil Dogs advanced with heavy feet. Two came straight at Roscoe, Mooch and Benny. The other two angled toward Rose, who crouched behind the Professor and Petard. This sudden development forced the three to momentarily abandon their teleportation protocol to defend themselves. The Professor and Petard both held Detainers, ready to meet the attack of legionnaires.

The Hag was ready for the assault. She reined the head of Hamish to point at the two coming at Roscoe, then kicked the basilisk's neck with her heels. Hamish unleashed a blast of fire that caught both of them in mid-stride, incinerating them instantly. She quickly swung the creature's head to the side and slapped the top of it. Its eyes glowed a ruby red as it zeroed in on the other two Devil Dogs. The two closed to within ten feet of Rose and her protectors before two laser-like red beams from Hamish's eyes hit them. They toppled to the ground like falling statues and shattered into pieces.

Roscoe looked back at Rose and her companions. The

tightness in his chest eased as he watched them teleport out of sight.

He looked up at the startled faces of Stuckey and Satan as cries of alarm swept through the legionnaires at the windows. A moment later a high trumpet call sliced through the din. It was followed by the massive sound of wings beating the air as Michael's archangels attacked through the roof and rear walls of the building. Taken completely by surprise, the stunned Devil Dogs scrambled back from the windows in desperate attempts to retrieve their tanks. A few of them managed to get them on before Michael's forces were upon them with their fiery swords. Three of the archangels were hit by the anesthetic and went limp with silly smiles on their faces, but Satan's men, without their tanks, were practically defenseless before the onslaught of Heaven's elite warriors. The screaming of the doomed men cut through the sounds of battle. Devil Dogs who were not vaporized by the flaming swords fled out through the second floor walls and windows, or dropped to the first floor and poured through the entrance. A handful of the fleeing legionnaires escaped by rocketing in different directions. The rest perished in the eye beams or withering blasts of flame from Hamish.

Bruno appeared at the parapet. He raised his fist in triumph and urgently beckoned Roscoe and his companions to join him. With Michael's recalibrated Detainer in hand, Roscoe quickly levitated to the roof. Benny and Mooch went with him. Benny carried the other recalibrated Detainer. Mooch was armed with the one taken from Oswald. The Hag remained on Hamish, stroking his back, calming him down.

"They're finished!" Bruno exulted. "Satan and three of his men zoomed off in that direction," he said pointing toward the wall in the distance. "By now they're probably on their way back down to Hell. But it won't make any difference. The Almighty will deal with them when he recovers."

"Did you see Stuckey?" Roscoe said.

"He and Taylor left a few seconds later, heading in the same direction. Cowardly bastards!"

Mooch said: "No question where Satan's going. He's

hightailing for the breach in the wall and the capsule back to Hell."

"And I'll bet Stuckey and Taylor will go with him...." Roscoe said.

"But those two can't escape the wrath of the Almighty down there, can they?" Benny asked.

"They can escape it for a time if Satan is willing to hide them in different guises. Like a shell game. Could be quite a long time before the Almighty gets them. But eventually he will," Bruno said.

"That bastard doesn't deserve even a short reprieve. I'd love to catch him with this Detainer before he gets into that capsule," Benny said.

"I know exactly where the breach is," Mooch said. "But Stucky and Taylor have never actually been to it. It might take them a little extra time to find it." Mooch did not need to voice the implication.

"Will Satan wait for them?' Roscoe asked.

Bruno shrugged. "Hard to say. If the archangels aren't hot on his heels, he might. But I can't see him waiting for long. If Michaels's men catch him, they'll beat the shit out of him with special Detainers only they have. He'd rather have the Almighty punish him in Hell. The punishment will be hard, but at least he won't be whacked about like a tennis ball."

It did not bother Roscoe that Satan would get away. Even if they caught him, none of them had the power to harm the mighty sovereign of Hell. His punishment lay in the hands of the Almighty alone. And that punishment would surely come.

But the thought that Stuckey might gain a temporary reprieve, perhaps even a lengthy one, set his stomach churning. Slim though it was, the possibility of catching the Colonel was irresistible.

Benny read his thoughts. "We're wasting time. Mooch, lead us to the breach in the wall." Mooch beamed. He didn't have to be persuaded to do it. He was finally going to get a chance to screw Stuckey big time.

In the confusion of the battle's last moments, Stuckey was

too desperate to escape to feel anger. But now as he and Freemont Taylor searched for the breach in the wall around heaven, anger flooded him with the bitter taste of bile. He reproached himself for not eliminating Duffy and the others when he had the chance. All the risks he had taken, all the hard work he had done, had come to nothing because of those meddling fools. He had almost achieved unlimited power as Satan's right-hand man...and now...he was a fugitive whose only hope was to flee to Hell! And even that bleak future might elude him if they couldn't find the breach in the next few minutes.

"I thought you knew where it is, you moron," he snapped at Taylor.

"I never actually went there," Taylor protested,"but its got to be here in *Theatris* behind a large bush."

"Behind a big bush! There's a goddamn big bush every twenty feet along this wall!" They passed bush after bush without finding the breach. Quite by accident, they passed over the open-air theater staging *Henry the Fifth* at the very moment an actor declaimed the king's famous rallying cry at Harfleur. "Once more unto the breach, dear friends, once more...."

"There, you hear that?" Taylor said.

"Hear what?"

"That guy says the breach is over there. See, he's pointing to it" He turned back and waved to the actor below who was pointing to the walls of Harfleur. "Thanks, pal," Taylor said. This sudden voice from nowhere startled the actor into forgetting his next line.

"You're crazy," Stuckey said.

"Let's just see."

They zoomed to the big bush Taylor thought the actor had indicated and, wonder of wonders, there was the breach hidden behind it. Taylor's ignorance of Shakespearean drama and plain dumb luck had proved a winning combination. And just in time. As they approached the gap in the wall they could see Satan ahead of them with three of his men about to enter the capsule. Stuckey shouted for them to wait. Satan turned around and saw them. He did not look pleased, but he stopped and signaled them to hurry up. Then his expression froze. His alarmed look caused Stuckey to glance back over his shoulder. Roscoe and the others were closing on him at terrific speed with Detainers.

Satan and his men rushed into the capsule, but the door was still open, with Stuckey only twenty feet from it. His initial rush of panic subsided. Duffy and comrades were closing the gap but they were still yards behind him. He would surely make it through the door before they caught him! Besides, the Detainers his pursuers carried were not calibrated to capture an official of his stature! Freemont Taylor lagged several feet behind the Colonel, not yet aware he was being chased. Stuckey glanced back at him, sure that Taylor was also protected against the oncoming sticky plates. He didn't bother to warn his accomplice, thinking he'd let Duffy swat Taylor and laugh in the detective's face when the device failed to work!

But his heart jumped to his throat when the impossible happened. Duffy raced up behind Taylor and slapped him squarely with the Detainer. With a plink Taylor instantly disappeared. As the detective drew almost close enough to swat Stuckey, the terrified Colonel managed a final burst of speed that carried him through the half-open door a second before it closed. The capsule jetted away into chaos before Roscoe reached it.

Roscoe slammed his Detainer to the ground.

"Son of a bitch," Benny said.

"Don't take it so hard, you two," Bruno said. "He's only bought time."

"At least we got Taylor," Mooch said. "Let's drop the bastard into Chaos."

"Sorry, Mooch. We can't do that. Regulations. The Almighty will decide his punishment," Bruno said.

The capture of Taylor was small consolation to Roscoe. He was still burning with anger that Stuckey had gotten away.

Chapter Nine

They traveled rapidly down through Chaos. Hideous forms swooped past the portholes, screeching furiously as they felt the sting of the electronic field protecting the large transport capsule. With only five persons onboard, there was plenty of room to sit on the padded bunk seats along the walls. The three Devil Dog officers sat a few feet from the Lucifer's side. Stuckey sat across from him, hunched forward, stunned by his narrow escape.

"I don't understand why that Detainer worked on Taylor," Stuckey muttered. "We were supposed to be protected from it...unless...

Satan glowered at him.

"It didn't occur to you that Michael would have recalibrated it for them in case they caught up with you? Another of your miscalculations, Colonel."

"I didn't think he would do it so *quickly*...."

Satan gave him a disgusted look.

Stuckey stared glumly at the floor.

"And that amulet around you neck that protects you from the furies...do you foolishly suppose Michael hasn't inactivated it?"

Stuckey jerked upright with alarm. He hadn't thought of that! He wrenched the chain from his neck and stared at the amulet as though looking at it would confirm its efficacy.

187

Satan snatched it from his hand. He held the chain in front of him and stared intently at the dangling amulet.

He nodded with a disdainful smile. "Of course. Just as I suspected. It's useless." He tossed it to the nearest legionnaire. "Keep this as a souvenir."

"You can tell just by looking at it?" the Colonel said weakly. Satan had no idea whether the amulet was still operative. He simply wanted to deprive Stuckey of it.

"Absolutely. But you won't need this anymore."

There was a strange edge in Satan's voice that made Stuckey tremble, but he clung to the hope Satan meant it would be of no use in Hell.

"Look, I'm sorry the coup failed...but it wasn't my fault...nobody risked more or worked harder for you that I did," Stuckey said. "I'm really grateful that you are standing by me. I always knew you would. You are an honorable soldier like me."

Satan smiled. *Honorable? The Devil honorable? What an amusing idea. You cost me the victory I had in my grasp, and you expect me to harbor you in Hell? Why should I hide you while things cool down. That would compound my offense in the eyes of the Almighty and make my punishment even worse. You're a bungling fool, Colonel Stuckey. I cannot stand the sight of you!*

Satan tipped his head sideways and smiled, closing his eyes and nodding slowly as if acknowledging their comradeship.

The Colonel felt reassured. He leaned back against the capsule wall. The Devil's harsh criticism of him could be discounted. He, Stuckey, was merely a convenient whipping boy, a someone on whom the Devil could spend his molten anger. It was to be expected. Stuckey had felt the sting of defeat in his own career and knew exactly how Satan felt.

The next few minutes passed in silence as the capsule continued to arrow down through Chaos.

Then Satan stood up, smiling benignly at Stuckey. "We're almost there. Time to attach ourselves to the wall magnets. The landing will give us a bit of a jolt and these act like safety belts."

The legionnaires slid sideways on the seat until each had his back aligned with a square metal pad on the wall.

"Sit over here next to me," the Devil said to Stuckey.

The Colonel crossed the aisle and seated himself.

Satan had already aligned himself with a magnet. Beside it were red and green lights and several buttons.

"Slide left until you're in front of that magnet," he said, pointing to the one he meant.

Stuckey did so.

Satan pushed a button activating the magnets and clamping everyone's back to the wall.

"Comfortable?"

The Colonel smiled. "Absolutely."

Satan's gaze lingered on Stuckey for several seconds. He gave the Colonel a reassuring wink. Then he pressed a button and a red light blinked. Stuckey had not noticed he was clamped to a pocket door in the side of the capsule. To the raucous sound of a warning horn, the door suddenly slid open into its pocket, scraping the uncomprehending Stuckey off its magnet and into Chaos. As the door closed, Satan heard his fading screams mingling with the banshee shrieking of devouring furies.

Satan grunted with pleasure. *The devil honorable?* After the strain of pretending to be a nice guy during the coup, it felt good to be his own evil self again.

Bruno left them at the wall. He zoomed off to help Michael track down the few Devil Dogs who escaped during the battle. Roscoe, Benny and Mooch returned to the Administration building. The ground in front of it was strewn with the stone rubble and ash piles of the fallen Devil Dogs. Roscoe wondered whether the legionnaires' atoms returned to Hell to regroup into the bodies they once had, or whether they would coalesce somewhere else into new, more hideous forms? He would have to ask Bruno.

They found the Hag standing beside Hamish, stroking his side. The basilisk had sunglasses and the codpiece on again. He acted like a big contented cat, nuzzling the Hag and emitting harsh gurgling sounds that appeared to be the basilisk equivalent of purring.

"He's spent all his power for the time being," she said. "There's no need to transform him back into Galoot. He'll go wherever I lead him."

Benny had little interest in this news. He hurried toward her, bleating pitifully and pointing to his throat. *Fix this! Please fix this!*

She cupped her chin in her hand and began tapping her cheek with her forefinger as she considered the problem.

"Hmmmmn....Don't worry. I'm sure it's something minor. Some little bit of the restoration spell didn't kick in...maybe I should have chanted it twice. Let's try that."

She took two deep breaths. She twisted her face into a scowl as she muttered the arcane words of the spell, and then repeated them.

Benny jerked backward as if he'd been shocked by a live wire. His cry was still a bleat--a startled bleat this time--but now he suffered an additional transformation. His hair had turned to sheep's wool.

"Oh, my god. What are you doing to him!" Roscoe cried.

The Hag ignored him. She shook her head, disgusted with the failure of her spell.

"Well, there is one last thing I can try. Benny, get down on your hands and knees."

"Do you know what the hell you're doing?" Roscoe demanded.

"Of course I do. All we need is a little adjustment."

With that, she walked to the rear of Benny, lifted her skirt slightly, and gave him a mighty kick in the ass. Her foot penetrated deeply into his etheric body, painlessly jostling most of his internal atoms. Instantly the head wool vanished and Benny let out a yelp that was definitely not a bleat. "Alright! Alright!" he rejoiced, bouncing to his feet. "Thank you. I'm fine." Roscoe released his pent-up breath. Mooch laughed. He said:"Damn! That's the way I used to fix my washing machine when it wouldn't work!"

"Old fashioned techniques, like old sorceresses, have their

uses," the Hag said with a satisfied smile.

"You won't get an argument from us, old girl. We couldn't have done it without you. We owe you," Roscoe said. His words pleased and embarrassed the Hag. She half turned away and flapped a hand dismissively, as if they were overstating the case.

Benny hugged her. She squirmed a little but did not resist.

Then Mooch said: "I wonder how the other three made out."

Roscoe's thoughts had already raced ahead of Mooch. *I'm coming Rose. I'm coming!*

Satan's defeat was greeted with universal rejoicing. No one, it now appeared, had really supported Satan. The excuse that quickly solidified among the masses, who hours ago had cheered the Devil, was fear: they were afraid of what might happen to them if they didn't appear to support him. Even those who had stood in the midst of the crowd, unable even to see the mermen on the distant perimeter, righteously insisted they feared these madmen with tanks would spray them at any moment.

The principal supporters who had taken the stage to justify the coup were already defending their actions to any audience that would listen.

"I had to do it," Jimmy Cagney said. He stood at the foot of the golden stairs, wearing a straw hat and a candy-stripe blazer. "Of course I knew he was evil as hell, but I had to defend the dirty rat. He was my *client*. Lying doesn't count when you defend a client, see. I was just doing my job." He flashed a self-congratulating smile and winked at the crowd he had attracted. "And I almost convinced you, didn't I!" His listeners applauded and whistled. He favored them with a twirl and another fragment of his *Yankee Doodle* tap routine.

The Preacher went on television. He clutched an open bible as he strode back and forth across the stage. A white-robed choir stood in the background softly humming "Rock of Ages."

"I deceived you, yes," he said, his eyes brimming with tears. "But I did it for your own good. Your faith in the Almighty had grown feeble. Your love of Him had grown weak. Your complacency and greed for "more" and "more" had sapped your righteousness." He paused and ran his fingers distractedly through his hair, shaking his head as if trying to cope with the enormity of their transgressions. His face darkened with anger.

"And you really thought I was in league with the Devil! How little you know me," he shouted. "I never *doubted* the coup would fail because the Almighty will *always* prevail. I only *pretended* to go along, mouthing the vile and twisted logic the Devil uses to ensnare doubting souls. I had to *show* you your weakness, your vulnerability to his wiles...and many of you succumbed, didn't you! Yes, brothers and sisters, you succumbed...but now you see your weaknesses and can pray for forgiveness from our merciful God. My friends, you were teetering on the edge of the abyss and I pulled you back!"

To make them think the burden of his effort had taken its toll on him, the Preacher wiped his eyes with a large white handkerchief, then blinked several times as if summoning new strength. He took a deep breath and smiled as the camera zoomed in on his face. Speaking in a confidential tone, he said "I tell you it was *very* difficult for me to pretend to be the Devil's advocate. But I would do it again if it meant your continued salvation...And I will continue to watch over you, but I need your support." He paused. "Send me a postcard saying how important I am to your spiritual life," he said, his tone now demanding. "I need thousands of these to persuade the High Council I serve multitudes, and therefore *deserve* what I have asked them for--expanded television facilities and a Worship Resort with all the recreational amenities that make praying a really fun experience."

He promised to send every contributor a "prayer plaster"--a virtual band-aid bearing a prayer he himself had composed. Wearing one was as good as actually praying, he said, and would be especially pleasing to the Almighty.

The Preacher raised his arms in victory. The choir burst forth with a rousing rendition of the "Hallelujah Chorus."

As for the Elder, he appealed to Jeremiah to intercede for

him. He conceded he had abetted the wrong cause but protested he did so for what he thought--mistakenly, he now saw--were the right reasons. He hoped Jeremiah could persuade the Almighty to show mercy to a befuddled old man who had recently lost a front tooth. Jeremiah, still recovering from the anesthetic, retained enough of the kindly optimism it induced to agree to make the petition.

Cronus put his case to the small number of gods and heroes who had responded to his call for a meeting on the highest mountain in the domain of the *Pagan Gods and Heroes*. He claimed he had been misled by that lumpen, Polyphemus.

"He told me he was in a play and they needed someone of my stature to speak a few lines. That's all I did--spoke the few lines they gave me. I never knew this was a real coup. I was told it was a satire on the Devil with a happy ending. The other gods who stood with me thought the same thing! And for this you condemn me? I eat my children and you say nothing, but when I make the tiny mistake of doing a walk-on in a bad production, you crucify me. Hypocrites!"

Blaming Polyphemus was mistake. Everyone knew the giant communicated only with grunts and gurgles. Cronus could read the scorn in the faces of his silent audience. The Big Lie hadn't worked. But give it time, he thought; tell it often enough and they will believe it. Their hostility did not undermine his confidence that he would survive this debacle. He was the oldest and most powerful of the pagan gods. What could they do to him? Plenty, as it would turn out. His listeners already knew his fate, and had come to take a last look at this once frightening god. Zeus had declared to them that, with the Almighty's approval, Cronus would be banished to the virtual domain of *Easter Island* and forced to devour every one of the stone faces. Each time he finished this task he would vomit them up and start all over again. Zeus figured this was only fitting. Cronus' punishment of Zeus had given him a bad liver. His punishment of Cronus would give the old bastard kidney stones.

The fate of the conspirators was not of immediate interest to the vast majority of Heaven's citizens, however. The Almighty would take care of them in his own good time. The thing now was to have fun in the festival of celebration going on all over the Golden City.

There were red and yellow and purple balloons on street lamps, and marching bands playing such pieces as "Under the Double Eagle," "Hail Britannia," "Oh Canada," "Darktown Strutter's Ball," " Washington Post March" and the Notre Dame fight song. Smart columns of marchers in identical outfits paraded down the avenue--matronly women in all-white outfits representing *Mom and Apple Pie*, girls in green woodland costumes marching in support of cookie sales, and among many others, a cadre of old men in bearskin hats representing *The Ancient Order of Pipe Smokers.*

Rollo Glotz and Lois Lane had trouble covering everything that was going on, largely because they spent their time eating the delicious offerings of the curbside food vendors. Glotz gorged himself on sweet Italian sausage, kielbasa, knockwurst with kraut, and white hot dogs. Lois was unable to resist fried dough, corn dogs, taffy and candied apples. The beauty part was that this delicious virtual food had no real calories and one could not get fat from eating it. The two spent so much time eating they gathered few significant notes, and by press time had almost nothing to write. Desperate to bulk out their meager story, they reluctantly included "Poem on the Defeat of the Devil" by Britain's worst poet. They never intended to publish the wretched piece but accepted it from McGonagle simply to be rid him. The poem was not written in the Cro-Magnon mode, the poet explained, because the occasion called for a more elevated style, one that employed many of McGonagle's charges at the *Permanent Shelter for Hapless and Abandoned Words.* It began:

Not screed nor scrivener's palimpsest can limn
The visage dark and sinister from Hell,
Who would the Almighty have usurped
Had not puissant Michael him did quell.

All is well, all is well.
Pricked on by faith and virtue rampant
The angelic host, with igneous blade
Forschimilled yon hoards of Devil Hounds
And foiled the plot they made.
    Sing we aubade. Sing we aubade.
Oh Hellish wight and scalawag vile
With naught but evil in thy heart
Begone, begone to Hadean fire
Where roast thy spleen into a tart.
    Horse and cart, horse and cart.

The poem wandered on for a dozen more epical stanzas with unrelated refrains. It managed to include such long-forgotten *PSHAW* residents as "collywobbles," " inveigle" "hoity-toity," "bastinado," "dodgy," "bubukle" and "fub."

"Poem on the Defeat of the Devil" further bolstered McGonagle's reputation as Britain's absolutely Worst Poet, and roused public sympathy for the *PSHAW* residents he bullied into forced labor. Never before had these hapless words been so abused as they were in the farrago that was McGonagle's poem.

   Tingling with anticipation of joining Rose at last, Roscoe plunged through the wall of Petard's house, along with Mooch and Benny. He found Petard, the Professor, and the Hag in the living room, but Rose was not with them. Before any of the others could speak, he rushed from room to room, searching for her, struggling to hold off his mounting anxiety. She was not in the house. He hurried back to the living room, fearing he might learn she had not made it back safely.

   Reading the look on Roscoe's face, the Hag said: "No. No. She's all right. She's just not here at the moment."

   "We got her here safely," Petard explained. "But I think she had a hard time getting over her close call back there. She kept pacing back and forth, wringing her hands and muttering. We tried to calm her down."

The Hag said: "A half hour later she left. Said she would be back shortly."

The Professor tried to ease Roscoe's obvious disappointment. "She's probably oot windin' down by walkin'."

"She didn't say where she was going?" Roscoe said.

The three shook their heads. Roscoe couldn't quell the growing sense that something was wrong. What was all her hand-wringing about? And the muttering? He tried to push these thoughts aside. Rose was okay, he told himself. She would offer a perfectly logical explanation when she rejoined them.

He felt himself winding down from the stress of the last few hours. The others were relaxing, too, as the knowledge they were truly safe reached gut level. The release of nervous energy set them all talking in high, excited voices, recounting what had happened to them. Mooch acted out the way Roscoe swatted Fremont Taylor and just missed the Colonel. Benny tried to make them understand the panic he felt when he could only bleat. The Hag confessed she had worried that Hamish would run out of fire, an admission that sent a shiver through the others as they realized how close they had come to being struck down by the Devil Dogs.

"That blast from Hamish came just in time," Petard said. He mimed the movements of a legionnaire raising his tank hose. "They were close enough to spray us but too far away for us to swat with the Detainers."

"Yes, but you stood your ground as they came at you. That's gutsy," Benny said.

"Noo, sheer ignorance," the Professor said. "We dint realize we wur at uh disadvantage until they wur gettin' ready tuh fire. My heart is still workin' its way down from my throat."

They were interrupted by Bruno's sudden arrival through the wall. He was smiling broadly and seemed pumped up with new energy.

"What a day this has been! I wasn't sure I gave Michael the

signal to attack at the right moment. From where I was, I couldn't see how many of the legionnaires were at the windows. But it all worked out. We've caught the few Devil Dogs that got away," he said.

"And everything's okay?" Roscoe said.

"Everything's fine. The rainbow is back in the clouds at the top of the stairs. It's a little faint because it'll take the Almighty a few more days to recover completely. But he's come back far enough to instruct Michael how to reward those who saved the day." He straightened up and jabbed his thumb toward his chest.

"Say hello to the new Head of Security. Chester Conklin will be my second in command and the boys back at the station house will be my security force. They'll have plenty of work now!"

"Congratulations, Bruno. You certainly deserve this," Roscoe said.

"Thanks. But we couldn't have carried this off without all of you, and the Almighty greatly appreciates what you did. Michael has authorized me to tell you how He has decided to reward you.

"For starters, all transgressions by Petard, Mooch and the Hag are forgiven. Your bravery and loyalty have redeemed you. Petard, you are now the Permanent Director of *Showtime in Heaven,* no longer answerable to any committee for your choice of theater pieces, and with authority to command all resources you need to produce them. The one change you may not like, however, is that you may no longer keep Hamish."

Petard did not seem upset. Having a basilisk was fun while it lasted. It was time to move on to something new.

Bruno turned to Mooch. "You have a choice. You can either become a Captain in my security force, or you can serve as Petard's right hand man on the *Showtime* staff." Mooch and Petard looked at each other with obvious delight. There was no doubt which option Mooch would choose.

"And you, my dear," he said to the Hag, " are free to live in Heaven without conditions. No more *Suds and Salty Tears* for you. What's more, your long years of loneliness are over. You are to have a loving husband."

The Hag gasped and covered her mouth with her hand. Her one large eye brimmed with tears. She timidly looked around her, but saw no one new. She gave Bruno a searching look.

"Everyone follow me," he said.

He led them down the cellar stairs to the pit where the Hag had placed Hamish. The basilisk sat calmly on its huge haunches. Its eyes were almost closed as if it were drowsing.

"By the power vested in me, I give you your husband," Bruno said, extending his arm toward Hamish. The Hag looked in disbelief and disappointment at the basilisk, and then at Bruno. The angel smiled at her. "No, no. Go down and stroke its neck," he said.

The Hag did not hesitate. She climbed down into the pit and moved confidently to the basilisk's side. She reached out and gently ran her hand along the creature's scaly neck. A sudden massive shudder rippled through its body, startling the Hag into lurching backward a few steps. The others watched in astonishment as the basilisk convulsed and seemed to coil in upon itself, growing smaller with each convulsion until, with a last giant spasm, it suddenly became a man.

A stocky, bearded one dressed in the leather jerkin and sheepskin leggings of a medieval peasant. This was the kind of man who would have courted the Hag in her maidenhood. He was not handsome. Bushy black eyebrows overhung eyes set close to a bulbous nose. His hair poked out in uneven black strands from beneath his goatskin cap. Because he was a newborn adult, his peasant face was not roughened and lined by sun and wind. The skin was smooth and pink, and he had strong, white front teeth with no gaps in them. He stood in the center of the pit, stunned, like another Adam awakening to life in a bedazzling world. He turned his hands over, studying their different sides and curling the fingers. He flexed his elbows and knees and seemed pleasantly surprised by how they folded and unfolded. He gently fingered his crotch, pulling, bending, lifting--puzzled that these parts did not seem to do anything.

Finished exploring the wonders of his new body, he looked

198

up. The first thing he saw was the Hag. Another strange wonder! He did not know what this other thing might be, nor could he yet articulate his feelings, but something in his heart, and a mysterious feeling in his groin, made him yearn for her.

The Hag moved slowly toward him, holding him in the gaze of her one good eye. He remained transfixed, an animal caught in sudden light. She cautiously extended her arms and embraced him. He instinctively responded by closing his arms around her and executing his first formulation of a kiss, which amounted to running his half-open slobbering lips all over her face.

"Well done, you two," Bruno said. "And now let us welcome Fenny Boggs, formerly a basilisk, once a mastiff, and now forever more, husband to the Blue-faced Hag of Glamis." Roscoe and his companions applauded.

"The Almighty could have made him from nothing," Bruno said, "but this way also rewarded Hamish by releasing him from appalling brutishness of being a basilisk."

"And he'll not retain any characteristics of the beasts in his lineage?" the Professor said.

"I was told he shouldn't, but that if he does they will be insignificant ones, like preferring to be bottle-fed by the Hag and pissing on fire hydrants."

Leaving Fenny and the Hag to get acquainted in the pit, the others returned to the living room.

Now it was the Professor's turn to learn of his reward. Bruno said: "You are free to continue your research. You will be given a staff and all the supplies you need. He already knows what good will come of your work but he will let you have the pleasure of discovering it yourself. What's more, you have been named Chief Scientist and will work to restore the good name of science in Heaven. The Almighty is tired of those overzealous nitwits who want to suppress it."

The Professor beamed.

"And now we come to you two," Bruno said to Roscoe and Benny.

He handed each a golden medallion on a chain. "These

199

guarantee safe passage though Chaos. We hope they will encourage you to visit us often before you come up here permanently...but there's more...Benny, there's an angel awaiting you back home who will bankroll your production of *Paradise_Lost*. This is a one-time deal, however. Something to get you started. In any future productions, you are strictly on your own."

"Oh, wow, oh wow!" Benny cried. "Oh, wow!"

"We'll do its out-of-town tryout up here. See what works and what doesn't," Petard said. "By the time it hits Broadway, it'll be a sure-fire success."

"Incredible. Absolutely incredible. Thank you."

Bruno turned to Roscoe with a broad smile. "Your reward is the most exceptional of all. You get what has never been granted before to a secular individual. The Almighty will allow Rose to return to the world with you. Reincarnated. A real woman!"

Roscoe's heart leaped. He lost his breath for a second.

Benny shouted "I told you it would work out, Duf. I told you!"

Petard brought virtual champagne from the kitchen. After toasting each other's good fortune they shook the bottles and sprayed each other like locker room athletes after a victory. By now the Hag and Fenny had joined them and received a good dousing. The abrupt encounter with more strange beings who were bent on wetting him down frightened Fenny into cowering in a corner. The Hag protected him with her body as best she could and, between delighted shrieks as she was sprayed, stroked his head and murmured reassuring words. The terrified look on his face made it clear he had not yet acquired language sufficiently to understand what she was saying. The Hag would have to begin naming things in a show-and-tell way until he could at least read *Horton Hatches the Egg* and *The Cat in the Hat*.

He was so engrossed with thoughts about Fenny's future it took him a few seconds to realize the others had fallen silent and were looking toward a far corner. Rose stood there, her arms limply at her sides. She did not look happy. But Roscoe hardly noticed that as he rushed to embrace her as the others cheered and clapped.

"How I've missed you," he said, putting his arms around her. She pressed her face against his chest, crying. He kissed her hair, then sought her lips. Her kiss was less passionate than he expected, but he thought that maybe she was still recovering from her ordeal.

"I've been worried about you. Petard said you were upset about something and just up and left. What was troubling you?"

Rose looked at him with red-rimmed eyes, but did not answer his question. She hugged him and said: "I'm so glad you're safe!"

Roscoe decided this was not the time to press his question.

"Anyway, I have wonderful, incredible news," he said. "Now we can be together. The Almighty will allow you to be reincarnated and return to the world with me. Can you believe that! Oh, Rose, what a life we will have."

He expected her to rejoice with him, but instead she broke out in large, choking sobs..

"What? What is it, Rose? Doesn't this make you happy?"

"No...no...it only...makes it...harder, Roscoe. Harder to tell you..."

"What? Tell me what?"

Rose took a step backward. She took a deep breath, and with hands locked tightly together in front of her, she began: "That night I didn't return to the bower...I said I stayed with a friend..." She looked away from Roscoe. "That was true. But it was a special friend who's here now...It was my lover, the Albanian shepherd...Our passion for each other is even stronger that it was in life...Oh, Roscoe, I didn't want to hurt you...I didn't confess this to you because I believed you would have to return to the world without me, and I wanted you to go back without the pain of knowing this. Forgive me, Roscoe, please...It breaks my heart to hurt you so...but I cannot bear to be apart from Habib."

Roscoe felt numb. "But...he treated you so badly...how can you go back to him!"

"Yes, I know. I know." She began weeping again. "I can't help it."

"Come back to the world with me and you'll get over him. You'll see. You just need time to realize we were made to be together."

She shook her head. "Perhaps in time I will realize that. But not right now...oh, Roscoe...I'm sorry, but it's best that we part...if you love me, please don't make this harder than it is."

"Rose..."

She sealed his lips with her finger and looked at him for a long moment. Then she slowly turned away and, with her head bowed, walked through the wall without looking back.

Oh, Rose, his heart cried out. Oh, Rose. He wanted to go after her, reason with her, plead with her, but he did not move. He knew deep down that it was useless.

No one spoke. Benny stared at the ground, unable to bear the pain in his friend's face.

Finally, the professor said in a quiet voice. "Ach, laddie, it just wasn't meant to be."To Roscoe, the words seemed to come from a great distance. They did not lessen the hollow ache in his chest. It was over. It was time to go home.

Roscoe and Benny stood in front of the Executive elevator in the Administration building. They could make the trip safely through Chaos with their medallions, but as a special honor, they were going to travel in the comfort of the elevator to the bottom of Chaos, where they would be let out precisely at the border of site 215.

Bruno had retrieved the clothes they came in. Benny once again wore his plaid pants, yellow shirt, blue nylon jacket and Yankee ball cap. Roscoe was back in his red bowling jacket.

A small group was on hand to see them off. McGonagle was there with a few of his charges–"huzzah," "a demain," "toodleoo," and "hip-hip hooray," all of whom waved little pennons and jumped up and down. Roscoe Conklin and his entire force stood in formation at attention. Conklin winked at Roscoe and gave him a thumbs up.

The Hag, leading Fenny by the hand, came up to hug Roscoe and then Benny. Then Fenny gave them both a slobbering kiss.

Bruno, his mutton chops neatly barbered and his portly frame smartly dressed in a new turn-of-the-century policeman's jacket and domed hat, stood beside Michael. He leaned close to the archangel and whispered in his ear. Michael approached Roscoe and said: "Sorry about your disappointment. Is there anything else we might do to show our appreciation?"

Roscoe thought for a moment. Then he said: "Well there is one small thing...may be a coincidence, I don't know...but every time it rains something bad happens to me. Could you look into that?"

Michael smiled at him. "Absolutely." Then he shook hands with Roscoe and Benny and stepped back. It was time to go. The two detectives exchanged wispy embraces with the Professor, Mooch and Petard.

Petard said to Roscoe: "You'll come for the tryout of *Paradise Lost*?"

"You can count on it."

Bruno pressed the button to open the elevator doors. "Well, my friends, this has been quite an adventure," he said. "I will miss you. You two are the world's best detectives. If you continue being detectives, and if there is any way we can help you, don't hesitate to call us. We'd be delighted to pitch in."

His praise left them a little giddy and at a loss for words. They simply nodded and shook his hand vigorously. Then they stepped into the elevator, waved farewell to everyone, and closed the doors. They were on their way.

The trip through Chaos, this time, was quite pleasant. At first Roscoe did not have the nerve to watch the hideous forms swarming around the elevator's window. The furies rushed at the heavy glass as though attacking, their mouths contorted with shrieks and howls, but neither they nor their fearsome sounds could penetrate the elevator. After a few minutes Roscoe and Benny felt secure and comfortable observing them. It was like being in a descending bathysphere and observing bizarre life in the deep sea. As an octopus-like creature passed the window Roscoe thought he saw a torn strip of camouflage cloth wrapped around one tentacle, but then decided that could not be, that it was an illusion created by the dim light and the swirling etheric mist.

"I feel like I'm in a Japanese monster film," Benny said. "I won't enjoy coming through here with just my medallion to protect me."

"You'll get used to it. You've already done it once with Bruno. It'll get your adrenaline pumping but you'll get through it okay. After all, you are now one of the world's best detectives. Best detectives are never daunted."

Benny laughed. "How about that. I wish our old colleagues could have heard Michael say it. But the important thing is that we know it."

Roscoe smiled and nodded. They were at last what they had always wanted to be: first-rate detectives. Bruno had confirmed it. Benny was right. Knowing that made all the difference.

The elevator slowed and came to a halt. They had reached site 215, the edge of Chaos. Roscoe did not open the doors. Although the amulets would protect them, he did not want an unpleasant encounter with furies that might attack even here at the brink of Chaos. He and Benny would depart through closed doors.

Back when he first instructed Benny in astral travel, Roscoe also outlined the procedure for returning home. It was the same one used to get here.

"You go first. I'll wait to see that you get off okay," Roscoe said.

"Piece of cake,"

"Better be, or Lotti will shoot me."

Benny lay down on the floor. "See you in a while," he said.

He crossed his arms and closed his eyes. He took several deep breaths as he visualized the interior of his apartment. Then he vibrated silently and disappeared.

Benny's smooth departure indicated he had followed the procedure correctly. Roscoe was sure his friend would be okay.

Then it was his turn to lie down and begin the journey home. In less than a minute he was once again traveling at blinding speed through a swirling vortex. Then he hurtled through a portal at the end of the vortex and lost consciousness. He awoke on his couch with his arms folded across his chest.

His muscles were a little stiff but otherwise he felt fine. The note he had pinned to his shirt was still there. He sat up and looked around. Nothing had changed in his apartment. How long had he been gone? A day? A month? He could swear his adventure in the etheric had lasted at least a week or more, but how long was that in worldly time? He found the answer in the pocket of his red bowling jacket. The two Krispy Kreme doughnuts wrapped in wax paper were still there. Their etheric forms had traveled with Roscoe, but their physical forms had remained behind in the pocket of the jacket. Loosely wrapped, they had been partially exposed to air, but they were almost as fresh as the day he bought them. He could not have been gone more than a day--or two at the most. Amazing! A weight in his pants pocket confirmed he was not dreaming. It was the gold medallion, solid and bright. All the events vividly in his memory had really happened.

He made himself a cup of coffee and ate one of the doughnuts. The taste of real coffee and the solidity of the doughnut were a little strange at first, but he quickly began to relish them.

Roscoe walked onto his balcony and looked down. The litter in the alleyways was still there. Three kids on skateboards hopped the curbstone, almost hitting an elderly woman. A man in a flat cap entered the liquor store on the corner. Beside the back door of the Chinese restaurant a kitchen worker smoked a cigarette. This was life as usual in his immediate world and its familiarity was comforting.

He thought about Rose. Had he given her up too easily? Should he return immediately and try harder to win her? Or should he wait a while, hoping she would tire of her Albanian psychopath? He could not answer these questions, but bolstered by new confidence in his judgment, he felt certain the right answers would come to him in time.

The sky began to darken with rain clouds, but this did not puncture his buoyant mood. He was beginning a new life. He decided to go uptown and treat himself to dinner at one of the city's finest restaurants. Afterwards, he might check in with Benny and compare notes.

It was raining hard by the time he hailed a cab. The driver spoke English and knew exactly how to get to the *Beef House*. After a scotch and water at the bar, he took a table looking out onto the street. It was almost dark. The rain was coming down in sheets. He had two glasses of the house merlot as he tucked into a goat cheese salad and the roast beef special with twice-baked potatoes and french filet beans. He felt wonderful. It was raining like hell and nothing bad had happened to him. This was indeed a new life.

He left the waiter a generous tip.

About the Author: William J. Kelly, Ph.D., has been a commercial journalist, a college English Professor, and editor of a natural history magazine. His humorous pieces and nature writings have appeared in a variety of publications. He and his wife live in a Victorian house in Mystic, Connecticut.

www.ingramcontent.com/pod-product-compliance
Lightning Source LLC
Chambersburg PA
CBHW050527260626
47157CB00004B/1500